CRAZY STU

Cassie ᴋᴏᴄᴄᴀ

CW0957287

About *Crazy Stupid Love*

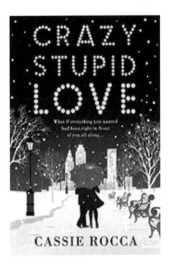

Are there written rules on how to find a soulmate? Or is it better to trust the hands of fate?

After enduring a string of dead-end relationships, Zoe Mathison has made a decision – to find a man who truly appreciates her. But this is turning out to be more complicated than she expected. Fed up of being surrounded by insufferably happy couples in love, her mission to find the perfect man starts to become an obsession.

Eric Morgan is pushed to his limits. Hopelessly in love with Zoe, who sees him as nothing more than a best friend to lean on, he can't bear seeing his hopes of romance crushed every time the sculpted pecs of a younger man comes along. But when a new girl appears on the scene, he is determined to prove that he can push his infatuation aside and move on. But is it as easy as it seems?

In the romantic and bustling city of New York, will Zoe and Eric's hilarious misadventures attract Cupid's arrow?

Chapter 1

The woman staring back at her in the mirror was the proof that she'd obtained exactly the effect she'd been aiming for when she'd started getting herself ready: her makeup, primarily targeted at highlighting her wide grey eyes, was perfect, her hair, smooth and dark, was held elegantly to the sides of her face by two ivory combs and hung down to her neck, and her dress – a soft woollen one with a round neckline – hugged her shapely figure without being too revealing. Okay, it *was* a beautiful bright red… but it was a longstanding tradition in her family to wear red for New Year's Eve. While she applied the final touch of all-day lip gloss, Zoe Mathison paid only scant attention to what she was doing. She was used to that face in the mirror – she knew that she was beautiful and she used the fact to her advantage, but managing her appearance and dressing up for special occasions wasn't really something she enjoyed any more: it was just something she did on autopilot, practically without realizing it.

And that seductive appearance of hers which magnetically attracted the male gaze meant that she was often the object of envy and spitefulness. Not that she looked like some airbrushed pin-up: she was slim and lithe, with a face that was attractive even without makeup. Her sensuality was something innate, something that emanated from her naturally, and only over time – and after several disappointments – had she learned how to use it in a way she was happy with. Nowadays, she knew how exactly how men worked and held the reins of power confidently, but when it came to women… Well, when it came to women she still had some problems.

Even as a little girl, Zoe struggled to get along with other members of her own sex. A lot of girls didn't like her because, without ever meaning to, she made them feel as though they were in her shadow. Others tried to imitate her, and others still spread gossip that she was easy just because she was always surrounded by boys.

None of them had ever wondered what exactly *she* thought about her good fortune. In all probability, the answer would have surprised them.

She was, of course, grateful to the heavens, or to her parents, or to whoever the heck it was who had made things turn out the way they had and ensured that she had a beautiful face and a beautiful body — but beauty didn't always produce positive results. In fact, it was often a double-edged sword, and other people's mistaken belief that having a pretty face automatically meant having a perfect life had begun to irritate her.

If her pretty face had actually been any use then maybe at that moment she wouldn't have been in her old bedroom at her parents' house, about to spend yet another evening celebrating with the whole family -- great-uncles and great-grandparents included – but without a man by her side.

For a moment she found herself thinking of Clover, one of her few friends, who at that time was in Ireland with her wonderful Prince Charming, the actor Cade Harrison. In less than a month, Clo had managed to meet the toast of Hollywood and make him lose his head over her, and now the two of them were practically inseparable. With her long red hair and her dimples and her straightforward soap-and-water beauty Clover was like some kind of elf, yet her simplicity had succeeded where Zoe, with her knockout body and perfectly sculpted face, had always failed.

And what about Liberty? Even the stiff, serious owner of Giftland, always tightly wrapped in her dowdy business clothes, had had a faithful boyfriend for years.

She was the only one who was single – and she had been for centuries! When men looked at her, they didn't lose their heads, it was just that the blood flowed off to a quite different part of their bodies... Ah, if only brains could speak...

Sighing in irritation for the umpteenth time, Zoe threw the lip gloss back into her vanity case and turned away from the mirror. That night, she would have given anything to be celebrating the New Year with a man, intelligent or otherwise, rather than with her family. But lately, interesting guys seemed to have become a bit thin on the ground – or maybe she was becoming more selective.

The sweet, public love affair between Clover and Cade had undoubtedly worked against her: it was hard to settle for some boring fling when right before her eyes there was that example of a perfectly matched couple. Just like it was hard to come back to the family home from time to time and see the boundless love that still glowed in the eyes of her mother and father for each other after thirty years.

Why hadn't she inherited their good luck in love, instead of their good looks? It would have been a much more welcome gift.

A discreet and familiar knock at the door distracted her from her gloomy thoughts. "Come in, Mom," she said, sitting down on the bed so she could slip on her stiletto-heeled black boots.

Claire Mathison poked hers head around the door, a sweet smile on her beautiful and still youthful face.

"Your grandparents have arrived."

"I'll be right down."

"Ah… you're wearing the red dress, I see," said her mother waveringly. Zoe looked up and blinked, puzzled.

"It's New Year's Eve, I thought it suited the occasion. Why?"

"Oh, nothing, you look great. But, you know, great grandmom has decided to join us tonight…"

Zoe jumped up, startled.

"That old witch is *here*? Mom, you promised me she wouldn't be coming!" she protested.

"Well, that's what I thought! They told me that she was in hospital, I never thought she'd make such a quick recovery… I mean, she *is* ninety-six, after all!"

Claire looked over her shoulder then walked into her daughter's bedroom and closed the door behind her, on her face an expression halfway between amusement and sadness. "It won't be that bad, honey. It'll be over before you know it."

"No it won't!"

Zoe went to the old dark wooden closet and began anxiously rummaging through the few spare clothes she had left at her parents' house.

"She'll be on my case all night! She'll sit there staring at me, decide that I'm dressed like a hooker and then she'll give me the third degree to find out if I've finally found a guy to start a family with, and she'll start telling me what women used to be like back in her day, and then she'll tell me how happy and satisfied with their lives all her other great-granddaughters are… Who, by the way, seem to have much more sex than I do, judging by the amount of children they keep producing!"

Her mother chuckled. "Oh honey, that has *nothing* to do with how many children you have – otherwise you'd have a *hundred* brothers and sisters!"

"Mom, *please!*" cried Zoe, raising her eyes to the sky. "This is already bad enough, I don't want to spend the whole evening not being able to get the embarrassing idea of my parents going at it all the time out of my head!" Resignedly, she let her arms drop to her sides. "I've got nothing decent to wear, I bought this red dress especially for the occasion and I didn't think I'd need an alternative. I don't have time to go home, right?"

"You could, but you'd still have to walk past Maude the dragon." Her mother stroked her arm. "I just wanted to warn you that great-grandmom was here, honey – don't get yourself into a state about it. Your dress is fine. So come downstairs with your head held high and just grin and bear it for a few hours: at the stroke of midnight she'll be off to bed and you can relax."

"Easy for you to say," thought Zoe, as she watched her mother walk out of her room. Her mother had a caring and loving husband to make everything more bearable.

That evening was going to be a disaster! She could already see herself, sitting at the end of the long table, listening for the millionth time to boring old stories until the dinner was over. Then, like every year, they would pass the time until midnight playing some old-fashioned board game that would mean having to pair off with the only single male present: her eleven year old cousin, Victor.

Groaning, she began to pace around the small room, trying to think of a way to get out of all this. She would rather spend New Year's Eve alone in her Manhattan apartment than see it in nursing a nervous ulcer thanks to a woman who had been

5

around for almost a century! The seventh daughter of a very large Italian family who had emigrated to America many years before, Maude Mathison's fragile, delicate appearance didn't fool anyone: those small grey eyes were penetrating enough to make your blood run cold and her sharp tongue could put even the most rebellious member of the family in their place. And Zoe was the most problematic of all her countless great-grandchildren, so it was upon her that her great-grandmother focused all her attention. If she had known that old dragon Maude would be at the party, Zoe would have found a way to get out of it…

Suddenly, a solution flashed into her mind.

Why didn't I think of that before? Wasn't he always the answer to all her problems?

She had avoided inviting him to dinner so as not to take advantage of his kindness. She'd already involved him in Christmas Eve, an extremely boring evening spent playing Monopoly with the over sixties, and she hadn't had the heart to ask him for an encore. Even he was entitled to a bit of fun.

But this was an emergency… She absolutely needed him.

She grabbed her phone and called Eric, praying that he hadn't decided to return to Boston to celebrate with his family. If he was in New York, maybe she could convince him to save her life…

"It's a bit early to wish me Happy New Year, you could at least have waited until eleven," he said, with his usual irony. "Or maybe you've got bigger fish to fry and you're getting this out of the way so you don't have to be disturbed at the stroke of midnight?"

"I need you!" cried Zoe, hand on heart. "Don't abandon me this evening!"

"What happened?"

"Maude's here." There was no need to say anything else. Eric knew all the members of her family by heart, most first-hand, and the rest from hearsay. And her tone left no room to wonder how desperate she was.

"What can *I* do about it?"

"If you're not in Boston with your folks, if you don't have a girl to spend New Year's Eve with and if you're not in the process of having the most wonderful night of your life, get over here to my parent's house and spend the evening being my knight in shining armour!"

"You do realize that's like asking a kitten to take on a fire-breathing dragon? From the little I know of her, your great-grandmother will eat me up in one bite," sighed Eric.

"Please, I'm begging you, I'm *begging* you! I'm wearing a bright red dress that's going to earn me a place in the old woman's prayers for the next six months, and I can't change because all I've got here is a tracksuit and a pair of jeans!"

"Not the same pair that ripped open at Christmas dinner two years ago, leaving your butt hanging out in front of your great-grandmother… right?" Eric asked, the amusement in his voice audible.

"I think those got thrown into the fire by Maude herself about sixty seconds after I took them off," Zoe muttered. "The old bitch… They cost me seven hundred dollars!"

"In any case, your relatives are already there and I'm not. How could I possible help?"

"Come as quickly as you can. I can put up with them and keep them at bay for a few minutes," said Zoe, letting out a sigh of relief. "You know how much I love you, right?"

"I'll be keeping that in mind. Sooner or later, it'll come in handy," Eric muttered, before hanging up.

Zoe lay on the bed, looking at the floral motif wallpaper on the ceiling, a satisfied smile on her lips.

Eric Morgan, her hero, was coming: now, she could relax!

The words of her great-grandmother would bounce right off her with no effect now that she had him at her side. In fact, it would actually be enjoyable to make fun of her great–grandmom's pronouncements with Eric. With her best friend's assistance, she could handle anything – she wouldn't have to feel alone and she would have a young and interesting person to talk to. Even playing Risk would be bearable, because when Eric got involved in strategy games he was really hilarious!

Sometimes she wondered how she would ever manage to get by without him. She had known him for ten years now, and they were inseparable, despite their completely different characters. Zoe was really lucky to have him in her life.

Eric was a living example of 'the good guy': smart, serious, mature, well-behaved. Besides having a large, scholarly brain, he also had a huge, honest and sensitive heart – and in a world chock full of bullies, hypocrites and assholes, he was a rare gem. He was never boring or dull and didn't take himself too seriously… Well, to be totally honest, he *was* terribly fussy and *did* have a bit of an old-fashioned mentality in some ways, but he also knew how to be witty, engaging and ironic.

In the reality she knew, which was made up of hungry stares and clumsy come-ons, Eric was the exception: he was the only guy who looked her in the eyes and not just in the cleavage, the only one who never got touchy feely, the only one who treated her as a woman with a brain, not just as a body to possess.

He was the only one who had never made a move on her.

Shortly after she'd met him, Zoe had found herself almost hoping he would. At the end of the day, he was so cute, with relaxed good looks that could be improved with a little attention to detail, and for sure he was someone you could trust. Eric was a 'serious relationship' guy, but the idea of offering her something more than friendship never seemed to have flashed in his brain, and eventually Zoe had accepted their relationship for what it was: a real connection, durable and free of ulterior motives.

You don't change a winning team. And none of her relationships had ever lasted as long as the one with Eric – not even the one with Stuart Harris, her longest lasting ex-boyfriend. So why complicate things?

She leapt up out of bed when she heard her father's voice calling her from downstairs. There was no time now to analyze her relationships with men, she had to go downstairs to entertain her family and help her mother get dinner ready.

But, before leaving the bedroom, she found herself hoping that Eric wouldn't take too long to get there.

*

"I have to go, guys," said Eric, returning to his friend Danny's living room.

"But we've just ordered the pizza!" Danny protested, looking up from the laptop on his knees.

Eric handed him the beer he had opened just before the phone rang. "So you'll have to eat a few more slices – that's no great sacrifice."

"It means having more beer to wash it down with too," nodded Kevin, who was stretched out on the couch with a bottle in one hand and the remote control in the other. "Where are you going?"

"Judging by the speed with which he's ditching us, Ms Mathison must have requested his presence," said Danny confidently. "Am I right?"

Well aware of how it was useless to lie to his friends, who had known him for years, Eric nodded. "She's got problems with her family and I don't want to leave her to face them on her own on a night like this."

"And so you'll quite happily ditch us. What a buddy you are!" muttered Kevin, finishing his beer and reaching out towards Danny, who passed him another without even looking.

Eric snorted. "In a couple of hours you won't even remember your name, Kev. I doubt you'll miss me much."

"I won't, but Danny will, since he's practically a teetotaller. This sucks, I'll have to entertain myself."

"Just make sure you don't overdo it. I'm not holding your hand while you throw up," warned Danny. "My New Year's resolution is to get my head straight and to find a nice girl to spend my time with. Locking myself away in the flat every night to play video games like some damn nerd is starting to get really tedious! God help me, this is the *last* depressing New Year's Eve I'm going to be spending!"

"Hey, I'm intending to find a girl tonight myself, so be warned: if I'm not already in an alcohol-induced coma by midnight, I'm going out to pick up a woman."

"Kev, the way you talk it sounds like you're going to be chugging gallons of alcohol, but we all know that a couple of beers are enough to get you babbling away," snorted Eric, as he placed his belongings in his backpack. "Dumbass."

"Hey, look who's talking! I'd like to remind you, Four-Eyes, that you're going to let yourself be used as a doormat by a woman who's had you by the balls for the last ten years – and without even supplying you with any relief!"

"Will you remind me why we let him join our gang?" Eric asked Danny, with a bored expression.

Danny shrugged. "Because his dad was the dean of the university and we couldn't have him as an enemy? And because he gave me an action figure of a mummified Ronald Reagan?"

"And don't forget that when I moved here and we threw that first party, I managed to get you a girl each," added Kevin. "Something which you've never done, Eric, despite all the hot chicks you surround yourself with at work."

Eric shook his head in amusement. "I told you: Clover and Liberty are already taken." And before his friends could reply to his last sentence, he said goodbye and left.

*

He went upstairs to his own apartment and began to undress, heading for the bedroom. Ten minutes later he emerged wearing a stylish pair of jeans, a blue shirt and a sweater of the same color. It was the best he could do at such short notice.

As soon as he had left the building and flagged down a cab, he began to think about what his friends had said, and he sighed deeply. They were right: when Zoe Mathison called, he went running like a lightning bolt.

But he wasn't a doormat, the way they all thought – he was just a good friend. If someone he cared about was in need of a helping hand, he was always there for them. After all, dinner with his friends wasn't such a rare event, especially since Danny and Kevin lived in the same building as he did. They had an evening of pizza, beer and board games at least once a month in any case, without needing a special occasion to celebrate. Zoe, however, would die of boredom if she had to spend New Year's Eve alone with her large, conventional family.

She needed him more than those two single nerds who would quite happily spend their New Year's Eve eating junk food and watching *Star Wars* for the thousandth time without him. That's why he was running off to save her.

"Oh, who the hell are you trying to kid?" he snorted mentally, staring at the bright panorama that flashed by outside the window.

If he went running off like a madman every time Zoe snapped her fingers it was because he was crazy for real: crazily in love with her.

Kevin had a point: ten years pining after a woman who held his emotions in her hands, albeit unwittingly. It was his own fault for having gotten her used to it, for spoiling her like a child, initially hoping to prove something to her, and later because he simply couldn't help himself.

He didn't know quite why Zoe had so much power over him. Yes, she was beautiful, charming and sultry and possessed every conceivable physical gift, of course, but what attracted him to her was something else. Under that glowing patina of perfection, Zoe was also sweet, sensitive, sometimes insecure, and had an immeasurable need to feel loved. A need Eric could have fulfilled for a lifetime and beyond, with all the love he had inside him.

Zoe, however, had no idea of this, even though he felt as if he had a flashing neon sign on his forehead. Perhaps because she looked at him with the same attention as she might some weird bug, or because she deliberately ignored the issue. In any case, the result was the same: apart from as a friend, she was not interested in him, and Eric had by now resigned himself to being exclusively her official confidant.

All things considered, he accepted the situation with good grace. Or at least, he did until he found himself face to face with her. When he arrived in Soho and rang the doorbell of the Mathison residence, it was Zoe who opened the door. Eric only managed to stop his jaw from falling right to the floor because she had mentioned what she was wearing when they spoke on the phone.

That red dress was… woah! It wasn't that it was vulgar or flashy, it was that she managed to turn it into something breath-taking with her shapely figure, cat-like eyes and smile that could have put a demon on the path of righteousness… or made a devil out of an angel.

"Finally!" she exclaimed, grabbing his hand and dragging him into the house. "I told them that there was someone coming, but I didn't tell them who, just in case you had a mishap or changed your mind or something."

"And how would you have explained the sudden absence of the mysterious guest if I had?"

"Oh, trust me, I would have found someone… even if it meant going from house to house knocking on every door and begging any available man on my knees."

Eric didn't answer, but he clenched his teeth. He had no doubt that such a plan would succeed: Zoe would have been able to convince any man within a one mile radius to go along with her just by batting her eyelashes.

"Well then, why did she call you?" asked a voice inside his head.

Maybe because it was easier. It wasn't necessary for her to promise him anything in order to convince him to help her.

His mind split into two, one part imagining enjoying Zoe's hypothetical thanks and the other rebelling against the idea that she would provide sexual pleasure in exchange for a favor.

Zoe wasn't what his mom would have called a tramp. Ok, she did date a lot of guys – but that didn't necessarily mean she went to bed with all of them. And yet it was difficult not to jump to that conclusion when just a casual look from her seemed to promise paradise.

"You're acting just like all those idiots who ask her out!" he scolded himself. Wasn't that the reason that he watched over her every day, like a mother with her cub? To avoid other men committing the sin of indulging in too much self-esteem and exceeding the bounds of decency? All it took was a smile from Zoe for them to start thinking they were one step from heaven, for God's sake!

His confused thoughts were interrupted when Zoe started to undress him... literally. She didn't merely take off his jacket, she started taking off his sweater too. When she put her hands to the bottom of his shirt, Eric grabbed hold of them, torn between incredulity and excitement.

"What are you doing?" he stammered. At the uncertain, wavering sound of his voice, he tried to pull himself together and hide his desire behind his usual tone of irony. "I thought you wanted me here as backup for dinner, not because you were so desperate that you were going to jump on me in your parent's hall."

Zoe laughed heartily. "I'm desperate enough to jump on you, believe me, but not right now, with great-grandmother on the warpath in the next room." She gave him a sly look, dug her fingers into the waistband of his jeans and pulled his shirt out of his pants. "Jesus, you look like the son of a pastor! My relatives know me, they'd never go for it if they saw you looking so prim and proper."

"Go for what?" Eric asked in apparent confusion as she ran her fingers through his brown curls to muss them up a bit.

At that moment, Zoe's mother joined them. "Eric, how nice to see you!" she smiled, and embraced him.

"Sorry for being late, Mrs Mathison," said Eric, handing her the bottle of wine he had bought on the fly just before coming upstairs. "I had… problems?" he said, glancing uncertainly toward Zoe.

His friend smiled gently and took his hand. "Don't worry, we were about to serve up dinner, you've come just in time"

As soon as they entered the dining room, Eric found himself the center of attention. Twelve people, including grandparents, uncles and cousins, were sitting around the long table, and all seemed to be waiting only for him to sit down.

'Well, it's natural, I suppose. I did arrive late," he thought, as he took a seat next to Zoe. However, the eyes of what he decided must be the dreaded great-grandmother Maude were fixed on him in a way that made him feel very uneasy.

While the first course of what had every appearance of being a sumptuous meal was put on the table, Eric leaned over toward Zoe. "The dragon keeps staring at me, it's starting to freak me out."

"Don't worry about it and enjoy the food for the moment," she murmured, passing him a plate. "The worst is yet to come."

"Thanks for making me feel better," he muttered.

The 'worst' arrived shortly after the starters. Once she had run out of anecdotes regarding the growth of Zoe's little cousin's baby teeth, Maude Mathison turned her watery grey eyes on Eric, who snapped to attention almost reflexively. It was absurd that such a frail-looking woman could inspire such fear, but she most certainly did. In her eyes, which must once have been like Zoe's, there was something harsh and unyielding despite her very advanced age.

"What's your name, boy?" the old woman asked, looking at him.

Eric grabbed his glass of wine, trying to appear confident and at ease. "Eric Morgan, ma'am"

"And you are planning on being my great-granddaughter's future husband, are you?"

Eric's wine seemed to go down the wrong way. Zoe came to his rescue, giving him none too delicate pats on the back while her parents smiled calmly.

"Grandma, you could be a little more tactful. Coming out with things like that can scare a guy," Zoe's father protested mildly.

"They tell me that you're thirty-one, is that right? I can barely hear in one ear, but the other still works fine," said Maude, turning her gaze back to Eric, who was still struggling to get air into his lungs. "Samuel, your daughter told me that he was a bright, serious young man. Why would he be scared at hearing himself called the future husband of the woman he has chosen to love? At his age, my poor husband already had three sons."

An awkward silence fell over the room, only to be broken by Zoe's grandfather. "I met Eric at Christmas. I can assure you that he's a very nice guy, mother."

'Well I do not know him and I intend to make my own mind up about him," said Maude, raising her white eyebrows and turning to Eric. "Do you love my great-granddaughter? Or have you simply been entranced by the physical charms she seems to be so fond of putting on display?"

"I would die for Zoe," said Eric, between one cough and the next. "And I think I'm already halfway there," he added, hoarsely. Zoe let out a chuckle and continued to thump him on the back.

"I don't want her ending up with some spineless wimp who only wants to marry her because she knows how to charm men's feet out from under them. From what I understand, you were friends until a few days ago. What has changed, so suddenly?"

Once he had recovered himself a little, Eric stared at his friend's great-grandmother.

"As far as I'm concerned, nothing – I fell in love with her right from the very first moment. But to differentiate myself from the other guys who were always chasing after her I decided to wait and to court her slowly."

Yeah, so slowly that she didn't even notice! he said to himself. But he went on. "I assure you that your great-granddaughter's appearance is simply the icing on the cake for me. When I first met her she was wearing a dowdy waitress's uniform, but I fell in love with her just the same. Zoe's charm lies inside her, not outside."

He didn't trust himself to cast a glance in the direction of Zoe. Everything that came out of his mouth was the absolute truth, but there was no need for her to actually read it in his eyes.

"If you like her so much and not simply for her physical appearance, then why don't you stop her from dressing so provocatively? Women who are always putting themselves on display often lack self-esteem, or don't feel sufficiently appreciated. Perhaps you are not fulfilling your duties as a boyfriend properly, despite all these fine words?"

Zoe made to cut short the embarrassing scene but Eric put his hand on hers, still staring at her great-grandmother. "Your great-granddaughter would look the same even if she wore a garbage bag, believe me. At first I tried to convince her to cover herself up as much as possible but, when I realized that other men would look anyway, I stopped being jealous. Let them look all they like at what I have and what they never will."

If only that were true…

"Now do you understand why I love him so much?" cried Zoe, a broad smile on her face. Then she bent over to kiss him on the cheek. "You're my hero!" she whispered in his ear, sending a shiver racing down his spine.

Eric didn't answer, so focused was he on challenging Maude the dragon to contradict him. After a silent staring match that lasted a few long moments, she bowed her head with a regal nod in acceptance of the situation, and Eric sat back to enjoy his victory.

Though there wasn't much to be happy about, to tell the truth: with just one look, a ninety year old lady had understood his feelings, while her twenty-nine year old great-granddaughter hadn't noticed in ten years.

The situation was extremely disheartening.

Chapter 2

"I want to go," Zoe whispered in Eric's ear as she leant against his back. She thought she could feel him tensing up, but she was so confused that she couldn't really be sure. God, she had drunk so much! Drinking was the only way she had managed to make it to the end of that dinner – plus, her cousin Sarah's meatloaf was so awful that you needed to get plenty of wine down you just to be able to swallow the damn thing. If Eric hadn't been there to distract her, she would have probably collapsed on a sofa long before midnight and wouldn't have been capable of raising a glass to toast the arrival of the New Year.

But he *was* there, luckily! And he was so sweet and so great at dealing with her noisy family that for a moment – but only for a very brief one, of course – Zoe had found herself wondering why she had never tried to hit on him. He had loved her for ten years now, although only as a friend... Could he have loved her as a boyfriend too? And, most importantly, could *she* fall in love with Eric Morgan?

"God, your brain must be really drowning in wine if you're even *thinking* about something like that," she said to herself. She had been single for too long, obviously. In other circumstances – that is, if she'd had a boyfriend, hadn't been half-wasted and if Eric hadn't spent the whole evening talking passionately about her to her family's great amusement – she wouldn't be wondering what it would be like to date her best friend, especially not while she was resting her boobs on his shoulder...

"Good God!"

She straightened up rapidly, and the sudden movement made her feel dizzy. Eric stopped playing Risk – at which he was actually, strangely, losing – and peered at her through his spectacles.

"You want to go? Aren't we supposed to be having a toast with your family at midnight?"

Zoe snorted and frowned. "I want to go and see the countdown in Times Square! There are gonna be a ton of people, and music, and fireworks! Toasting the New Year in the middle of all that chaos would be cool... And staying in the house without being able to shout because you're not allowed to scare the old folks is definitely not."

"In that case, tell your parents that we're going and we'll get off," agreed Eric, shrugging his shoulders.

Zoe leaned towards him again. "You should be the one to tell them – they adore you already. You managed to stand up to the old dragon so they see you as some kind of hero now. They'll go along with anything you ask." Eric gave her a skeptical look and she smiled back at him. "You touched my grandmother's feelings, my aunt is already organizing my bottom drawer and my cousin asked if she can help me to look for my wedding dress. Even my parents started treating you like my real boyfriend at some point. I was almost about to start believing it myself!"

Eric didn't reply, and for a moment they stared into each other's eyes. Zoe felt dizzy again and blinked a few times. She wasn't sure that the wine was the only thing responsible for her feelings. But it had to be, right? Because the guy in front of her was just Eric!

He stood up and went to converse in a low voice with her parents, who nodded in approval. A moment later, Eric took her hands to help her to her feet and said: "Let's go, honey, we're going to go to see in the New Year in Times Square."

Zoe was as happy as a little kid; she grabbed his arm and let him lead her to the door, where Eric helped her on with her heavy jacket.

"Cover yourself up, it's going to be freezing in Times Square… and what you're wearing doesn't look particularly warm."

"You're not going to start getting 'possessive' now, right?" she joked, remembering what Eric had told her great-grandmother about the way she dressed.

"Your great-granddaughter would look just as great even if she wore a trash bag… When I realized that other men would look at her in any case, I stopped being jealous. They can look all they want – I don't care, because I know they will never have her."

Even though they weren't true, those words had touched her. Eric could be even fussier than Grandma Maude when it came to her clothes, but for a moment she had pretended to believe that he was the type of man who was proud to show off how beautiful his woman was, and she had enjoyed it.

"You're right, let's go then. I can't wait to show everybody the hottie I'll be seeing midnight in with this year," he said, with a strained smile on his lips.

*

They walked to the metro station chatting casually about the funniest moments of the evening. A few times he had to take her by the elbow because she was about to stumble in her high heels. Zoe was finally feeling free, although as tipsy as hell.

She loved her family, obviously, but she wasn't comfortable around them. Apart from her parents, who knew her and had always supported her, she often felt left out and different. Maybe they expected too much from her. They had always been very close to each other, linked by deep and long lasting affection. All the women in her family had married very young, none excluded. They had all started families and remained forever loyal to their men, with no regrets, ever. And their partners loved them too, unconditionally. Zoe hoped that one day she would enjoy the same happy destiny. Because, on the contrary, she was almost thirty and had never had a long-lasting, idyllic relationship. Her longest relationship had lasted for two years, with some highs and plenty of lows, and had ended so disastrously that ever since she had been steering clear of strong emotional ties. But that had been a long time ago, and she missed having real feelings, confusing emotions and a partner to shower her with attention and love.

What the hell! She had dated plenty of guys, but somehow she hadn't met the right one yet – was meeting a decent man *really* so impossible? And admitting her failure to her relatives got harder each time.

"What are you thinking about?" asked Eric as he helped her out of the metro.

"About my family. Clover's always been very envious of all my nosy and noisy relatives, who are always desperate to snoop into every detail of my life. While I would much rather not have anyone to answer to."

"Right, so is this the reason why you have temporarily promoted me to being your future husband?" he asked ironically.

Zoe smiled. "I was sick to death of feeling like the Mathison family's black sheep, so I thought that if I told them I had settled down with a boyfriend they would finally leave me alone. I'm constantly neglecting their hopes for me, and the situation is really starting to get unbearable." She looked at him with a contrite expression on her face. "Sorry for dragging you into this without even warning you beforehand… but you handled it brilliantly! Not even Cade, the great actor, could have done better than you!"

"Hmm… Yes, I must admit I acted perfectly… especially when I almost choked on my wine!"

Zoe chuckled and took his arm as they walked towards the crowded square together. "Maybe you could have avoided that, but even so, the evening was without a doubt better than usual, thanks to you. You really are my hero, Eric Morgan."

"And you really are drunk," he sighed.

Times Square was usually packed with tourists, but that evening the crowd was massive. Thousands of people filled every possible space, and they all stood looking towards a stage that had been set up at the foot of the central skyscraper; there, at six in the afternoon, the famous crystal ball had started ascending. Once it reached the top, the ball would start climbing down again for the countdown. Colorful maxi-screens lit up the faces of the crowd, the music was loud and the noise was infernal.

Conversation started to get difficult, but Zoe didn't mind: all the activity made her feel as though she was somehow coming back to life! New Year's Eve was one of the few celebrations she actually liked, probably because it wasn't a sentimental one and it gave her the sensation that something new was about to begin. Every year she would mentally list her resolutions, and, although she never actually kept any of them, she liked to think that in another twelve months she could take up the challenge again and possibly change her life for the better. She had often let someone talk her into leaving a note at the Victor Center, on 7th Avenue. All the colorful notes that people would stick on the Wishing Wall would then be turned into confetti and sprayed onto the crowd at midnight: that rain of hopes and dreams would apparently bring good luck.

That year she had forgotten to leave her wish there, but to be honest she didn't have any specific requests to ask of the universe. Maybe that was the reason why her dreams never came true: she wasn't sure of what she really wanted.

That night, though, maybe thanks to the alcohol she had drunk or because of the absurd situation at her parents' house, she decided to send a message to the sky.

"Let me find a decent man!" she wished, with her eyes closed.

Someone bumped into her, and she turned rapidly towards them. It was a guy, clearly pretty drunk, who turned to look at her too when he realized he had hit someone. He stared at her for a moment, and when he was finally able to focus he laughed stupidly. "Wow, you're hot!" he exclaimed.

"A man with whom I can fall in love, not the first idiot who comes along," Zoe added mentally, raising her eyes up to the sky.

As soon as the countdown started, she forgot about her melancholy thoughts and focused her attention only on the euphoria of the moment. She shouted, counted the seconds with the crowd, and laughed happily like everybody else. But when midnight came, accompanied by all the chaos, the shouts, the fireworks and the rain of confetti, she felt her eyes tearing up.

Almost everyone around her was kissing someone. It was a good luck ritual that she had performed quite often in the past with whichever man she had happened to be with. But that time, when she really needed it and wanted to give that ritual a deeper meaning, she was alone...

Eric found her hand and held it, and his smile warmed her. Dear, sweet Eric. It was almost as though he had some special kind of radar which allowed him to always know exactly when she needed comforting.

"Happy New Year!" he shouted into her ear, trying to avoid a group of partying people behind him who were about to stagger into them.

She saw his pale eyes behind the lenses of his glasses and felt her affection for him triple.

"Oh, what the hell!" Zoe thought suddenly: she was single, but there was a handsome guy with her. And she was desperate and drunk enough to do something stupid, like grabbing Eric's jacket by the collar, pulling him towards her and plastering her lips on his.

She had only wanted a chaste little kiss, nothing more. Some lip action that would make her feel less alone in such an exciting moment.

But Eric's mouth was so soft and warm... She hesitated one moment too long and suddenly the situation was out of control. She was squeezed among shouting people who were jumping up and down, trying to catch the colorful confetti while the lights of the fireworks illuminated their faces, and all they could hear was the American national anthem. All Zoe could think about, though, was the taste of Eric's lips, which were both soft and questing at the time.

He was kissing her... he was really kissing her!

She sighed in surrender, hugged his neck and lifted herself up on the tips of her feet to get closer to him. Even though she was tall and was wearing high heels, Eric was far taller than her. Strange, she thought in a quick glimpse of rationality, that she had never noticed how tall he was…

Eric's warm hand started caressing her hair and then the back of her neck, while his mouth opened wider and his kiss became more passionate. Zoe felt as though she was spinning in dense foggy pleasure and let a satisfied moan slip from her lips. She hugged him even closer and felt his arms surrounding her and almost lifting her off her feet, which provoked a pleasant feeling of lightness.

Wow… that was some kiss!

She almost didn't realize that a young guy had banged violently into her, until she was brought back to earth by feeling Eric pulling away and, although he was still holding her by the hips, taking a step backwards. Only then did her mind slowly start reasoning properly again.

She felt very embarrassed and confused and couldn't do anything but look him in the eye hoping to find some indication of what she should do. But what kind of sign was she looking for? Did she even want to find a sign at all?

Eric's face was as immobile as stone. He wasn't showing any emotion and his spectacles provided a good shield for his eyes since they were reflecting the light from the fireworks. What was he thinking? Was he as surprised as her by what had happened?

"Happy New Year!" she shouted to break the silence, remembering that a moment before she jumped on him, he had wished her the same.

He nodded and turned to watch the show, and the weird moment passed. But Zoe's confusion didn't. All the alcohol, sadness, music and chaos had already blended into a fatal cocktail for her, but the final touch had been that fabulous kiss… no wonder she was so out of it now.

When they managed to slip away from the infernal crowd and could finally walk side by side without being jostled by anyone, and when the noise started to fade into the distance, Eric looked at her. "Do you want me to take to you back your parents'?"

"No, I'd rather go to my place. I don't even think I can walk to Soho," Zoe mumbled. She really needed to be alone and sort out her thoughts, and her apartment was only a few minutes away.

They walked a few blocks, remaining close to each other but without touching. Eric had his hands in his jacket pockets and kept looking straight ahead, and Zoe couldn't really understand what mood he was in. She could have asked – they were friends, after all – but for the first time in many years she felt hugely ill at ease in his presence, so she didn't dare speak.

When they reached her apartment in the heart of Manhattan, Eric accompanied her to the door, but didn't look as if he wanted to go through it. Zoe looked at him while holding the door open, unable to decide whether to talk now, when she had still some alcohol in her veins, or to postpone any discussion to another time.

"Do you... do you want to come in?" she stuttered, playing for time.

Eric hesitated, and then shook his head. "Better not."

He was right, it was better if he didn't come in. But Zoe couldn't help but feel slightly disappointed by his refusal. Eric was a friend and the last thing they needed was to complicate things between them, especially knowing the state of mind she was in. All the events of that night had contributed to creating a surreal situation which really shouldn't be taken to its logical conclusion. What would she think of herself, and of Eric, if she woke up with him in the morning? She would probably regret it. She couldn't remember how many times she had felt bitter when she had woken up with some guy she couldn't care less about, and who she had only used to try and fill the emptiness she felt inside.

Eric was different. He was an important presence in her life, she couldn't just use him to fulfil her sudden need for company. And he had just shown her that he obeyed a strict moral code: he would never take advantage of her sudden weakness, not even if he was desperate or completely mad about her... Which, of course, he wasn't.

So she forced herself to smile and took a step backwards. "I'll call you tomorrow then... If I manage to wake up! I'm starting to get a huge headache so I guess I'm going to be asleep for most of the day."

"Sure," he replied, "talk to you tomorrow."

Did it really sound like a threat or was she just being paranoid?

Eric mumbled 'goodnight' and left, leaving her finally alone and able to breathe again, but her hands kept shaking and she really needed something to calm her down.

The only thing she had in her fridge was a bottle of white wine, so she poured herself a full glass of the stuff and while she sipped at it she leant on the windowsill and stared at the fireworks from various areas of the city that were still lighting up the sky, although without really seeing them.

What had gotten into her? Was it possible that a vague sense of melancholy and some inner solitude had been enough to make her behave in such a horrible way? And with Eric! The only person she really trusted, the only one she would never, under any circumstances, want to hurt. She would never forgive herself if their relationship was spoilt because of a reckless kiss.

But he did kiss me back, a voice in her head said. "Well, yes, that doesn't mean anything. He's still a man," she grumbled. And she knew men well enough to know none of them would ever miss the opportunity to put their hands on a woman. But the idea of Eric being just as much of a pig as the rest of them was still upsetting. Maybe she had idealized the guy too much, and now imagining him responding to a purely physical impulse was disturbing.

Taking her glass of wine with her, she walked over to the sofa and sat down. She stretched out on the soft white leather and switched the TV on in an attempt to take her mind off things. She continued to sip her wine, only now directly from the bottle. She was feeling cold and somewhat nauseous, and her head kept spinning. She knew that drinking more would only make things worse and that she would sorrowfully regret it the following morning, but every time she thought of calling it a night and going to bed, the chaos in her mind suddenly vanished to make space for only one thing: the memory of the breath-taking kiss she had exchanged with Eric, and she felt more and more like crying. So she held on to her bottle and watched the flickering TV screen until she passed out with exhaustion and fell into a dreamless sleep.

*

He felt as if he had been staring at his phone for the whole day. He had actually managed to sleep, but not for long enough and not well. At some point during the day, he had even eaten while watching the TV… but he couldn't remember what, or even what he had been watching. His mind was focused on only one thought: he had kissed Zoe.

He had really kissed her… passionately! And she had kissed him back, moaning in pleasure in a way that had almost made him lose his mind. But the most incredible thing was that Zoe herself had kissed him first. She had made the first move.

Eric got up from the sofa and ran his fingers through his messy hair. He had tried to find a plausible explanation for what had happened, because he didn't want to get his hopes up only to have them dashed, but his heart kept pounding in his chest and it was hard to control it. He knew that he had to stop feeling so happy, though, and get his feet back on the ground.

First of all: Zoe had been drunk, and for this reason hadn't really known what she was doing.

Second: he had helped her with her family by pretending they were a couple, so there was a chance she had just been showing her gratitude.

Third: celebrating New Year's Eve in Times square was a particularly easy way to let yourself get carried away by your emotions, and that could be another reason why Zoe had decided to observe the tradition she had always observed in the past – that of kissing a man at midnight.

All three of these explanations seemed plausible, which also made them depressing. Moreover, his illusions had been systematically shattered over the past few years, so he doubted very much that things would be different this time.

He sat back down on the sofa, discouraged. He knew very well that Zoe hadn't suddenly fallen in love with him. He had just found himself in the right place at the right time. It was a sad hypothesis, but definitely the most probable one.

The thing that made him anxious was not finding out that their kiss hadn't meant anything to her, but realizing, instead, how important it had been for him.

He had been dreaming of kissing Zoe for ten years. Ten! Only a few hours ago his dream had seemed unreachable, something that could exist only in his fantasies. And sometimes you're even scared of a fantasy turning into reality, because you know that it might disappoint you.

But that kiss hadn't disappointed him at all. On the contrary, it had been far better than he'd imagined it would be. For all those years he had been trapped by his feelings for a woman to whom he could only be a friend, and now that he knew the taste, warmth and softness of her lips he felt even more like a prisoner than before.

He was hopeless.

"Why are you getting yourself down this way? She must have enjoyed kissing you, judging from the way she kept at it," he thought to himself, in an attempt to be optimistic.

Why would Zoe ignore what had happened? They were inseparable and they shared a deep affection for one another. She trusted him and asked for his help every time she had a problem. She had told her family that they were engaged, then she had kissed him… She had even invited him inside after he had walked her home. After all that, why would she find the idea of making their relationship more intimate strange?

Maybe because she never seems to have wanted that before?

Having convinced himself of the impossibility of a happy ending of any kind, he now had to think about what their relationship would look like from next Monday onwards – how would it change? Zoe had the excuse of having drunk too much alcohol, but how could he justify the fact that he had kissed her so passionately right in the middle of a crowded square?

He had given her all that he had in those few instants. And she would surely have understood everything by now and decided to keep him at a distance so as not to give him any false hope. In conclusion, their relationship was ruined forever.

That was the reason why he had never admitted his feelings for her. He'd preferred to have her as a friend rather than not have her in his life at all.

"Ok, you need to come up with an excuse of your own," he sighed, covering his face with his hands. He could say that he'd been a little tipsy too, even though he was practically teetotal. Or he could say he had only gone along with the kiss out of gallantry...

"And anyway, she kissed me first!" he muttered.

But that didn't mean that you were allowed to put your tongue in her mouth!

He didn't stand a chance. He was totally screwed.

His mobile phone vibrated in his pocket, and his heart missed a beat. It was her. He was absolutely sure that it would be even before he saw her name on the screen.

He cleared his throat and answered the phone, trying to sound casual.

"Hey, finally..."

You damn fool, now it sounds like you couldn't wait to hear from her! he scolded himself.

But it's the truth – you couldn't, the usual annoying voice in his head reminded him.

"I didn't think I'd ever manage to get up today. What time is it?" murmured Zoe, in a voice so hoarse that he shivered when he heard it.

"It's five in the afternoon."

"Wow... I slept for fifteen hours straight! That's why I feel so completely out of it now."

"Are you ok?"

"I have a headache, nausea, I feel like I ate my own socks, my bones ache because I fell asleep on the sofa and on my cheek I can see the mark that the neck of the bottle left. And I have no idea how a bottle ended up on my sofa."

Eric had a sudden suspicion.

"So you don't remember if you carried on drinking after you arrived home, right?"

"Apparently not. Did I drink that much yesterday evening?"

"I guess about a bottle of wine during dinner, and then there were a few toasts after that."

"Jeez, I'm not used to drinking that much. I mean, I like a glass of nice wine every once in a while, but yesterday I must have drunk *way* too much. Do you understand the effect that family reunions have on me now?" sighed Zoe. "By the way, I guess I didn't tell them that I was not going back to their place. That would be why my mom filled up my answering machine with worried messages. In the last one she finally said you told them where I ended up."

Eric was sitting stiffly on the sofa. "Yes, your mother called me early this morning. I should have called her last night... but I forgot."

"You shouldn't have to do anything at all – I'm a grown up, I should solve the problems I create myself. I already forced you to take part in that farce to keep mad Maude quiet. I guess you were exhausted too last night."

"God, yes... I was so all in I was barely myself."

Great, good move. If the subject comes up you can use that excuse to justify the passionate kiss you gave her! he thought.

But it seemed as though she didn't remember it at all... or was she just play-acting?

"I can never thank you enough for covering my back. I promise I'm not planning on accepting any invites for dinner from my relatives on your behalf! I am going to let a reasonable amount of time pass, then I'll let them know we decided to go back to being friends like we used to be. In the meantime, I hope I'll have solved the problem. I mean, ok, I might look like a zombie today but I'm not usually that hideous, am I? Sooner or later I'm going to find a man who actually wants to be with me."

If she had stabbed him in his chest it would have been less painful.

Eric's hand clenched tightly into a fist and he closed his eyes. "I am sure you will," he forced himself to reply, even though he would have rather have smashed the phone against the wall and not spoken for a month.

"By the way, I think I dreamt of you last night," Zoe laughed. "And it was a pretty peculiar dream!"

"Was it? What did you dream?" asked Eric, suddenly paying attention again.

"I don't really remember the context, I only remember we were kissing each other. I know, crazy, right? Wine and parties obviously have a weird effect on me."

Eric didn't reply, and his silence made her curious.

"It was a dream, wasn't it? Don't tell me that the alcohol made us do something stupid… right?"

Her voice sounded almost frightened. Why? Was the thought of kissing him so horrifying for her?

"God, Eric, say something! Your silence is scaring me. Did we really do it then?!"

"We didn't, don't worry. I was just going through yesterday evening in my mind and I can't remember doing anything like that," Eric lied, despising himself for it. "I'd had a few drinks too, though less than you, and you know very well that two glasses of wine are enough for me to feel like I'm practically Superman. But I think that if you'd jumped me I'd remember it pretty clearly. I mean, I even remember the moment your uncle fell asleep and his face ended up in his plate…"

"Hey, babe, it's not *me* who jumps men – it's usually the other way round…" snorted Zoe in an irritated voice. "So, yes, it must really have just been a dream, then," she added, sounding relieved, and that made Eric suspicious.

"A nightmare, you mean. It must have been horrible to dream that you were kissing an awkward geek like me," he said, trying to muffle the bitterness in his voice.

"You couldn't be more wrong. It was an *awesome* kiss! Maybe I should actually give you a try! I'm missing a nerd in my collection of men." Eric hesitated, wondering if, by any chance, she was in fact testing the water, but then Zoe laughed. "I'm joking, Eric! Hey, I hope I didn't make you uncomfortable and that you're not blushing right now! You can relax, I like our relationship the way it is and I wouldn't change it for the world."

Inside him, he heard a noise that sounded like the shattering of his dreams.

"Ok, I guess I'd better hit the shower and get back to being human," continued Zoe, blissfully unaware of just having pierced his heart with her stilettos. "Do you want to come over here for dinner later?"

She had just made a casual proposal, like so many times in the past, and only a few hours earlier Eric would have surely accepted it. Not that night though, he wasn't really in the mood. He needed time to work through all that had happened and hide his silly ideas back inside the armour he had built up around himself over years of resignation.

"I can't, I'm going out with some friends tonight. I dumped them yesterday to come and help you, I can't do the same today too."

"God, I'm such a selfish bitch. One day, you'll get tired of me and tell me to go to hell," sighed Zoe. "I promise I won't behave like that any more."

"Great, that's good to hear! Because I am not your freaking doormat, and I won't always be there ready to jump every time you snap your fingers only to be thrown aside like an old shoe when you don't need me. It's about time you found yourself another servant!"

At least, that was what he *should* have replied to vent all the anger and bitterness consuming him inside.

What he *actually* replied, however, was, "Don't worry, I'm happy to help. Anyway, that's what friends are for isn't it?"

"The only thing I remember for sure about last night is saying to you that you're my hero. And I can confirm it, Eric Morgan: you are amazing. And I am such a lucky person to know you."

Zoe blew him a kiss and hung up, leaving him staring at the phone with sad eyes.

That was what he had wanted, wasn't it? To not have to explain why he had kissed her so passionately, not ruining their relationship forever and beyond any hope of possible recovery, not feeling rejected. Zoe had given him the perfect alibi, since she thought she had just dreamt the whole thing.

Problem solved, then. He could go back to pretending he was just a friend without either of them having to feel embarrassed. So why did he feel as if he'd been hit by a truck?

A truck which had then reversed back over him?

Chapter 3

"I hate Valentine's Day," echoed Zoe's voice around the shop, which was temporarily silent. Her colleagues all turned to look at her.

Clover stopped decorating the window with cloth hearts to glance at her in amusement. "Yeah, right – you're saying that only because you don't have a boyfriend to celebrate it with."

"Hey, dating a super-cool actor doesn't entitle you to make fun of your friends," protested Zoe, pulling a threatening face.

"It's what you say every year, Zoe. And every year, I reply in exactly the same way," smiled Clover. "Valentine's Day is just an excuse for people to show their feelings."

"It's stupid. People should show their feelings every day, not just once a year. Every Valentine's Day, the average American man spends hundreds of dollars on dinners, boxes of chocolates, flowers and cards. Are you telling me that women wouldn't appreciate that type of stuff in January or July too?" demanded Zoe, crossing her arms over her chest and shaking her head in disapproval. "Women should be courted every day, all the time. You shouldn't just be romantic when circumstances force you to."

"Oh, I agree with all of that. All that I meant was that it's nice to let yourself get carried away by the romantic atmosphere of Valentine's Day. Same goes for Christmas: the right atmosphere can make all the difference."

"Yeah, well I hate Christmas too," Zoe reminded her friend.

Clover rolled her eyes and went back to decorating the shop window.

Zoe leaned on the counter and gave a long sigh. "And anyway, not having a boyfriend for Valentine's Day is really depressing."

"That's your problem, Zoe: you don't know what you want," burst out Eric, without lifting his eyes from the pack of pictures he was checking. Zoe spun round towards him, her grey eyes half closed.

"So even our little nerd here has a theory, apparently."

"You'd have one too, if you just stopped moaning for five seconds."

Zoe frowned. "I'm *not* moaning, I'm just saying things the way they are."

"What is the problem, anyway?" asked Liberty, sorting the piles of photos in front of her into four separate groups. "You could have all the men you want, if you wanted them, and you don't like Valentine's Day anyway. So what the hell are you griping about?"

"Because in two weeks everybody will be off having their little romantic dates and I'll be all on my lonesome again!"

"So you're saying that I'm right," said Clover. "Even though you think Valentine's Day is a completely manufactured way to sell cards and teddy bears, you *still* think that it would be nice to celebrate it with a romantic dinner."

"You're better off on your own than in bad company," muttered Eric, glancing over at Zoe. "And given your terrible taste in men, I'm pretty sure that spending Valentine's Day alone can only be a good thing for you."

"Oh don't be so melodramatic. The men I date aren't *that* bad."

"Let me just remind you of the last two: Jordan Edwards and Tommy Parks."

Clover pretended to throw up and even Liberty coughed lightly at the sound of those names. Zoe waved away their reactions with a hand, as though they were making a fuss about nothing.

"Ok, Jordan might not have been exactly what you'd call classy and Tommy was maybe a little obsessed with my butt, but…"

"Not exactly classy and only a *little* obsessed with your butt?" asked Eric with a smirk. "The first one was always burping in public."

"He couldn't help it, it was an accident…"

"And the second one kept his hand on your ass as though he thought he might fall over if he didn't. As well as not being able to lift his eyes above the level of your cleavage. I bet he wouldn't even have been able to tell you what color your eyes are!"

"Come on, you're talking about the two most extreme cases, they were certainly not the rule," snorted Zoe.

Eric raised his eyebrows over the tops of his spectacles. "Those were just the ones you went out with last *month*. I could go on for hours."

"Do you really remember all the men that I've dated?" she asked, looking perplexed.

"Yes, because I like to train my mind, not my biceps," mumbled Eric, turning his attention back to the photographs.

"Of course, our pet scientist! But remember that girls like muscles, so maybe you should think about improving them too and not just your brain."

"I think that I can aim for something more in life than a girl who faints over a set of sculpted deltoids."

"Like who? What kind of girl would you like in your life?" asked Zoe. She smirked. "Let me guess: an intellectual like you is bound to be looking for another bookworm. She'll have to have a Master's degree, of course, and not be too bothered about her looks, and she must know absolutely nothing about makeup and clothes. And she'd better always be ready to launch into conversations about science, computers, philosophy and even politics! Just to sum it up: she must be deadly boring. You don't want her to be a virgin too, do you?"

"You know what, Zoe, you don't have to be unattractive to be intelligent or to be able to talk about politics. Stop putting yourself down," said Eric with fake kindness.

"And stop putting us down too," added Liberty. "Clover and I are pretty *and* we're intelligent, and I guess I could even say the same about you."

"You *guess*?" asked Zoe pretending to be outraged. "You're going to pay for this when you least expect it. Anyway, yeah, I feel intelligent enough, even if I *don't* have a Master's degree."

"In that case, the problem must lie elsewhere," cut in Eric. "Maybe you think that a guy with underdeveloped muscles like me can't attract intelligent girls who are pretty too, hmm?"

Zoe turned to look at him in surprise. "I never said anything like that," she said in shock. "And anyhow, you're not that bad, dear Brainbox, even if your glasses *do* make you look like some stuffy high school teacher!" she added, giving him a wink.

She wasn't lying – Eric actually was really cute. He was tall and had a slim, athletic figure, brown curly hair and blue-green eyes. He had plenty of potential but just didn't seem to be interested in showing it off. The glasses that made him look like a laboratory researcher were constantly perched on his straight nose while his body was always hidden under casual clothes. As a result, he looked like the stereotypical serious and intelligent good guy, and that made him appeal to many girls. Unfortunately, he was too shy to take advantage of the fact.

While Eric was mumbling something incomprehensible in reply to Zoe's comment, Clover finished off fixing up the shop window and looked at her sweetly. "Why don't you prove your intelligence and stop dating men just because they happen to be good looking? If you aim a little bit higher, sooner or later you'll be bound to find a man to spend Valentine's Day with."

"Coming from the woman who's currently dating one of the most lusted after men in the U.S., that advice rings a teensy bit hollow," muttered Zoe.

"There's more to Cade than just being handsome."

"It's pointless trying to convince her, Clo," sighed Eric. "She has to go out with guys who pump themselves full of steroids and have absolutely nothing in their heads, otherwise she can't control them."

"What do you mean?" hissed Zoe.

"I mean that the self–confident mask you wear when you meet people hides a very insecure person who prefers dealing with vacuous guys so that she can feel better about herself. And since the only man you've ever actually fallen in love with wasn't dressed like an asshole and didn't have pumped-up muscles but a Master's degree in Medicine, you decided that cavemen are more suitable for your needs because they don't have enough brains to hurt you." Eric looked her straight in the eyes with a serious expression on his face.

"If it's a man's intelligence that scares you then you should know that Harris had a lot less of it than you credit him with – otherwise he wouldn't have done what he did to you. Maybe it's time you let go of your past and started looking to the future."

Touched by those words, Zoe didn't reply.

Eric was right. Who knew her better than him, anyway? He had been listening to all her complaints and putting up with her outbursts since university. Lately, though, he'd been a lot less patient with her and they seemed to be arguing for no reason at all.

Sometimes she thought it was strange that their relationship had lasted so long. They couldn't have been more different from one another! But they had bonded immediately, no matter how strange it seemed: she was a pretty waitress, always surrounded by suitors, while he was a lonesome physics and informatics student, taciturn and shy. He had quickly become her best friend and the only one who had supported her on every occasion. He had consoled her when Stuart Harris, the only guy she had ever fallen in love with in her whole life, had broken her heart by cheating on her repeatedly with her best friend and since then had been putting up with her, and especially with her hysterical hunt for a man – an obsession that had led her into ruinous relationships with the wrong men.

Maybe he had finally had enough and didn't want to babysit her any more. Was that the reason why he had been so touchy lately?

The idea was terrifying to her: Eric was the only person she trusted unconditionally. She didn't get on particularly well with other women and apart from Clover and Liberty she didn't have many friends, so losing Eric's affection and support would have left her feeling desperately alone.

His unusual coldness and distance were hurting her. It wasn't normal for him to be like that, and he would never usually have spoken about such delicate matters in public.

He seemed to have read her mind and gave her a rather contrite look. "Hey, sorry – I went too far."

That made Zoe feel a lot better – how could she feel hurt by someone who would apologize for just telling the truth? Her good mood restored, she smiled at him brightly the way she always did – and the way that allowed her to conquer the heart of any man of any age. "I'll accept your apologies when you do something for me," she joked.

Eric suddenly raised his brown eyebrows. "Something like what?"

"Well, if I can't find anyone to go out with in the next few days, you could take me to dinner on Valentine's Day."

Eric looked up to the sky. "Right, like I've never done *that* before."

"Hey, don't act so smart, it would be a mutual favor. It'd be a fun evening between friends and people would think that we were a couple, and that way we'd both save face."

It was almost a tradition: when both of them found themselves single, they spent their time together. Zoe couldn't remember how many times Eric had stepped in to stop her getting drunk alone. He had put up with accompanying her to family celebrations, stepping in for dates to take over from some partner who had stood her up at the last minute, to Valentine's dinners all those years when they were both single, and they had even gone on holiday together! In other words, Eric Morgan was the man she had spent the most time with – he was her longest lasting relationship… and they hadn't even slept together!

She felt the need to demonstrate her affection to him, so leaned down to kiss him on the cheek. "I don't know what I'd do without you."

Eric pushed his glasses up his nose the way he always did when he was embarrassed.

"You don't need to sweet-talk me – I'll take you to dinner."

Their conversation was interrupted by the sound of the bell indicating that someone had come into the shop.

Zoe raised her eyes and smiled at the new client, and when she saw that it was a handsome blond guy of about six feet tall, she immediately smoothed out her wool skirt and primped her dark bob haircut.

"God, look how *cute* he is! I'll deal with him."

Liberty sneaked out from behind the counter and headed to the upper floor. "We had no doubt that you would," she giggled with a weird smile.

Zoe turned to the client. "Welcome to Giftland! How can I help you?"

The man looked her over from head to toe and smiled. "There are a lot of things you could help me with, but right now your smile will do just fine," he said playfully.

Zoe chuckled and went into seduction mode.

"So I guess I'm going to be free the evening of Valentine 's Day after all," muttered Eric as he walked past her on the way to his office.

Clover followed him.

"Let's not make snap judgements – maybe she won't like him." But at the sight of the look Eric shot her, she sighed. "OK, I'll just shut up."

Zoe ignored her colleagues' comments and stood in front of the new customer, smiling all the time. It had become a habit for her: she would feign interest in any attractive men who happened to enter the shop, flirting with them and doing her best to appear attractive. It was almost like a sort of hobby and a way of boosting her self-confidence. Lately, she'd really needed it.

The New Year hadn't started out great, to be honest, and over the last few days she had felt really agitated and restless. New couples seemed to appear out of nowhere and seeing them everywhere made her feel lonely. And what was worse was that her relatives couldn't stop congratulating her on the 'fantastic new boyfriend she had found', and it felt like an unbearable weight in her stomach.

*

It had been a mistake to pretend that Eric was her boyfriend. Doing it had meant actually finally satisfying her family's expectations, but it was all thanks to Eric and not to her. He was a perfect old-fashioned gentleman and had behaved impeccably, saying all the right things at the right time, and he had managed to do it all so naturally. Zoe was sure that was the way he usually treated his girlfriends, although she had never seen him with any of them. He didn't have new relationships as often as her, but when he did, she was sure that he put a lot more into them than she did.

Zoe hadn't informed her relatives that she and Eric had 'broken up' yet – she was waiting to find a real boyfriend to take home to them first. But it was absolutely impossible to find someone even more perfect than her best friend.

And most importantly, it seemed as though it was impossible for her to fall in love again.

It had just never happened again after Stuart, although, thinking about it rationally, she wasn't even sure if she had ever really loved him either. The slimy pig had managed to seduce her with thousands of words and with his charm and his fancy clothes, with candlelight dinners and surprises... But then he had ended up in bed with her best friend right under her nose. Any feelings she'd had for him had disappeared the moment she had found out, together with all her trust in men. From that moment on, she had protected her heart – probably *over*protected it, to be honest – and she had never trusted intelligent and charming men again – she knew that they were able to wound her in subtle ways she had no defenses against.

What she needed were less polished, rougher guys. They were the best company for someone looking for some fun, and they wanted what everybody wanted from her: a bit of gratifying sex and a nice trophy to show off to their friends. The difference was that they were honest enough not to pretend they were looking for something more. With them she could always be in charge and always be the one who dumps the other first. Obviously she wasn't exactly over the moon about her love life. Ok, those brief, meaningless relationships were fun, and sometimes even physically satisfying, but they didn't really give her anything. Even though she was well aware of all that, though, she seemed to be incapable of finding herself more serious relationships. It was true that she found it hard to really let herself open up nowadays, but it was also true that nice guys seemed to give her a pretty wide berth. They were probably intimidated by the apparent self-confidence, the beauty and the sex appeal that she seemed to emanate almost unconsciously.

Take off her makeup and her sexy dress and you'll see, she's not that special.

Women like her aren't good in long-term relationships; they're never going to be satisfied with just one man for the rest of their lives!

A woman like that has nothing except her looks to use to get a guy!

She'd heard people whispering things like that so many times over the past few years, especially women. It had hurt her at first, but then she decided to ignore those malicious voices and not to change just to please others.

Anyway, she wasn't doing anything wrong: she was a grown-up who was perfectly entitled to take whatever life had to offer to her for as long as she wanted to. What the hell was wrong with going out with a handsome guy? It wasn't like she was married or engaged, she was completely free and she was responsible. She could choose for herself, that's why she would select her prey and take the best from each of them before moving on to the next. And dating a lot of guys was also a way to try and find someone who she thought deserved her love. How else was she supposed to find the right one? There was no point just standing in a corner and acting like some shy virgin with a head full of silly romantic dreams.

She pushed all those useless thoughts out of her head and focused on the situation at hand. The guy in front of her was tall and muscular with a charming face and very beautiful dark eyes. His voice was mellow, his hands big and his smile captivating. He looked like many of her ex-boyfriends, especially in the way he dressed and behaved like a predator. That predictability, though, was reassuring for her. Flirting with men like that was easy – a few moves from her were enough to snare them and she could pick up all the information she needed with a couple of questions. Sometimes she didn't even need to sleep with them to work out that they weren't suitable for her needs. Contrary to her reputation as a huntress, the number of men she had actually slept with was less than half of the number of men she had dated.

The customer told her his name was Evan, and the piercing looks he gave her, the classic lines he came out with and the mannered gestures made it clear right from the off that he was interested. He was obviously one of those men who are only looking for fun. She could have gotten rid of him in two seconds, because it was as plain as the nose on his face that he wasn't the type of man to fall in love with. But Valentine's Day was getting close... And she just couldn't stand the idea of being alone on Valentine's Day again. She had never had a really good one. Every Valentine's Day, she always ended up settling for any guy who had dared to ask her out, or she had gone out for dinner with Eric. Spending the evening with her best friend had always turned out to be far more stimulating than a night out with another stallion in heat – at least Eric and she knew how to have fun together.

After observing Evan's expression she almost thought of giving up immediately and opting for pizza with Eric, but the idea of having to beg for her friend's attention again was enough to convince her to go through with the farce. She had already asked too much of him on New Year's Eve, and the fake relationship with Eric had only intensified her desire to have a serious relationship with a smart guy. While she'd been acting she'd almost felt as though it were possible to actually be someone's special person – and the idea of it had even made her have that outrageous dream about Eric! She couldn't risk becoming dependent on the poor guy, nor could she take advantage of his kindness every time she felt alone. If she wanted to go out with someone she had to roll up her sleeves and get to work.

She smiled, half sad and half amused, while she focused on her new prey. Her know-it-all colleague was most likely back in his office celebrating, she thought, having realized he didn't have to take her out to dinner for Valentine's any more…

*

The pile of photographs landed on his desk with a thud, his chair was dragged back abruptly and a drawer yanked open too violently. He knew he must look gloomy, just like he knew that Clover's big eyes were looking at him kindly.

"Not a word," he ordered, without even looking at her.

Clover was leaning against the door of the office, watching the corridor with one eye. She smiled sweetly. "You know it's not going to last."

"Of course I know it's not going to last. She's going to sleep with him a couple of times then dump him. There's no need to be upset over something so trivial," said Eric sarcastically while he switched his computer on.

"Maybe she won't even sleep with him. You heard her: she just doesn't want to be alone for Valentine's Day. I was half expecting her to force herself to fall for the first flashy guy she bumped into. It's not the first time she's done something like this."

Feeling his usual headache coming on, Eric pinched the top of his nose just under his glasses between his thumb and index finger. "I was expecting the same thing."

Clover took a step towards him. "Eric, you should do something."

"Like find a new job, move away from New York and forget all about her once and for all, right? Yes, I agree with you: I should."

"*Or…* you could tell her how you feel and keep the escaping option as plan B in case she gives you an answer you don't want to hear."

"Why would I make a fool of myself for nothing? We already know what she thinks of me." He remembered Zoe sighing in relief when he told her she had only dreamt that New Year's Eve kiss and felt an awful acidic burning in his stomach.

"She adores you, and you know it."

"Sure, as a stand-by." Eric steepled his fingers in front of his nose and stared straight at his computer screen. "To her I'm just some sort of cute teddy bear to hug when she feels alone or scared. A comfort blanket. The kind of guy she is really attracted to is the one she's talking to right now!" he said, pointing to the door. "I'm not athletic enough, or blonde enough, and maybe not even manly enough for a woman like her."

"Don't say that…"

"It doesn't matter, really. I've been watching the same crappy movie for years now. Sometimes it bores me, sometimes it upsets me, but at the end of the day, I'm the one willingly choosing to watch it, right? I'll be ok in a minute."

Clover heard the sound of footsteps coming down the corridor and shrugged.

"Whatever you say."

Liberty entered the office to assign them their tasks for the following morning. Even if it was still only early afternoon, she liked to organize their work ahead of time, because that way she could have everything under control and avoid disappointing their clients.

When she saw only Eric and Clover, she peered around in search of their other colleague.

"Is Zoe still flirting in the shop?"

"Yes, she is," answered Eric. "Actually I was meaning to ask you if you could please keep her away from me for the rest of the afternoon: I don't think I can bear to hear all the gossip about her *wonderful* encounter with the latest stud."

"You're supposed to be going to Mrs Morrison's house to fetch those photo albums, remember? So go and get them, if you want."

"Great." Eric forced himself to smile at Liberty, who didn't have a clue that he was in a bad mood, and set about quickly finishing off some stuff he had to do before leaving Giftland. He really wanted to go before Zoe had a chance to come into his office and start telling him all the juicy details of her chat with Mr Muscle. A few minutes later he walked across the shop floor and slowed down when he was about to reach the door. She was still there, flirting with that idiot among the shelves and wearing a wool dress that revealed all her curves, totally unaware that she held his heart in her beautifully manicured hands. And why should she suspect, come to that? He had managed to hide his feelings for her pretty well for all those years.

Once outside, he took a deep breath of the bitter February air and let the New York crowd absorb him.

The cold air, the people coming and going and the stroll cleared out his mind and allowed him to think a bit more rationally.

Zoe Mathison was a wonderful girl, and not just physically. She was extremely beautiful, sexy, chic, funny, and she even smelled good... But she'd only turned into a femme fatale in the last few years when she had started to devote more time to her looks, her attitude and even her facial expressions. Eric had known the younger Zoe, though, the waitress at the Boston

University coffee shop, the same girl who used to work until late in the hope of saving enough money to be able to move to Manhattan. He had learned to value the insecure Zoe, the one who had trouble relating to other girls of her age and who didn't know how to react to boys' attention.

Back then he'd just been a poor nerd and a creature of habit who would visit the coffee shop every afternoon at the same time. He used to go there to study… and to look at her in secret.

He had fallen in love with Zoe about an hour after meeting her for the first time, or maybe even less. It was probably the same thing that happened to all the newbies like him who found socializing difficult, as well as to a lot of less weird guys. But unlike all the others, he had nurtured that love for her and kept it intact for ten long years.

And for all that time he had always felt the same resignation that he felt right then, which was the reason why he had gone out with other girls over the years. But even so, the total adoration he felt for Zoe had never waned in all that time, and even though Clover thought his loyalty was the sweetest thing ever, he thought it was just plain ridiculous and he was starting to be ashamed of it.

He felt stupid. Zoe was destined to end up with some handsome, self-confident guy – the type of guy who could take her any time and anywhere, without hesitation, not some cerebral intellectual who was almost afraid to even touch her.

For all those reasons, there was absolutely no point lusting after her and dreaming about her, just as there was no point having flashbacks all the time to moments they had spent together – and particularly to their kiss in Times Square. And it was useless to get angry or jealous about her love life too. If he couldn't have her for himself, though, he hoped that she could at least find a man who was worthy of her.

Zoe deserved all the love in the world and a partner who could make her forget about her doubts and uncertainties. A man who could give her all the attention she needed. And instead she surrounded herself with testosterone-headed cavemen who were able only to keep her happy in the sack and then show her off like a trophy to their friends.

"Well, if that's what she wants then you have to let her have it. It's probably what she deserves," his mother would often repeat to him. Apart from Clover, she was the only person who knew of his real feelings. Maybe she was right, or maybe she just couldn't bear seeing her only son so sad. Sheila Morgan, of course, thought Eric was extremely handsome and the type of guy women should be fighting to get their hands on.

Blind motherly love.

"Zoe adores you," Clover would repeat to him, though, and that tiny, feeble spark of hope that she was right was probably the reason why he was still so patient.

If there was even the smallest chance that Zoe would eventually fall in love with him, he couldn't afford to waste it. And he didn't even care if in the meantime he was wasting all other chances to build his own emotional life.

Zoe was more important than anything else.

Chapter 4

"You're very quiet this morning," mumbled Zoe, sneaking up on Eric. "Although to tell the truth, you've been quiet for a while now."

She noticed that he started in surprise and lifted his head slightly, despite stubbornly keeping his eyes on the shelves.

"I've never been much of a talker, you know that."

"True, but you've never been totally mute either. Is there something wrong?"

"I have a headache and I didn't sleep at all last night."

"How come? Did something happen?"

"Not that I know of," said Eric, dumping some books into Zoe's hands. "Since you're so thoughtful, you can help me with these."

Zoe looked at a few titles and turned up her nose. "Love manuals… Bah! As if this stuff is any good for finding a soulmate."

"Plenty of people have been asking for these things lately. They're looking for aphrodisiac recipes, Wiccan spells to find the love of their life, the rules to follow to avoid being dumped…" Eric shrugged his shoulders. "Sometimes you can actually find an idea or a suggestion in a book."

"Have you ever read any of these?"

"I'd need a miracle – some dumb book wouldn't do the job for me," he muttered, heading back towards the counter.

"Don't underestimate yourself, hon," she said, giving him an honest smile. "Under that striped pullover of yours you're quite a catch – and you're even honest too. You're not going to be single forever."

Eric peered at her from over the top of his glasses, making Zoe wonder for the umpteenth time why he bothered wearing them if he wasn't going to look through the lenses.

"You're right. One day pigs will sprout wings and take to the skies and sweet, sexy, intelligent women will suddenly start being interested in nerds like me."

Zoe fluttered her eyelashes. "Since when have you been looking for a sex bomb?"

"Hey, if I'm going to ask for divine intervention, I might as well aim high."

"Well, the best things are often the simplest too," she replied, thoughtfully.

"Yeah, tell me about it."

They worked together in silence for a few moments and then Eric cleared his throat. "So how did it go yesterday? I had to leave before you could submerge me with the usual vacuous gossip about your new toy."

Zoe winked and her red lips curved into a half-smile. "If you think it's just vacuous gossip, I won't tell you anything."

"Oh, no, please do. You know I've been a masochist for years, I need my daily dose of idiocy or I'll start suffering from withdrawal symptoms," said Eric with a smirk. "Come to think of it, that might have been what was causing my insomnia last night."

"Funny guy!" She finished putting some books on the lower shelves, and then walked over to the counter. "Anyway, there isn't really much to say. Evan is… nice? He's a football player, but not a professional one."

"Who would have guessed? A sportsman with a competitive, aggressive temperament – just the kind of guy you prefer! Be careful not to let him crush you in those big arms of his: he might even kill you by accident and then just think that you had passed out after being overcome by the overwhelming pleasure of being in his company."

"What an asshole you are," laughed Zoe, shouldering him amicably. "Hey, it's not like I'm going to *marry* him! He's just a bit of fun like all the others."

"Have you ever tried reading? Or signing up for a dance class? Or doing some voluntary work? Or Yoga? They're all much more instructive alternatives and they might help you clean up your karma."

Zoe laughed. She was used to Eric's stinging sarcasm, and actually found it comforting. The way they constantly mocked each other was really helpful for her, especially in days like that one.

Since she'd woken up that morning, she'd felt totally drained of energy. The combination of the approach of the dreaded Valentine's Day, being single, and the cold and the rain had filled her with deep melancholy. The emptiness she felt inside was getting deeper every day and it couldn't be cured by friends, family or boyfriends, and that was why knowing that she could still count on Eric's affection was comforting.

Yes, he could be preachy and bit judgmental of her behavior, but she knew that he loved her and cared about her. Over the years he had told her more than once that he only wanted her to be happy, and that was why he used to analyze and criticize all of her wannabe boyfriends. And after the awful experience she'd had with Stuart, Eric had become even more careful and protective.

Sometimes she had actually thought that Eric was jealous, but then she had told herself that if there were any stronger feelings between them, they wouldn't have remained friends for so long.

Suddenly, confused and baffling images of the breathtaking kiss she and Eric had exchanged in her dream emerged from the fog of her memory, but she hurriedly pushed them aside. If it had been a real kiss instead of a drunken mental fantasy, she would have listed it among the best kisses of her entire life, but it hadn't, and that only reinforced her belief: if Eric had been interested in something more than just friendship, he could have taken advantage of the situation and tried to make her think that it had really happened. But he hadn't done.

Anyway, judging from the girls she remembered Eric being interested in in the past, she was certain that she wasn't his type. He was too intelligent and sensitive! She would have driven him crazy after just a couple of days together. Her inner insecurities were always making her lose her self-control and turning her into a spoiled, shameless – and even selfish – person. For Eric it was hard enough to put up with her as a friend, she would have been a *terrible* girlfriend for him.

She stood for a time staring silently at the wet road outside the shop window. Business was unusually quiet today, probably because the hard rain was keeping all the potential customers away. Liberty was in her office working on some poems commissioned by clients, and Clover hadn't even arrived yet. It was a really weird day.

But he was there, though. He was always there.

Standing by Eric, Zoe smiled self-consciously at him. "Thanks," she said in a soft voice.

Eric raised his eyebrows and looked perplexed. "Thanks for what?"

"For being a friend. You always care about me, put up with me and make me laugh when I need it. It means a lot to me."

"Ok, I get it – you're having a bad day," he joked, pulling a fake haughty face. "When you start being all saccharine with me it's because you're about to get depressed."

"You're right, you shrink, but I did actually mean what I said."

"Then would you mind saying it a bit more often? It would be good for my ego."

"No, you wouldn't like always being given compliments. You're not like me."

"You don't need to be given compliments all the time either. A couple of genuine ones every once in a while would be enough. Especially if they came from someone with at least one functioning neuron."

"Find me a guy like that and I will be forever in your debt," sighed Zoe, resting her elbows on the counter.

After a moment of silence, Eric cleared his throat.

"Zoe?"

"Yes?"

The door opened just as Eric was about to speak, and Clover and Cade came in, both holding his raincoat over their heads to protect them from the rain.

"Jeez, what awful weather!" said Clover, extricating herself from her fiancé's arm and taking off her wool hat, which was soaked with rain water. Her red hair lay flat down her back like a wet blanket and Cade spontaneously caressed it almost without noticing what he was doing.

Zoe noticed that gesture and felt slightly envious. She would have loved to have a man like that by her side – someone so deeply in love with her that he couldn't keep his hands off her.

"Good morning guys," Cade smiled. "Yep – this is one of those days when I really miss L.A."

"And that's why he's heading there tonight," mumbled Clover, without turning towards him. Cade smiled and grabbed her by the waist to try and get her attention.

"If I remember correctly, I did ask you to come with me but you didn't want to."

Clover stared into her man's blue eyes and emitted a trembling sigh. "It's almost Valentine's Day, there are too many things to do. I just can't leave right now."

Zoe stared at them and suddenly felt worried. "But you are going to be back by the 14th, right?" she asked Cade, looking at him menacingly.

"Of course," he smiled. "I'd never be able to come back to New York at all if I missed a date as important as that. Clover would probably hire a hitman to take me out in California!"

"Oh, you know me so well even though we've only been dating for two months," Clover sniggered, looking at him with eyes full of love.

Eric pretended to wipe the sweat from his forehead. "I'm so relieved, Cade. The idea of taking them *both* out to dinner for Valentine's Day was really scaring me."

"You can relax, we're not even going to be in New York that night," laughed Cade.

When she noticed that her colleagues were looking at her questioningly, she said with satisfaction, "He's taking me to Paris!"

Zoe crossed her arms over her chest and frowned graciously. "It's official: I hate you," she said, then she looked at Cade seductively. "Are you absolutely sure that she's the one you want to be with? I would be quite willing to forgive you for choosing her if you just admitted that you were wrong and had decided you wanted to start dating me."

"I'm not ready to change my mind just yet, but I did actually come here today to talk to you," Cade smiled at her as he held his girlfriend's hand tightly.

Zoe winked. "I like that. Go on."

"A colleague of mine, Brooke Samuels… I guess you've heard about her…"

"The blonde actress who was your co-star in *Nobody's Land*? Of course I have!"

"Great. She's coming to New York the day after tomorrow and she's looking for a photographer who can help her create a calendar for a friend of hers. I told her about Giftland and you and she said she would like to meet you."

"You mean Brooke Samuels wants to meet *me*? Wow!" Zoe smiled. "It'd be an honor to work with her! And could you tell Patrick Dempsey about my work as well, if you get a chance?" she added with a wink.

"I'll see what I can do. But let me warn you: Patrick is happily married."

"Damn it! I'm always just that bit too late!" she snorted.

"Do you think you'll be able to help Brooke out before Valentine's Day? I know you're pretty busy."

"Don't worry, I'm sure we can squeeze your famous colleague into our schedule."

Clover looked at her watch and sighed. "I'd better go. That kid is probably already in Macy's waiting for me."

Cade frowned. "What kid?"

"My first client of the day, who was also my last client of yesterday. He's looking for a special present for his girlfriend, because Valentine's Day is also going to be their first anniversary."

"How romantic," smiled Zoe. "But they're really just kids, so finding a special present for them shouldn't be too difficult. When you're that age, everything always seems amazing, and that's probably how it'll go on being... at least until he cheats on her with her best friend."

"That doesn't necessarily have to happen," Eric said without looking at her.

"Well, except for my parents, I don't know many couples who are actually as much in love with each other as they were when they first met. Maybe the guy won't cheat on her but he will eventually lose interest in finding the perfect present for his partner – and for some couples, routine can be even worse than betrayal," said Zoe, shrugging her shoulders.

Clover stared at Cade with threatening eyes. "Do you promise never to get into a routine, to be faithful to me and to still surprise and love me even in thirty years time?"

"Do I have an alternative?" he joked.

"No."

"Ok, well I'll do my best then."

Clover smiled at him brightly, said goodbye to her colleagues and headed towards the door with her boyfriend. Eric and Zoe observed them through the shop window and Zoe smiled sweetly at the sight of them hugging each other and kissing.

"They're really a cute couple, aren't they?"

"Yes, Clover has been so much happier since she met him."

"They were made for each other."

"They've only been dating for two months, let's give it a bit of time to see how it goes."

Zoe turned to look at him. "Don't you believe in love at first sight? I mean real love, not just fleeting crushes."

"Of course I believe in love at first sight," he mumbled while he fiddled with a small bottle of water.

"I'm glad to hear that even someone as rational as you thinks that it's possible. These days I really need to believe that stuff like that can actually exist. Stuff like real love, and stories of love at first sight, and endings like 'and they lived happily ever after'."

"Where's all your pessimism gone? Not long ago you were saying that you hated Valentine's Day, lately you've barely been able to look at a happy couple without saying how much you hate them."

"It's just envy, that is all," grumbled Zoe. "Just mean, insidious envy. And I'm sure that I'm going to get even worse unless I find a boyfriend as soon as possible."

"Oh, my God. Every man for himself!"

Zoe leaned her elbows on the counter, cupping her face in her hands and staring over at the window, against which the rain was pounding. "Don't you miss it?"

"What?"

"Being in love."

"Sometimes it's better not to be in love," replied Eric enigmatically.

Zoe stared at him curious. "What do you mean?"

"I mean that there isn't much point being in love if the object of your desires doesn't feel the same way about you."

"Are you talking from personal experience?"

"Well, I am actually human, even though you and your girlfriends seem not to have noticed the fact," said Eric sardonically, cutting off the conversation with a gesture.

But Zoe was now too thirsty for details to let it go, and kept her grey eyes on him.

"Spit it out, mister! I want to know the whole story!"

"It's something that happened to me and to the vast majority of people on the planet. What do you want me to tell you about it?"

"A lot of things! Who is she? Do I know her? When did it happen? And what, exactly, did happen?"

It took Eric so long to reply that she thought he would never answer at all, but then, never moving his eyes from the little plastic bottle of water he was holding, he shrugged.

"I fell in love with her while I was at college. She was absolutely gorgeous, really sweet, and way smarter than me. We used to see each other every day and she thought I was… funny. But she never looked with anything like passion, even though I'm pretty sure my eyes must have gone heart-shaped every time I was around her. I practically drooled every time she walked into the room."

"And did she know about your feelings?"

"Of course not. A girl like her could have had any man she wanted – what use could she have had for a nerd like me?"

"You coward!" she snorted, while shaking her head. "You let her slip away just because you were scared to confess how you really felt about her."

"Yeah, maybe – but at least I avoided hearing the usual answer."

"Which would be?"

"Oh Eric, I'm really, really flattered but we can never be anything more than friends," he mimicked with a smirk. "It's not because of you, of course, you're wonderful. It's all my fault… I'm just not really sure of what I want from life yet. Can you ever forgive me?"

"And how many times have you heard that garbage?"

"Never, but I've heard plenty of other people tell me about when they heard it."

"Well, I'll admit I have dumped guys that way a few times, but…" When she saw Eric glaring at her, she raised her chin pugnaciously. "Hey, I only say stuff like that when I need to get rid of idiots. And anyway, that doesn't make you any less of a coward. What was her name?"

Eric hesitated a moment before saying, "Stephanie."

"Right. Now you'll spend the rest of your life wondering if Stephanie would have said 'yes' or 'no' to your proposal. You might have missed out on the chance of being with the love of your life just because you were scared of being turned down!"

Neither of them spoke for a few moments and then Zoe looked over at her colleague again. "And haven't you ever been in love since her?"

"No."

"That's more or less what happened to me too. I haven't allowed myself to feel any emotion since the disappointment I had with Stuart. I didn't want to suffer any more so I just threw myself into all these pointless relationships. And what did it get me? Having a hundred numbers on my contact list doesn't make me happy."

"A *hundred*?!"

"More or less," replied Zoe quickly, ending the discussion with a shrug of her shoulders. Suddenly, her eyes began to twinkle and she stood up straight.

"You know what? We should do it!"

Eric had just taken a sip from his bottle and almost choked at her words. "Do it?"

"Yeah! I mean let go of the past and look forward to the future," smiled Zoe. "We're young, good-looking and intelligent, we deserve something more than the occasional empty relationship. Don't you agree?"

"Uh huh."

"We should start seriously trying to find our soul mates."

"Ah," Eric put the bottle down. "And how do you propose we go about that, exactly?"

"We should go out more, get to know new people."

"You already know half of New York," cut in Eric. "Do you know what I think you should do instead? *Stop* going out with men! Take some time off from dating and think seriously about what you really want from life. You go out with so many guys that it's almost become your second job. The way you're going, you won't even know when you do meet someone you like!"

Zoe wrinkled her nose. "It's too late to try out your method – I want a boyfriend by Valentine's Day! And since there's only two weeks left, I need to seriously get to work on finding one."

Eric pushed his spectacles back up his nose without turning to look at her. "I guess I'm free for that evening then, right?"

"Keep yourself available for me in any case – you never know… OK?" joked Zoe, kissing his cheek. "I'm going to go and talk to Liberty about Brooke Samuels. I'll be right back!" she added, before running off up the stairs.

Keep yourself available for me, you never know…

When he thought again about what she had said he felt his jaw clench.

What was he for her? Just a spare tire to keep in the trunk in case she needed it?

Eric ran his hand through his hair, feeling almost overwhelmed by the increasingly intense waves of anger washing over him. He wasn't angry with Zoe though – he was furious with himself.

Zoe wasn't aware of the pain she caused him every time she talked, she didn't know about the pain of loving someone in silence. It was all his fault, because he was a coward, just like she had said a few moments before. He had adored her for ten years without saying a word, he had indulged her and had managed to always have time in his life to dedicate to her. When Zoe needed him, he was there, always available, day and night. The most important things for Eric were knowing that she was happy and being able to enjoy her presence. So how could be blame her for not considering him a man, seeing as how he behaved more like a faithful dog?

"Pathetic," he muttered as he rummaged about in the drawer of the counter in search of some aspirin.

He had tried to stop being in love with her and to put her out of his thoughts. He had gone out with other women and listed all the things he didn't like about her, hoping that it might help him like her less. But nothing had ever changed, because Zoe Mathison was in his blood. He was in love with all of her neuroses and obsessions, her frowns and the cold, superior mask she would wear in public to hide her vulnerable side. And after New Year's Eve it had gotten even worse, and living a life independent from Zoe had become totally impossible.

Clover was right – he should just talk to her and put an end to it all, one way or another. Even though things might go wrong – and he was pretty sure they would – he could always just pack up and move back to Boston. He could start a new life, without having to see her every single day.

"And what if things go right instead?" his friend would always say.

But how *could* things go right? Zoe had never realized what he felt for her and that couldn't simply be because of his talent as an actor. She just didn't listen to him enough, she never really looked in his eyes. That's why she had never noticed the devotion in his face when he looked at her. However there was also a chance that she *did* know and pretended not to.

Both options were pretty depressing. No, he couldn't confess his feelings and risking ruining everything, the stakes were too high. He would embarrass Zoe and it would ruin their friendship and make being together uncomfortable.

He had to find a way to get her out of his mind.

The shop's door swung open wide and, walking backwards while trying to close a big umbrella, a figure entered. Eric put aside his thoughts and tried to focus on his job.

The client turned out to be a very pretty blonde girl who was now approaching him with an apologetic look on her face.

"I'm dripping water all over your floor, I'm such a disaster!"

Eric smiled gently. "Don't worry, you're not the first to do that today. How can I help you?"

"I'm looking for a funny book for a friend of mine and someone told me that you have a good selection of strange titles here."

"Oh yeah, we have *quite* a lot of strange things here," said Eric as he accompanied her to the books section.

He helped her reach the ones which were on the highest shelves and after reading through the blurbs on the back of several, the girl decided on one and then gave him a curious look.

"You know, you look familiar… Do we know each other from somewhere?"

"I wouldn't know. I meet so many people every day that it's kind of hard for me to remember them all, despite my analytical mind."

"You look like a guy who used to attend the same classes as me at M.I.T. Is your name Morgan?"

"Yes, Eric Morgan."

The pretty blonde smiled and held out her hand. "Steffy Parker. You helped me with a project once."

"Parker… Yes, that sounds familiar," lied Eric. "I'm sorry, but M.I.T. was so long ago…"

"Oh don't worry about that, I understand – and I've changed a lot since then, too." Steffy put the book on the counter and waited while Eric gift wrapped it properly. "I've only just arrived in New York, and I never thought I would bump into a familiar face so soon."

"I've already lived here for five years. It was always my plan to move here."

"Yes, I remember that." When the girl noticed the perplexed way he was looking at her, she waved a hand and blushed adorably. "We talked a few times. I… had a crush on you. I always used to try and sit near you and I used to make notes in my diary about any conversations we had, even the completely unimportant ones. Anyway, now you know. Are you happy?"

Eric opened his eyes wide behind the lenses of his glasses. "Well… I don't get to hear things like that often, so I'd say yes, I'm happy about it."

His reply made her laugh, and that made her look even prettier.

"You were already pretty cute back then but you've got even cuter, even though you haven't changed much. You've still got the same adorable nice guy look."

"Now, that's the type of compliment I get more often," mumbled Eric, with an amused smirk. "But if you'd told me that my nice guy look could have an effect on female hormones I would have passed out, so I guess it's for the best that you didn't."

"Maybe it does," she said, fluttering her eyelashes. "For some girls, being sweet is much more exciting than a lot of other things."

Eric hoped he hadn't blushed. Was this girl actually trying to hit on him? It wasn't the first time that a girl had done, of course: some girls actually seemed to find him attractive despite his serious bespectacled look, but this girl was really pretty…

"I didn't mean to embarrass you, Eric," mumbled Steffy, biting her lower lip. "I'm sorry if I did."

He shook his head. "Don't worry, you can say whatever you want. I mean… I don't mind."

"And would you mind if I invited you out?" Eric didn't reply right away so Steffy pulled in her shoulders. "Look, I mean, no big thing, we could just have a chat. Like I said, I just moved here and I don't know anyone yet… It would be fun, don't you think? I mean, if it's not a problem for you, of course." Suddenly a look of shock appeared on her face and her green eyes opened wide as an awful thought occurred to her. "Oh my God! Please tell me that you don't have a girlfriend already and save me from looking a total idiot!"

Did he have a girlfriend?

He suddenly thought of Zoe and felt his stomach clench agonizingly, but feeling guilty for cheating on someone who didn't even notice he existed was just plain ridiculous and there was no way on Earth it could be a valid reason to turn down the invitation of a very pretty girl who was interested in him.

"No, I'm not in a relationship," he managed to mutter. If he wanted to forget about Zoe, he should really welcome some distraction, and this blonde was not bad – not bad at all.

"OK." Steffy Parker leaned on the counter, picked up a pen and looked him squarely in the eyes. "I'm going to give you my number. Do you have a piece of paper?"

"Err…" A panicked Eric looked around him in confusion, but Steffy was quick to react. She grabbed his hand while still staring at him, then pushed up his sleeve and rapidly wrote her telephone number on his forearm.

"There you go. This way you'll have to call me soon, otherwise you'll end up washing it off," she said, with a smile. "And if you *don't* call, I can always tell myself that it's because the number got washed off by mistake and not because you're not actually interested in me."

She gave him a wink.

Eric nodded, distracted by the footsteps he heard coming from the stairs. He had learned how to recognize the sound of those sensual, confident and unhurried steps very well.

"Lib says that it's OK with her and that it'll be a good way of getting our name out there! I really can't wait to…" said Zoe, before shutting up as soon as she reached the counter. She had apparently noticed the blonde girl's hand still holding Eric's forearm, the pen in her hand and the telephone number on his skin. "Ah, sorry for interrupting you, I hadn't realized we had customers."

Eric pulled his arm back. He hated himself for feeling guilty about having let Zoe walk in on that situation.

"She's a friend from back at college," he said vaguely while he finished wrapping the book.

The blonde offered her hand to Zoe. "Hi, my name's Stephanie Parker. My friends call me Steffy."

Zoe fluttered her eyelashes, then smiled and grasped the girl's outstretched hand. "Stephanie! I think I've already heard about you."

"Have you really?" said Stephanie, giving Eric a look.

In that moment he wished he could vanish into the shelves behind him. Damn it all to hell! When he had told Zoe about his unreciprocated crush a little earlier, he'd just said the first name that had come into his head because he hadn't wanted her to realize that he was actually talking about her. And the name he had come up with had been none other than Stephanie!

Zoe must be convinced that she was meeting Eric's old flame…

"I've known Eric since college too," continued Zoe, "so he probably mentioned your name to me."

"Yeah, that's probably it. Though he didn't seem to be too interested in me back then," said Steffy, giving Eric a smile. "But, hey – things can always change, can't they?"

Eric coughed and handed her the wrapped package. "Here's your present."

"Thank you. So… Speak to you soon, then."

"Sure," he mumbled, feeling Zoe's eyes staring at him.

Zoe gave Stephanie a friendly smile. "Drop by and say 'hi' to us."

"I will!"

Once Stephanie had left the shop, Zoe leaned on the counter and stared at Eric. "So was that her then?"

"What?" he said, trying to play for time while he tidied up the counter top.

"I guess it must have been, seeing how jumpy you are. It's absolutely crazy: you mention her to me and a moment later she pops up in our shop as if you'd summoned her!" Zoe sighed. "That is really romantic."

Eric didn't reply. He couldn't admit that he didn't even remember the girl, because that would shatter all his good intentions about moving on from Zoe. Stephanie could be a real help in proving to Zoe that he wasn't just some idiot who was always at her beck and call, but it was a real struggle for Eric to lie about things so shamelessly.

"She's really pretty. I didn't know you were into blondes. You've always dated brunettes so I thought you preferred them. Or maybe you didn't go out with blonde girls because they reminded you of your first love, is that what it was?"

"Quit overthinking it. I couldn't care less about hair color. When I go out with a girl it's because it feels like there's something special about her."

"She wrote her number on your forearm, that's a pretty clear message! If all she was interested in was just being friends with you, she'd have asked for a piece of paper or she'd have used her mobile phone, but she didn't want to miss out on the opportunity to touch you. She wants you," said Zoe. Then she frowned, and started playing with a pen. "I'll confess, I'm a little jealous."

Eric felt his heart do a backflip in his chest.

"What?"

"Yeah. I mean, we've been friends for so long and you have always been there for me every time I've needed you... Now your big love re-appears from the mists of time and she's going to get all of your attention. I won't have you all to myself any more."

"Real friendships don't just end because one of you gets romantically involved with someone," said Eric without looking at her.

"Wow, are we really talking about getting romantically involved already? This Stephanie is really lucky to be loved so much," she muttered. "Anyway, you're right, friendships don't just end. But I always noticed how all your exes used to glare at me like they hated me. Girls don't like me, you know that. She'll ask you to steer clear of me."

"Ok, but did anyone ever manage to keep me away from you, though?" joked Eric. All his ex-partners had instinctively felt an aversion towards Zoe, perhaps because they understood his real feelings for her. Luckily for him, none of them had ever decided to avenge themselves by telling Zoe the truth.

Zoe took his hand, unwittingly sending his heartbeat rocketing.

"No, you're right. None of them did, and I'm truly thankful for that – you've always been a really wonderful friend."

Eric grunted some reply, and when Zoe pushed up his sleeve, lightly touching his skin with her smooth fingers, he gasped slightly. "What are you doing?"

"Write down that number before any of it gets rubbed off, giving you a good excuse not to call her," she said gently. "Fate's given you a second chance, so don't waste it: you deserve it.

If you really think that I'm so wonderful and if you're so damn envious of the girl of my dreams that you feel jealous at the idea of losing my attention, then why the hell you don't want me for yourself? thought Eric in frustration.

For a moment he felt like saying it out loud just to see what would happen. He was sure that her initial reaction would be shock. But then? How would she react after the initial surprise?

The same old doubts started tormenting him and forced him to abandon the idea.

Feeling like a complete idiot, he quickly wrote Stephanie's number down on a post-it.

Chapter 5

Everyone always has such high expectations of Hollywood stars, and that had certainly been the case with Cade Harrison the first time he had entered Giftland looking for Clover. Everybody had expected him to be somehow 'different', but in the end he had turned out to be a charming, easy going, funny, regular guy who – apart from being rich – seemed to be just like everybody else.

And it seemed that Brooke Samuels was equally pleasant and easy going. She was tall and blonde with a face that was just as capable of seducing you in person as it was on TV. She arrived at the shop wearing a huge pair of sunglasses and a baseball hat over her curly hair and had walked straight over to Eric, giving him a frank smile.

"Two attractive blondes smiling at me in less than twenty-four hours," thought Eric when he saw her approaching him." They must have sprayed something strange in the air."

"Hi, I'm Brooke. I was supposed to be arriving tomorrow, but I took an earlier flight and I just couldn't resist coming to meet you in person," said the actress in a carefully modulated voice that made it clear why there would have been no point trying to dub her voice in movies. "Cade told me that you can help me."

"Of course, Ms Samuels. It's a genuine pleasure for us," smiled Eric, coming round from behind the counter to shake her hand.

"Please, call me Brooke. Ms Samuels makes me feel so terribly old."

"Whatever you prefer."

"So should I talk about my calendar idea with you?"

"No, not with me – with the photographer, Zoe. She'll be down any minute."

With perfect timing, Zoe appeared from the second floor, her camera hanging from her neck. She recognised the actress immediately and came running down the stairs, trying to fix her clothes and untie her hair from the very small ponytail she had tied it up in as she went.

"I *thought* I heard someone say my name," she said as she approached them.

Eric introduced her to the actress. "Brooke has arrived a day earlier than expected and would like to know if she can talk to you about her project."

"Of course! I will be done taking pictures with my client in about ten minutes, then you can have my undivided attention, Brooke." Zoe held out her hand to the woman in greeting, and Eric stared at the pair of them: a blonde and a brunette, both fabulous looking. His friends wold have paid anything to have been in his place. The truth was that they were always pestering him about his attractive friends and trying to get him to hook them up with his colleagues, but now Clover had a boyfriend and Liberty had been engaged for a while. And Zoe was, of course, totally out of the equation.

She went back upstairs, leaving him alone with Brooke. Eric noticed that she was looking at the objects around her with interest so he forced himself to try and make conversation. He was usually very discreet and preferred to let his colleagues keep the customers entertained, but he couldn't let Brooke Samuels hang around killing time and not even try to keep her company.

"Cade told us something about your idea for the calendar," was the first thing that came to mind as an attempt to try and get the woman's attention.

"Did he? Well, what happened is that my friend Sydney was dumped by her idiot boyfriend just a week before they were supposed to be getting married. She was really cut up bad about it, but finally, a year later, she's starting to go out and meet people, and that's why I wanted to get her a funny present – something to distract her from the unpleasant anniversary of the break-up," smiled Brooke. "Cade told me a lot of good things about this place... Although I think part of his enthusiasm is due to a particular woman who works here and has managed to make him totally lose his head!"

"Yes, Clover can have that effect," Eric joked. "She's got so much energy."

"Yes, Cade told me that too. He's completely besotted with her."

"I really hope so. Clover's like a sister to me – knowing that he feels the same way about her as she does about him makes me really happy."

"Oh, you can bet that he does. What's your name?"

"Eric Morgan."

"And do you own the shop?"

"No, the boss is Liberty Allen. Zoe, Clover and I are just her devoted slaves."

"This place is just enchanting," said Brooke, looking around her again in amazement. "You have so much cute stuff!"

Eric nodded. Giftland was truly a paradise for anyone who was looking for a present – a place where you could always count on finding an endless amount of funny, original ideas to surprise your friends with. Apart from selling all kinds of objects, they also offered special services upon request: he would create videos and short films using material provided by the clients, Zoe would take photographs to use in a hundred different ways; Liberty, who managed the shop, could also write poetry and stories, and Clover's job was to accompany and advise clients while she took them shopping for the perfect gift. They were a team, and the shop's reputation was based on their ability to work together. And since Clover had stolen the heart of Hollywood's prince, moreover, their business had increased significantly. Brooke Samuels was their second celebrity client, and that could only bring them even more good publicity.

"So what kind of calendar were you thinking of for your friend?"

"Something funny that'll make her laugh. What I want to do is bring her here on some pretext and then surprise her with a photo shoot designed exclusively for her. I'm sure she'll be comfortable with it – Sydney is a model, so she's used to being photographed."

"And I am sure Zoe will manage to come up with something original that'll put a smile on your friend's face. She's an amazing photographer and on top of that she's a woman, so they'll understand one another perfectly. It's a bit of luck that it's not up to me to think it up – I wouldn't have the first clue about how to console a girl with a broken heart."

"You wouldn't even know how to break a girl's heart in the first place," said Zoe as she came back down the stairs. "You're too darn nice to be able to hurt anyone."

"And he's also very cute," added Brooke. "Maybe we could use him for the calendar." She studied Eric for a moment, nodding and pondering. "If he loses the glasses and we muss up his hair a little…"

"…I would look exactly like a scruffy mole," interrupted Eric, who was starting to feel embarrassed, "and that, I can assure you, wouldn't cheer *anybody* up."

Zoe, who had in the meantime had walked over to stand next to him behind the counter, gave him a kick and then smiled at Brooke and said, "He's such a shy, self-effacing guy!"

"He's adorable," agreed the actress.

Zoe invited Brooke to her office upstairs to discuss the details of what they were going to do, thus saving Eric, who was finally able to breathe normally again. For a moment he had feared they were actually going to drag him into the project, and the idea was just terrifying to him. He didn't have a particularly good relationship with cameras, and would freeze in embarrassment each time he found himself in front of a lens, which would inevitably lead to disastrous results. Making a fool of himself in front of an actress, a model *and* Zoe would really have mortified him, but he was even more scared of how angry Liberty would get if he refused to satisfy the request of such an important client.

Suddenly the shop's front door was flung open violently. For a moment, a pale ray of sunshine illuminated the room until it was blocked out by the silhouette of a well-built man. He Man had made his appearance.

Eric glowered at the new arrival, quickly trying to think of a way of getting rid of him before Zoe could see him.

"Can you get Zoe for me?" said the man, putting a big hairy hand on the counter.

"I'm sorry but she's busy at the moment."

"I'm sure that if you tell her that I'm here she'll find ten minutes for me. My name's Evan."

His arrogant tone irritated Eric. "Evan what?"

"Evan Lewis."

"Hold on a moment." Eric grabbed the phone and called Liberty's office's extension, hoping to interrupt her right in the middle of a moment of pure inspiration. That would annoy her so much that it would give him the perfect excuse not to tell Zoe that her pet troglodyte was looking for her. "Lib, there's a guy here who would like to see Zoe, but she's with Brooke at the moment… Should I call her anyway?"

He heard Liberty snort at the other end of the phone line. "How the hell should I know? If it's someone important you can try and call her – if it isn't, you can tell him to wait his turn."

"He says his name is Evan Lewis, but Zoe's never mentioned a client with that name to me – do you know anything about it?" continued Eric, enjoying the annoyed expression on the man's face.

"Hey, I'm not a client," he cut in. "Me and Zoe are dating."

Liberty heard his reply. "Tell him that he can wait for Zoe to finish or kick him out. And the next time that you interrupt me for something as dumb as that…"

Eric hung up before Liberty could finish her threat. "Zoe can't come down right now, so I'm afraid you'll just have to come back later. Or you can wait, if you like, but you might be waiting a long time."

"I'll wait then," mumbled the hulk, before heading off to browse the shelves.

Eric had hoped that the meeting between Zoe and Brooke Samuels would last forever but, unfortunately, Mr Steroids only had to wait twenty minutes before the two women came back down the stairs. Brooke gave Eric a gesture of thanks and then rapidly vanished, since she had noticed that there were a few people in the shop now, while Zoe went over to Eric with an enthusiastic smile on her face.

"It's going to be so much fun! I'll have to ask Lib and Clover to get *me* a present like that the next time some asshole breaks my heart!"

"Yeah, well seeing how smart *this* guy is, I'm guessing you won't have to wait for too long," grumbled Eric as he watched Evan Lewis walking towards them.

Zoe noticed Evan for the first time, and her expression immediately became seductive.

"Hey handsome! I wasn't expecting to see you today."

"I've been here for half an hour," he replied, putting his arm around her waist. "I thought I'd just pop in and say 'hi', but apparently it's impossible to distract you when you're working."

Zoe gave Eric a perplexed look, and he gestured towards Liberty's office with his head and ran his thumb across his throat.

"She's in a *really* bad mood today," he explained, absolving himself of any responsibility.

Zoe shrugged and dragged the football player off to a secluded corner at the back of the shop.

Eric quickly dealt with the rest of the clients, as he was anxious to keep an eye on the pair of them. Knowing that they were hidden away behind shelves busy doing who knew what was driving him crazy.

When he was finally free, he grabbed a handful of things that needed sorting out and walked towards the place where the two lovebirds were hiding. He always tried to keep an eye on the situation when she was with a man. The problem wasn't her, it was the men that she always dated. Zoe had the power to make them completely lose their minds and make them feel like they just had to take her, throw her against the wall and… kiss her passionately while they ran their vulgar hands all over her body… which was exactly what Evan Lewis was doing right now.

Eric's vision became blurry and he only managed not to throw all the things he was holding at the asshole because he didn't want to look a complete fool – but, God, how dearly he would have loved to!

From where he was standing he couldn't see Zoe's face clearly, but whatever expression she wore, the fact was that she was allowing that caveman to grope her!

He saw her pulling away, mumbling something that he couldn't hear, but Evan didn't seem to be particularly interested in what she had said, because he leaned over her again in an attempt to pick up from where he had been interrupted. Zoe took a step backwards and that was enough to convince Eric that she wasn't particularly eager for Evan to start kissing her again.

He didn't need to see anything else to realize that the guy was being insistent – though as far as Eric was concerned, just coming to the shop the way he had could have been interpreted as being too pushy.

But then, looking almost resigned, Zoe let him kiss her again…

Consumed with anger, Eric punched a shelf. It broke, sending everything on it crashing to the floor, and leaving his right hand full of splinters of wood. He bit his lip to muffle the swear words but the pain made him want to shout and he rushed away as quickly as he was able to, as he was sure that the couple would come over to see what had happened.

Zoe arrived to find him kneeling down, picking up books and brightly-colored frames from the floor.

"What happened?"

"A shelf broke," he muttered, without looking at her.

"How the hell did *that* happen?"

"I don't know. It's wood, maybe it got damp and couldn't take the weight."

His arms full of objects, Eric stood up, and Zoe noticed that his hand was covered in blood. Her eyes opened wide.

"Evan!" she called, taking some of the books out of Eric's hands.

The caveman appeared in an instant. "What's up, babe?"

"Hold these for a moment." Zoe gave him everything that was in Eric's hands, then took Eric's arm. "Come with me, hon, let's disinfect that cut."

"Don't worry about it, it's just a scratch. I'm not going to pass out over something as stupid as that," snorted Eric, annoyed at being treated like an infant but at the same time enjoying the perplexed expression of Evan Lewis, who was standing on his own in a corner, his arms full of gifts.

"How the heck did you manage to hurt yourself?" continued Zoe as she stubbornly tried to drag him towards the office.

"I was trying to stop those things from falling," he answered.

Like a mother hen, Zoe set about medicating his wound. "I'm so sorry. If I'd been helping you…"

"You were busy."

Zoe bit her lower lip in mortification. "I told him he could take part in Brooke's project and… well, he was very happy about it."

"Too damn happy," thought Eric, gritting his teeth at the memory of how intensely Evan had been kissing her. Zoe noticed his expression and peered into his eyes.

"Does it hurt?"

"Not much."

"Stop being a hero! I know you're not crazy about the sight of blood."

"I'm sure your friend loves it, though. It's a good thing that you got me out of his sight or he might have gotten even more excited than he already was."

Zoe narrowed her eyes. "Were you spying on us?"

"I didn't have to spy on you, I could hear your moaning from all the way across the shop."

"Come on, he was only kissing me."

"Well it sounded more like he was eating you, to be honest. Though, after all, he had been waiting for almost half an hour. I guess his libido had already gone through the roof."

His tone was starting to annoy her, and she put the band-aid on with an angry gesture. "Well, I'm sorry if we offended your sanctimonious sensitivity. You've obviously forgotten what it means to be attracted by a woman, or to kiss one passionately… if you've even ever done it, that is!"

"Yeah, well not all women like being shoved against the wall in front of everybody, Zoe."

Those words hurt her, as Eric realized when he saw her eyes turn dark and her cheeks go pale. Another time he would have apologized, and in fact Zoe was probably waiting to hear him say that he was sorry, but he was so angry that he had no intention of doing anything of the sort.

She said nothing for a few moments then let go of his hand and walked away, her face a mask of cold indifference.

When he was alone Eric had to stop himself from punching something else. He didn't want to lose any more blood even though punching the shelf had released some of his frustration, and in addition it had stopped Evan Lewis from fondling Zoe.

He shut the door and sat at his desk, Zoe's words whirling around in his head.

Did she really think he was that pathetic? A loser who didn't know how to deal with women just because he wasn't constantly pawing at them in public?

And was that what Zoe wanted from a man? Because in that case he didn't really have a hope in hell with her. He just wasn't that type of guy. He knew how to be passionate without feeling the need to put it on show before the entire world. As far as he was concerned, the kind of macho-man public display he'd seen Evan engaged in a few minutes earlier didn't really mean you desired someone – there were classier ways of demonstrating you were attracted to someone. And the thing the girls he had gone out with had liked most about him had always been how classy he was!

But Zoe was convinced of the opposite, evidently.

His attention was drawn to the yellow post-it he had written Stephanie's number on. Steffy Parker was the perfect example of what he had just thought: Zoe wasn't interested in a discreet and well-mannered guy like him, but someone else appreciated him.

"Fuck it," he muttered as he grabbed his phone.

If Zoe wanted a gorilla as a boyfriend then she would be spoilt for choice. He was aiming for something better, though.

*

"So can I see you this evening?"

"No." Zoe realized that her reply had sounded too categorical, so she smiled. "I'm sorry, Evan, but I've got some work to finish and I think I'm going to have to do it at home.

We've got a backlog of orders at the moment and I just don't have time to go out."

"Whatever you like. It's a shame though, because you've got me thinking about some stuff that…" he said allusively as he moved closer to her.

Zoe slipped out of his hug, praying that some customers would appear to back up the excuse she had just given him. "I really am too busy."

"OK then. In that case, I'll see you for the photo shoot with Brooke Samuels." Evan shook his head, still over the moon at the idea of posing for a calendar. "My buddies are never going to believe me when I tell 'em that I'm going to be posing with one of the hottest actresses in Hollywood!"

"You're not actually posing with *her*," sighed Zoe. "The calendar is for a friend of hers, who's a Canadian model."

"Are you sure that you don't want to 'instruct' me? If we met up tonight you could take some warm-up shots of me. We could hook up at my place, or at yours if you prefer, it's fine with me either way."

How slimy could a man be when all his blood was flowing to the area directly beneath his belt buckle? Zoe was starting to regret having suggested that Evan pose for the project. Brooke's idea had been to photograph her friend Sydney with twelve good looking guys, hoping that it would make her realize that she could have any man she wanted, any time and in any way she desired, in the place of her vile ex-boyfriend. The actress had asked her to find attractive male models and when Zoe had gone back downstairs and seen Evan, she found it natural to ask him to participate. He was blond, sexy and handsome and would be perfect in the role of Cupid for February's picture.

Evan had reacted to that proposal with just a bit too much enthusiasm, and for some reason it had annoyed her. Wasn't it women who, according to the stereotype, loved that kind of exhibitionism? How could a guy get so excited at the idea of posing half-naked for a calendar? Over the last few years she'd increasingly had the impression that – both in private life and at work – men and women had switched roles. Nowadays, more and more men seemed to love being photographed half-naked in sensual poses, and some of them had even asked her to use her camera in the bedroom to take even more explicit pictures! At first, the novelty of it had amused her, but then she had gradually grown bored of it and learned how to avoid that type of guy.

Just the idea of spending an evening doing stuff like that with Evan really gave her the creeps.

And it was all Eric's fault.

He had made her feel awful about herself, as though she was a superficial hussy, just like a lot of people thought she was. He had poured out all his resentment on her in that patronizing, puritan way of his, ridiculing the guys she dated and criticizing her life choices. Well nobody was allowed to tell her what to do with her life, not her father and certainly not Eric!

"Yeah, but your father doesn't know what you do to feel less alone," whispered an insistent voice inside her head, "and Eric does."

Well, even in that case, he still didn't have the right to judge her!

She got rid of Evan and dealt with a couple of clients, and as soon as she found a quiet moment, she went upstairs to Liberty's office. She needed to talk to someone.

When she opened the door, Liberty stopped her in her tracks with a hand gesture. "Wait a minute," she said abruptly, staring at a page on the desk in front of her. Zoe walked over and sat down nearby. When she was writing, Liberty's face took on a remote expression and it was very dangerous to interrupt her when she felt inspired. She saw her friend's pen rapidly tracing words on the paper while her computer sat unattended in a corner, and smiled. Liberty loved written words deeply, you could practically see it in her face.

When she finally raised her head, a satisfied expression on her face, Zoe gestured to her notebook. "Why on earth do you keep writing by hand if afterwards you have to copy everything onto your computer anyway?"

"It's a question of intimacy. A pen and paper are more closely linked to the words that come into my mind," said Lib, caressing her face and primping her blonde hair into shape. "Did you come all the way up here just to ask me that?"

"No, I came here to avoid bursting into Eric's office and breaking his other hand!"

Zoe jumped to her feet, suddenly feeling the same irritation she had felt a few minutes earlier.

"Did Eric break his *hand*?!"

"No, but he hurt it. A shelf broke and he decided to sacrifice himself and save the objects that were about to fall. What a hero, right? Or maybe he was scared that you would make him stay behind after school," she said venomously.

"That's good: I'm pleased to hear that he's scared of me. But how did the shelf crack?"

"You should ask him! I'm sure he has some interesting theory involving the chemical composition of the wood and how it changes when in contact with atmospheric agents."

"You two spend *way* too much together," snorted Liberty, organising the pieces of paper on her desk. "Sometimes you even talk like him."

"Exactly – we've known each other for a long time and that should have taught him something about me, right? Instead he's always finger-pointing and judging me, without taking into consideration the possibility that he might actually be hurting the feelings of the person he's talking to."

"Can you get to the point, please."

"Evan came by to see me."

"I know, Eric told me. And by the way: find somewhere else to meet next time?"

Zoe rolled her eyes. "I didn't *ask* him to come, he just decided to turn up here. He waited for me to finish the meeting I was having upstairs with Brooke Samuels and when I went downstairs, I took him off for a couple of minutes to say 'hi' and ask him if he wanted to take part in the calendar project. Evan was over the moon about it, so he demonstrated his enthusiasm with a kiss… a passionate one, to be fair."

Liberty raised her eyes. "Dammit all, Zoe, do you really have to be making out in my shop?"

"It was only a kiss! Hasn't Justin ever grabbed hold of you and kissed you passionately?"

This time Liberty lifted an eyebrow. "Justin is a reserved, elegant man. He would never dream of necking in a public place, and that's one of the things I like about him."

"Yeah, and that's why Mr Perfect downstairs gets along so well with your boyfriend."

"Zoe, what's the problem?"

"Eric made me feel like a slut – like someone who just throws herself at every man she meets."

"And is that what you were doing?"

"It. Was. Just. A. Kiss," said Zoe, glaring at her.

"OK. But if it was only a kiss and you like being kissed that way, what the hell are you so angry about?"

"Because Eric knows very well that I'm not some nympho who lets everybody and anybody feel her up, especially in public!"

"Did he call you a nympho?"

"No, but the way he said it made it sound like that was what he thought."

"In that case you should clear things up with him. Tell him to mind his own business and to stop judging your choices."

"That's exactly what I was thinking," grumbled Zoe.

Liberty looked at her for a long time. "I'm guessing that's not all, or you wouldn't still be here with that miserable expression on your face."

"It's just… I don't want Eric to have such a low opinion of me. It's really upsetting."

"I don't think he has a low opinion of you. He just wants you to have the best in life and, since he knows you like the back of his hand, he also knows that what Evan Whatshisname has to offer you isn't what you need."

"I told him that he only reacts like that because he's incapable of kissing a woman passionately," mumbled Zoe.

She felt genuinely guilty for hitting below the belt like that. What did she know about the way Eric kissed women anyway? Except for that kiss in her dream, of course…

"It's nice to know that my employees spend their time on the clock insulting each other," sighed Liberty. "So anyway, at the end of the day, Eric said you were slutty and you insulted his masculinity. I'd say you two are even."

"I only said it because I was angry."

"Well maybe he was too."

"About what?"

"Maybe because he had just hurt himself and was pissed off about it? Or maybe because he cares about you and worries about you?"

"In other words, you're taking his side. So I am the easy woman who puts out behind the shelves, leaving her colleague to do so much work that he even ends up hurting himself…"

Liberty smiled, unable to hide her amusement.

"Zoe, if you feel guilty about not having helped him and you know that you were behaving in a way that's not like you then why don't you just go and apologize to him?"

Lib always knew how to get straight to the point. Sullenly, Zoe crossed her arms across her chest. "OK."

"Good girl. Now get the hell out of here and let me work."

Zoe stopped at the door. "Do you think that I'm just a shallow, spoiled kid, Lib?"

"I think you're a woman who craves attention and who comes on strong to hide her weaknesses. I know how hard it is to show your feelings, Zoe, but there's absolutely no need to hide them behind weird behavior."

"You mean it's better to pretend you don't have any feelings at all, the way you do?" said Zoe, smiling sweetly at the surprised expression on her colleague's face. "You are either the most self-confident woman on Earth, Lib, or you've just given me a piece of advice that you refuse to follow yourself. In any case, thank you." Leaving a stunned looking Liberty sitting there, Zoe closed the door behind her and walked downstairs. Her boss was right, she was feeling guilty both for having left Eric alone to manage the shop and for having let Evan treat her like some needy girl who lets people fondle her in public, and that was why she had reacted so aggressively.

But she hated getting caught out.

She had to apologize to Eric. Even though he was a hateful know-it-all, he was right about one thing: not all girls liked to be thrown against a wall in a public place. And she didn't either, even if she pretended she did in the hope that it would make the men she dated like her more.

*

The afternoon turned out to be a long and tedious one and she longed for the working day to be over. On quiet days like that, there was nothing worse than having to work on your own, knowing that your best friend was mad at you.

When she saw him coming out of the office to help her close up the shop, as usual, she was overwhelmed by tenderness.

His expression was stern and his jaw tense, but he forced himself to be kind anyway. Even when he was angry, Eric was never so predictable that he would sulk or sink to seeking some kind of petty revenge. His good manners and respect for others were evident even in those simple things, and the affection he felt for her wasn't diminished by a stupid argument.

Zoe hung the 'CLOSED' sign on the door, then leant against it staring at him.

"I'm sorry."

"Sorry for what?" asked Eric, averting his gaze.

"You know very well for what." Zoe walked over to him, forcing him to look at her. "I didn't mean what I said. Unlike you with mine, I know nothing about your sex life. But precisely because you know every single thing that's happened to me in the last ten years you should know that I'm not that kind of girl."

"I do know it, but not everybody else does. So don't waste your time explaining yourself to me – explain yourself to the people who haven't worked out that your behavior is just an act."

"Maybe the others don't actually care what I'm like. But I care about your opinion, and that's why it hurts me when you get angry with me."

"If you really think that the others don't care about who you actually are then why the hell do you waste your time with them?" he burst out, throwing his hands up in frustration. He was almost ready to start one of his lectures, but at that moment Zoe smiled and Eric gave a shamefaced smirk. "It doesn't matter, though – it's none of my business."

"I'm happy to know that you care about me, really I am. I reacted badly because... well, because I felt guilty for having left you alone. And about Evan – it's true, he was a little rough, you're right, but I'm used to dealing with guys like him, and in fact I've already dumped him."

"Meaning that you won't be seeing him any more?"

"Meaning that I'll have something else to do tonight and that in the future, we'll see."

"Well I guess that's already something," he answered grouchily.

Now that they had cleared things up, Zoe felt more relaxed. She rubbed her hands together and said, "What if I buy you a pizza as an apology? If we get a move on, we might find a table even though we haven't booked."

Eric hesitated, then shook his head. "I can't."

Zoe fluttered her eyelashes. "Why not?"

"I have a date."

"Oh," Zoe stared at him in confusion. "With Stephanie?"

"Yes. She'll be here soon."

"Got it. OK, we'll have a pizza another time then."

Zoe finished organising next day's orders, but she couldn't stop thinking about Eric's refusal.

It was absolutely normal for him to be going out with that girl. He'd had an unrequited crush on her when he was younger so obviously he wanted to make up for lost time. She just wasn't used to having to take into consideration the fact that he might be busy. He'd had other relationships in the past, but none of them had ever interfered with their friendship.

"And this one isn't going to interfere either," she reasoned, frowning at the thought. "Eric is still my friend."

Even though she knew that, the realization that she wasn't going to be able to spend the evening with him made her feel… excluded.

They both turned their heads at the sound of two light taps on the window. Stephanie was standing outside, her cheeks red with cold but still smiling beautifully. She seemed excited about the evening ahead. Zoe turned to Eric, who was putting his jacket on, and forced herself to smile happily.

"Have fun! Show her what she's been missing all these years!"

"I'll do my best."

"We're ok, right?" she asked, a moment before he reached the door. Having caught his attention, she looked into his eyes. "I don't want to go home thinking that you haven't forgiven me yet."

"Don't I always forgive you?" sighed Eric, an indecipherable expression on his face, before saying, "See you tomorrow," and leaving the shop.

Zoe watched the couple walk away along the road. They were really cute together and she was genuinely happy that Eric finally had the opportunity to fulfil his old dreams of love.

Or at least, she knew she should have been.

But what she was actually feeling was an almost overwhelming sensation of sadness, envy and regret, and when she realized it, she felt lonely, selfish and mean.

She finished tidying up the shop with a lump in her throat, thinking all the time that she really deserved to be lonely.

Chapter 6

"So – did you two do it, then?"

Eric almost fell off his stool at this.

Zoe giggled at his embarrassed expression. "Come on, you can tell me. Am I or am I not your best friend?"

"I don't think that gives you the right to poke your nose into my private affairs."

"But I always tell you what I get up to with my boyfriends!" protested Zoe.

Eric got off the stool and began to walk away. "Exactly."

Ignoring his sarcastic tone, Zoe followed him. "Come on, tell me! It's driving me mad!"

"Mind your own business."

"Please! *Please?*" begged Zoe as she grabbed hold of him, an exaggerated pout on her lips.

"What difference does it make if you know all the details?" he sighed.

"None whatsoever, it just gives me something to gossip about. I did it with Clover, remember?"

"If you think I've come here to discuss intimate stuff about Steffy, you can think again."

"Oh, for God's sake!" snapped Zoe, starting to lose her patience, "I don't want to know *everything*!"

"Well you asked Clover for all the details."

"Yeah, but she'd just got it on with a film star from Hollywood! And anyway she never actually told me, the bitch!"

"Why all this interest in Stephanie? You've never given me the third degree before. You didn't seem particularly interested in the other girls I went out with."

"This is different, this is special. She's the woman of your dreams, isn't she? Or at least she was when you were twenty."

Eric began to sort through some of the collectibles on display in the showcase. "That was years ago, we've both changed since then."

"Uh-oh," said Zoe, shaking her head and looking totally unconvinced. "That sounds a bit weird."

"Why?"

"Because I thought you were over the moon but instead it's starting to sound like you're putting the brakes on. Hasn't Steffy lived up to your youthful expectations?"

"We've only been on one date, for God's sake!" said Eric, rolling his eyes.

"Well sometimes that's all it takes."

"I'm a big believer in rationality, remember? I need time to figure out if I really like a person."

"But when you were a kid you fell in love at first sight."

"It might have been better if I'd just been struck by lightning," he muttered. Zoe returned to the counter, deep in thought. After the argument with Eric, she had spent all night thinking about what she had really felt after seeing him walking off with Stephanie Parker and she had felt so bad that she'd promised herself she'd behave like a perfect friend for the rest of her life. She didn't want her own regrets to make her jealous or bitter or spiteful towards one of the people she loved most in the world, nor did she want to continue being treated like an object by men. She wanted to start seriously working on herself – to try and become a better person, stop hanging out with people who didn't deserve a moment of her time and be a better friend to her friends.

She wanted Eric to feel free to ask her for advice or to let off some steam any time he wanted to. He was a special guy and he deserved a special girlfriend.

When she caught up with him, she started again. "Listen, I just wanted to remind you that you can tell me anything. If you need advice, reassurance, whatever, I'm here," she said, seriously. "Agree?"

"Is there something I should be forgiving you for?" said Eric with a puzzled look, and Zoe took his right hand and stroked the plaster on it.

"This, for example. If I'd given you a hand with the work yesterday, instead of wasting time with Evan, you wouldn't have hurt yourself. I felt really guilty about it."

Eric didn't move, just stood there staring into space, his hand abandoned in hers. "It doesn't matter. It was just me being clumsy, as usual."

"Yeah, Mr Troublemaker!" cooed Zoe, giving him a slap on his wrist.

"My mother should *never* have told you that nickname," he muttered, adjusting his glasses.

Zoe laughed heartily. "She only told me as revenge for you not going home to her for Christmas."

"You used your whole arsenal of dirty tricks to persuade me to spend that evening with your family instead of mine. It should have been you she punished you, not me!"

"But I know how to make you forgive me," said Zoe, pursing her lips and fluttering her eyelashes. "I'm adorable and irresistible, aren't I?"

Eric grunted.

"Am I interrupting something?"

At the sound of those words, they both turned around to find Stephanie staring at them with a puzzled look on her face. Zoe realized that she still had hold of Eric's hand, and so she slowly released it. She wasn't doing anything wrong and therefore didn't intend to behave as if she had been caught with her fingers in the till.

"Hello, Steffy."

The girl looked from one to the other, a tight smile on her lips. "I was just passing and I thought I'd drop in for a quick chat. Have I come at a bad time?"

"Of course not."

"You were absolutely right to come," Eric said, smiling at her. "You okay?"

"Yes, of course. I have a job interview in twenty minutes and I'm early."

Eric walked around the counter to join her, and Stephanie leaned over to give him a kiss on the cheek, very close to his lips. Zoe realized that they were not yet intimate enough to kiss each other on the mouth in public, and for a brief moment she felt heartened. Then, scolding herself for acting crazily and remembering her good intentions, she moved away to give them a bit of privacy.

The shop door opened and Zoe set off towards the customer, but Eric rushed in front of her, apologizing to Stephanie before abandoning her there alone in the middle of the room. Seeing the sad look on the girl's face, Zoe walked over to her.

"There is always a steady stream of people here. They've managed to whisk him away from you in less than a minute."

"Yeah. But I can't expect him to devote all his time to me and to stop him from working," Steffy shrugged. "I turned up here without letting him know I was coming, so I wasn't expecting him to only have eyes for me – and it's now clear that he doesn't."

The last sentence, spoken with a hint of bitterness, made Zoe raise her eyebrows. "What do you mean?"

Stephanie stared at her, "Can I ask you a question?"

"Shoot."

"Did you and Eric ever go out together?"

"What?" Zoe was stunned. "Me and Eric… no! Why do you ask?"

"You seem very close. When I came in just now, neither of you noticed the door opening and… Well, I mean, I just want to make sure that I'm not facing any… you know, unfair competition."

Unfair competition? If I had wanted Eric, you'd have already lost him, girlfriend!

That thought appeared so suddenly in Zoe's head that it gave her the creeps.

She couldn't feel that she was in competition with Eric's girlfriends. That was crazy! She laughed, but it sounded a bit hollow.

"We've been friends for a long time."

At that moment, Eric returned and Zoe dragged him into the conversation. "Can you reassure your girlfriend, please?"

"About what?"

Stephanie interjected, giving him a hesitant glance. "I'm sorry – I embarrassed Zoe by asking her if you two had ever been a thing."

Eric took off his glasses and rubbed his eyes with one hand. "What made you think that?"

"You seem to be very close."

"Anyone would be close after being friends for ten years."

Zoe stepped back when Steffy took hold of his hand. It wasn't the first time that one of Eric's girlfriends had looked at her suspiciously for the complicity they demonstrated when they were together, but it was the first time that one of them had confronted the situation head-on. She had to admire her for it: it was obvious that she really cared about Eric, and Zoe couldn't help but be happy for them.

"Don't worry, I'm going out with someone too, at the moment," she said.

"Oh, cool! I mean, I'm happy for you – I wasn't trying to insinuate anything, I hope I haven't said anything weird!" exclaimed Stephanie, almost breathlessly. "You're just so pretty that it makes me feel insecure, you know? It sort of makes you wonder if any guy would be interested in an ordinary girl after spending the whole day with you."

Zoe dismissed the idea with a wave of her hand. "Thank you for the compliment, but there's no need to be worried. Eric has known me for ages, and if nothing has ever happened between us I would imagine that it must be because he's immune to my charms."

She tried to catch Eric's eye, but he looked terribly uncomfortable. He turned and smiled at Stephanie. "And anyway, you're beautiful girl, too," he said.

"Thank you. I'm sorry if I've embarrassed you."

"Don't worry about it."

"Listen, Zoe? We're going to the opening of a new restaurant tonight. Why don't you come along with your boyfriend?"

Zoe hesitated. She looked at Eric, who looked as if he had just swallowed a live toad, and shook her head.

"Thanks, but I really can't tonight. Enjoy the evening by yourselves."

"I'd really like you to come, honestly. After that blunder of mine a moment ago, the least I can do is try and be friends with you. I'd like to get to know the people who are important parts of Eric's life, and you're certainly one of them." Stephanie looked at Eric searchingly. "You wouldn't mind if Zoe came, would you…?"

"I don't really think Zoe wants to spend the evening with us. I'm sure her boyfriend has made other plans for tonight."

Zoe's mobile phone began to vibrate in her skirt pocket. She pulled it out and gave a sigh. "Speak of the devil…"

She walked away from them to answer the phone, but Eric caught up with her before she could.

"Come with us," he said in a serious voice. "We've never been on a double date, before."

"Can you put up with Evan for the whole evening?" she asked.

"Maybe if I get to know him better I'll end up liking him," said Eric in the same tone before returning to Steffy.

Zoe felt a strange sensation as she answered the phone.

Eric was right – they had never been out together with their respective partners before. It seemed that their relationship existed only outside their own romantic liaisons.

Yet it was natural to introduce your partner to your friends. That was what Clover had done with Cade, and Liberty had done the same with Justin. She and Eric, however, had never officially presented any of their amorous conquests to one another. Perhaps because none of them had ever seemed worthy of the privilege?

She suggested having dinner with two friends to Evan and, as she'd expected, he wasn't too happy about it. They had only been out as a couple a few times and he was more interested in devoting their time together to doing other things. Feeling slightly annoyed, Zoe found herself insisting. She wanted a normal relationship with a guy and an evening with friends was her idea of normality.

Sensing that he might end up not even getting to first base that evening if he decided that he didn't want to go along, Evan agreed to have dinner with Eric and Stephanie and Zoe hung up with a satisfied smile.

"He said 'yes'," she said as she walked back over to them.

"Fantastic – we'll have fun!" smiled Stephanie. Zoe couldn't tell if the girl's enthusiasm was genuine or dictated by a desire to repair the faux pas she had committed earlier. Obviously, she didn't want to antagonize Eric's best friend but it was equally understandable that she didn't trust her completely.

Zoe found herself looking forward to the evening ahead – after all she would have the opportunity to study Eric's new flame and decide whether she really was suitable for him or whether she should consider her an enemy like all the others. But above all, she would be able to observe her shy and reserved friend in a situation outside of their own friendship. And that was something she was very curious about.

*

What a dumb idea.

How could he have pushed her into accepting that reckless invitation from Stephanie? He should have made her understand that she wasn't welcome and pretended that he wanted to dine alone with his girlfriend... but the idea of making Zoe feel like a third wheel seemed absurd even to *his* brain cells.

Did Zoe understand now why they had never been out on a double date before? For him the reason was clear, but apparently that little detail had never occurred to her before this evening. At that precise moment, though, she must certainly be thinking about it, given the lacklustre conversation that was taking place at their table.

He and Evan had nothing in common. All the football player spoke about was sports and cars, two topics that Eric had always found tedious. Without Zoe acting as an intermediary and without Stephanie's forced cheerfulness, silence would have fallen on the group a minute after they'd been served with their starters.

The two girls were pretending to share a camaraderie that didn't really exist. In reality they were observing each other like two cats competing for the same fillet of fish, although for quite different reasons, and that made for a heavy atmosphere.

In short, it was a disastrous evening.

Eric understood Stephanie's doubts about his relationship with Zoe – he had already been through the same thing with previous girlfriends. All of them, without exception, ended up feeling threatened by the looming presence of his best friend, even if Zoe didn't actually do anything to fuel their suspicions. It wasn't her fault that she was gorgeous and sexy as hell and that he couldn't help but desire her every time he laid eyes on her. Although he worked hard at not showing the world how he felt, even a corpse would have picked up the vibrations that his body gave off whenever he was around Zoe. As long as the corpse wasn't Evan, of course – all *he* could come up with were a few monosyllables and a whole load of lascivious glances at Zoe's seductively tight pants and white T–shirt that left a glimpse of velvety skin, from her neck to her shoulder which would have been enough to awaken the vampire in anyone.

Every time Evan looked at her or touched her, Eric felt as though he was going to die of jealousy. The effort of not staring him out, or stabbing him with a fork every time he reached out to her, or telling the pair of them off like some bitter old prude each time Zoe gave Evan a peck to keep him quiet was killing him.

To counteract the bitter taste of bile in his mouth, he focused as much as possible on Stephanie, who looked as pretty and fresh as a daisy in her peach-colored dress. It really was a shame that Zoe was so ingrained in his head and in his heart, because Steffy was a sweet girl who really cared about him and clearly wanted to please him and to show him how happy she was to be going out with him.

Why couldn't he just fall in love with her? It would have been so much simpler.

Zoe glanced continually in their direction, partially sating her curiosity, intrigued as she was with the idea of seeing him in action with a girl.

Eric knew what was going on and that was why he was trying to behave as naturally as possible , even though he felt uncomfortable playing the role of the boyfriend in the presence of the woman of his dreams. But that wasn't the only reason why Zoe was watching them.

Knowing her as well as he did, Eric guessed that what really bothered her was being monitored by Stephanie as though she were some kind of explosive device. Some of his former girlfriends had tried to break them up and Zoe wanted to make sure that this newcomer wasn't yet another threat to their friendship.

Eric would have laughed at that nonsense, if he had only had the strength.

"So did you get the job?" Zoe was asking Steffy, as they waited for dessert.

"Yes! As of next week I'm going to be Dr Leitman's assistant."

"Doctor? Weren't you a sort of scientist?"

On hearing that, Eric stared at Evan, a sarcastic quip poised ready on his lips. The chump had a brain as big as a peanut.

Stephanie, always polite, feigned amusement. "I *am*. It's not just doctors who are called 'doctor' – a lot of graduates are called 'doctor' too."

"The name Leitman sounds familiar to me," said Zoe.

"He was one of our professors at M.I.T., but nowadays he's completely dedicated to research, and I will be working for him."

"I must have heard his name when I was helping you with your studies," said Zoe, smiling at Eric.

"Probably. He was my favorite teacher back then."

Stephanie looked at Zoe." Did you study at Boston too?"

"No, I worked in the campus cafeteria. Eric came in every day at the same time and when things were quiet I used to go over and sit with him and give him a hand." Zoe looked down at her empty plate. "I wasn't really helping him, I just listened to him going over his notes – physics and computer science have never been my forte."

"What did you graduate in?"

"Oh, I didn't go to college."

"Zoe knew what she wanted to do when she was twenty," said Eric, intervening to try and prevent his friend from feeling embarrassed. At the mere mention of university, Zoe always tensed up. "She worked really hard while half the guys on campus spent all their time getting wasted at parties and joining weird secret organizations. Her dream was to move to

New York and attend one of the most prestigious courses in photography in the United States. She was right to go her own way – she didn't need a degree to become the talented photographer she is now."

Zoe's sweet smile threatened to send him into raptures even though he hadn't said what he'd said with the intention of making himself look good in her eyes. Zoe had always felt inferior in front of people like him who had a degree in some subject that was considered difficult. She had nothing in common with graduates and that made her feel left out when people started talking about college and prompted her to seek general approval by focusing on her other skills.

"I just partied the whole time!" laughed Evan, who certainly seemed to have no problem showing his weaknesses. "I went to college for a year, then I left to play football."

'You went to *college? You?!*' thought Eric in amazement. "So what faculty did you attend?" he asked, trying to restrain the level of sarcasm in his voice.

"Ah, I don't know – one of them. I can't even remember, my dad picked one out for me."

"I thought it was strange," said Eric, letting out a tired sigh.

He was grateful when the waiter brought them the dessert. Only a few more minutes and they would be able to leave, finally.

"Eric tells me that you're going to be doing a special in-store photo shoot in the next few days," said Steffy while she took a spoonful of cake.

Zoe nodded. "Yeah. We're going to do a racy calendar for the girlfriend of one of our customers."

"And the customer is Brooke Samuels!" exclaimed Evan.

Zoe and Eric gave him dirty looks, but Stephanie didn't notice.

"Seriously? The Hollywood actress? That's fantastic!"

"It will be, but it's information that we only usually give out once we've finished when we're working with a particularly well-known client," Zoe said, giving her a meaningful look. "You know, for privacy."

"Oh, sure. I guess it's a hassle to have to deal with all their fans crowded outside the door."

"Exactly."

"You should be used it. One of your colleagues is dating an actor, right?" interjected Evan.

Stephanie stared at Eric. "Liberty or Clover?"

"Clover," sighed Eric. Since Mr Muscle couldn't keep his mouth shut, he might as well clarify the whole situation immediately. "She's seeing Cade Harrison, who has worked in the past with Brooke Samuels. That's why she's coming to us tomorrow."

"Cade Harrison, wow! He's absolutely gorgeous!"

"The story was all over the papers. How come you didn't know about it until now?" Zoe asked, puzzled.

"Oh, I don't usually pay much attention to that type of gossip."

"Just like Eric. Do you always have your head buried in a book all day too?"

Thanks to the radiant, happy smile on her face which diluted the content of her words, Zoe's slightly sarcastic tone went unnoticed, but Eric noticed it and grimaced.

"That's why we are such a well-matched pair," he said. "We've got the same boring interests."

At his words, Stephanie's eyes lit up, sparking a twinge of guilt in him. He knew that he had only really complimented her in order to take some petty revenge on the other girl at the table.

How sad.

"I quite like the world of showbiz," Evan said, finishing off his dessert in a flash. "Those guys get a boatload of perks, who *wouldn't* want to be in their place?"

"And do you have any aspirations in that field?" asked Eric, getting more and more bored.

"I never really thought about it seriously, even though I always enjoy appearing in the newspaper after a game. But I'm pretty excited at the idea of being one of the models for the calendar. Hey, I'll get to meet two famous women!"

"Excited, really? I had no doubt about that whatsoever." His mumbling earned him a kick under the table from Zoe, who was trying to hold back her laughter. The idiot, of course, didn't pick up on the sarcasm in his voice.

A very good-looking but rather gaudily dressed woman passed by their table and stopped dead when she saw Lewis.

"Evan? Is that you?"

He looked up and his face broke into a smile. "Luanne?"

As the two, speaking almost simultaneously, embraced and kissed one another on the cheek, Eric looked over at Zoe, who was staring at the newcomer like a scientist observing a cell culture under a microscope.

Whatever degree of interest she actually felt for her partner of the moment, Zoe – his beautiful and smart Zoe – always seemed to end up feeling increasingly threatened by other women.

How ridiculous – that bleached blonde with fake boobs wasn't even *half* as pretty as she was.

Evan, though, seemed to appreciate her and his slightly lascivious interest in her neckline made Zoe get up from her chair.

She walked over to the pair of them and placed her hand on Evan's back, sliding it down his spine in a gentle caress which was aimed at attracting his attention.

Eric could not speak for Lewis, but his body reacted immediately and unmistakeably. He looked away from the pathetic scene and tried to concentrate on his dessert, even though it felt as if he were eating shards of glass.

"Aren't you going to introduce me to your friend?" Zoe said sweetly. In less than two minutes, she had already started competing with the new arrival – it usually took her longer. Did that mean that she liked this nobody more than others?

"This is Luanne. She was my old college girlfriend," explained Evan. "Lu, this is Zoe. We've been dating for a few days."

Zoe and Luanne reached out and shook hands. If they had been in a science fiction movie there would have been the sizzling sound of high voltage sparks flying from that handshake.

"She's jealous, huh?" Stephanie murmured in his ear, distracting him.

"Who are you talking about?"

"At a guess I'd say both of them are, but mostly Zoe. When a man's ex-girlfriend and his new girlfriend meet for the first time, they're always pretty hostile. They observe each other and wonder what he found so interesting in 'the other girl'."

"Well, personally I can't see anything exciting about that woman," Eric said. "Perhaps it's my affection speaking, but I don't think Zoe has anything to be jealous about."

"You're very loyal," Stephanie said as she stroked his cheek and gave him a quick kiss on the mouth. "And you've got no reason to be intimidated by Zoe's boyfriend either, you know? He is so…"

"What? Stupid? Vulgar?" proposed Eric, with a grimace.

"I'd probably have been slightly more magnanimous in my description, but I'd say you've hit the nail on the head!" she laughed.

Unable to help himself, Eric glanced again in the direction of Zoe, who continued to drape herself over her little toy in order to mark her territory. Feeling more and more irritated, Eric suddenly got up from the table.

A puzzled expression on her face, Stephanie looked up at him. "What's the matter?"

"I just need to make a quick phone call," he improvised. He gave her a kiss on the head, to reassure her. "I'll be right back. And then I would like to go, if it's ok with you – I really don't want to spend the whole evening with them."

"I agree," she smiled, her green eyes glinting mischievously.

Eric walked to the exit and, once outside, leant against the stone wall of the restaurant.

What a rotten evening. He would need to convince Stephanie not to have any similar ideas in the future. Their relationship had to run parallel with his relationship with Zoe, otherwise it would be a total waste of time.

Hadn't he decided to go out with another woman so that he could *forget* about his colleague?

Seeing her showing an interest in that idiot just to avoid being pushed out of the way by Miss Silicone Tits made him mad. Zoe Mathison with her fantastic figure, Zoe Mathison who could have any man she desired, whose brain was as keen as her face was pretty, was so desperate for attention that she ended up making a fool of herself. He had always hated that about her and his ability to put up with it had dropped off sharply over recent weeks.

He was finding it increasingly difficult to control his feelings.

He took a deep breath to calm himself down, then went back inside. Luanne seemed to have vanished, but Evan and Zoe were still standing up and that gave him hope that the end of the evening was in sight.

"We're leaving," said Zoe, without looking over at him. Evan was smiling from ear to ear… and had a conspicuous bulge in his pants.

On the verge of throwing up, Eric pulled back Stephanie's chair as she stood up and helped her put on her jacket. "Yes, we are too."

They left the place in silence and, once they were outside, Steffy smiled at Zoe.

"Thank you for accepting our invitation, it was nice getting to know you better."

"It was for me too," said Zoe, looking somewhat distracted.

Evan handed her a helmet, then climbed up onto a huge motorcycle that Eric hadn't noticed before. "Get on, baby. We'll be home in a jiffy on this bad boy."

"Does he even know how to ride that?" Eric asked Zoe, his fists clenched in his pockets.

"Sure. He goes a bit too fast, but… who wouldn't with a bike like that?" Zoe climbed on behind Evan then turned towards him. "See you tomorrow!" she shouted over the noise of the revving engine.

"If you're still alive," Eric muttered, taking Stephanie's hand as they headed for the taxi stand.

"It wasn't a great idea of mine, was it?"

Eric tried to smile at his girlfriend. "It doesn't matter, it's over now."

"I'm sorry. I felt bad about the impression I'd made on Zoe and I just invited her on impulse to try and make up for it," Steffy said, biting her lip and sounding mortified. "I shouldn't have asked her that stupid question about the two of you being together, I should've asked you or just have minded my own business. But I wanted to know whether I should be worried about her or whether I could trust her."

"Fear Zoe?" said Eric with a bitter laugh. "Didn't you *see* the kind of man she likes?"

"She does have rather unusual taste."

"Yeah, that's one way of putting it."

Stephanie stared at the road ahead, suddenly looking melancholy. "Listen, I hope I didn't give you the impression that I'm some kind of crazy jealous fruitcake, but it's hard for me to trust people. Years ago I fell in love with a guy who was really close friends with this other girl – they'd been family friends since they were at kindergarten together. As far as he was concerned she was like a kid sister or something, but then we started dating and she got jealous and she kept throwing spanners into the works until we eventually split up. I hated the way she was always meddling in our relationship and it ended up driving me nuts, but at the same time my boyfriend was still too attached to her to tell her to buzz off – he didn't want to hurt her," she said as she observed him from under her long lashes. "So can you understand now why I wanted to make sure that Zoe wasn't another rival? Us women always tend to make the same type of mistakes in love, and this time I just really want to avoid doing that…"

Eric was silent for a moment, feeling more guilty than ever. But if Steffy needed reassurance about there not being anything going on between him and Zoe he could give it to her without lying. He was the one who was hopelessly in love with

Zoe, not the other way round, and he was determined to remedy the situation with Steffy.

"You heard what she said today – if nothing has ever happened between us in all the years we've known each other, you have nothing to worry about," he said, gallantly opening the door of the taxi for her, then following her in and sitting beside her.

"I'm really happy to hear that," she murmured with a smile, pulling him closer to her.

"Where to?" the driver asked.

Steffy looked at Eric, a clear invitation in her eyes.

"The night's still young. You want to come back to my place?"

He hesitated a moment, feeling confused, and then the image of Zoe on that pig in heat's bike appeared in his mind.

"Good idea."

Chapter 7

Things were buzzing at that time in Giftland. To cope with the constant demands of customers, Liberty had recruited a couple of extra girls so as to let her, Zoe, Eric and Clover get on with their own jobs.

That particular day, however, the situation was even more chaotic than normal. In addition to the usual customers – of whom there were more than usual because Valentine's Day was approaching – there was a Hollywood star and a listed Canadian model in the store, and confusion reigned supreme. The employees wanted to take a look at the celebrities and the customers jostled to admire the fantastic models parading up and down the shop's stairs for hours.

Intent on adjusting her camera, Zoe waited for Brooke Samuels to explain the purpose of the photo shoot to her astonished friend Sydney. She and the actress had met the previous afternoon to choose twelve faces from among those the model agency had made available, and to assign roles for each calendar month. Now, the same models were gathered in a corner, almost ready to start, but Sydney was still shaking her head in disbelief and amusement.

The phone rang and Zoe answered it without thinking. "Giftland," she said, still staring at the settings on her camera.

"Hello, this is Cade. I'd like to speak to my insane girlfriend!"

"No chance that you'd rather speak to me, then, I guess?" joked Zoe, peering around her in search of Clover. Her friend had stayed in the store to help choose the costumes so she couldn't be far away.

"Stop hitting on me – you'll make Patrick jealous!"

"Patrick?"

"Dempsey. I've got his autograph for you. He didn't put his phone number on it, unfortunately, but it's better than nothing…"

"Oh, Cade, you're the best!" laughed Zoe, as she located Clover. "I'm going to try with all my might to get between you and that darn redhead – who, incidentally, doesn't deserve you. You've only been away only a few days and she's already replaced you, did you know that?"

"Oh, really? Who with?"

"With a bevy of oily, half-naked models. She's over there schmoozing them right now. I don't know if I'll be able to drag her away," she cooed, smiling at the look in Clover's eyes once she realized who was on the other end of the phone line.

"What the hell are half-naked models doing in your shop?" growled Cade, affecting a stern voice. "I thought it was safe to let her work there!"

"I know – but hey, what can you do, we're about to start doing a racy photo shoot and Clover immediately offered to lend us a hand. She's completely shameless!"

"Send me the photos of these guys – I'll show them to my team of hitmen so they know who they need to take out."

With a grin at Zoe, Clover snatched the phone from her and said, "See what happens when you're away from me? If you hadn't gone to Los Angeles, I wouldn't have needed to try and forget how lonely I felt with the help of twelve hunky strangers!" she said as she walked away.

How sweet, thought Zoe as she returned to her desk, looking around her as she went.

The large room in which she worked was unusually full of people: twelve models, four costume designers, the makeup artists, Brooke and Sydney, Clover and Liberty, and even Eric. Samuels had asked for him in fact, and they had also requested a backstage film that showed the most entertaining moments of the photo shoot, and so Eric was working hard with cameras and microphones.

Zoe allowed herself a moment to observe him. Since the awful evening they had spent together with their respective partners they hadn't been alone for a minute and so they'd had no chance to talk about it. In fact, he seemed to be keeping his distance. Perhaps he had other things to think about – his new relationship, for instance. Had his sweet girlfriend already begun to brainwash him about not getting too close to her?

Zoe gritted her teeth at the thought of yet another girl who was going to try and get between her and her best friend. What was it they were afraid of? If Eric had had any interest in her he would have shown it by now, wouldn't he?

She remembered the thoughtful, sweet way he had acted towards Stephanie during dinner and let out a sigh. Now *that* was a normal couple. Whatever it was that she and that sex addict with ambitions to break into the world of entertainment had definitely couldn't be considered a *relationship*!

She looked around for the man in question and when she spotted him, intent on admiring himself in the mirror before getting ready for the photographs, she grimaced. Their relationship had taken a weird turn after the evening at the restaurant – a sexual one that Zoe wasn't really into. But she had made the mistake of giving him one steamy night to try and regain the ground she felt she'd lost when she'd seen Evan staring admiringly at his ex-girlfriend, and now keeping him at bay had become even more difficult than before. She was ashamed of the awkward strategy she had adopted so as to avoid being pushed out of the way by that walking pair of fake boobs. On the other hand, the thought of being single and desperate around the couple of the year made her feel like crap, and that was why she was carrying on with this stupid relationship, hoping to get something positive out of it. But the task was proving more difficult than she'd expected.

Against her will, she turned her eyes back to Eric. He looked distracted and quiet. His face looked relaxed, which she read as a sure sign of sexual satisfaction, but his eyes weren't shining the way Clover's were.

Wasn't he happy with his girlfriend?

He turned and Zoe met his gaze. She wanted to ask how he was, how his new romance was going, or just spend some time chatting to him, teasing each other the way they always did, just to make sure he wasn't trying to put some distance between them, but she wasn't sure that he was willing to confide in her – and anyway, at the moment she was too busy to be thinking about this stuff, so she forced herself to put the whole thing out of her mind until a later date.

Evan emerged from one of the makeshift cubicles that had been put up to give the models some privacy, dressed – or rather, *un*dressed – as Cupid. A piece of white fabric was draped over his private parts, from his back sprouted a pair of white wings and in his hand he carried a bow. There was no denying that he was genuinely attractive and very sexy, though perhaps the makeup artist had gone a bit overboard with the body oil. Every single muscle was highlighted, glossy and quivering, and his blond curls were artfully arranged.

Zoe saw him approach Brooke and Sydney and swore under her breath. She had told him to stay away from them,

117

but it was evident that he hadn't listened to her. On his face was the same expression you might see on the face of a kid going into a toy store, as he stared at the two women almost adoringly.

Sickened, she approached Liberty, who was absorbed in choosing the background music. "I've never seen a man brown-nosing the way Evan is doing right now with those two," she muttered.

"Is he trying to become a male model?"

"I have no idea."

"What do you two talk about when you are together?" asked Liberty, without looking at her.

Zoe shrugged. "That's usually left up to me."

"I see."

Eric stopped next to them with a bundle of wires in his hand, trying to arrange them so that they wouldn't get in the way.

"Be careful with those, I wouldn't want someone to trip over them," Liberty reminded him. "We'd have to pay the agency if one of their models got hurt."

Zoe grimaced. "The only one who can get hurt without it being a problem is Evan, he doesn't belong to any agency – at least, not the moment."

"Cupid has wings so I don't know if I can trip him up. But I can try," quipped Eric, ducking under a table to hide the tangle of electrical cables. Brooke and Sydney came over. "Zoe, can we have a word?"

"Sure, girls, what's up?"

"It's really fun, and I absolutely love the idea," smiled the model, turning to her friend and giving her an affectionate look. "I just have one teensy problem."

"Tell me what it is and we'll try to sort it out."

"Cupid." muttered Brooke. "Can't you just get someone else?"

An amused snort coming from under the table made Zoe smirk. She tried to restrain herself. "What's the matter with Evan?"

"He's a little... insistent!" said Sydney, rolling her eyes. "All he does is smile and keep giving us compliments. I have a feeling that he's trying to get me to put a word in for him with my agency... Either that or he's angling to get a date. But either way, I'm not interested and he's getting on my nerves."

"What we mean is that we would have preferred someone a bit more delicate for the part of Cupid," said Brooke.

Zoe blinked in surprise. "I'm sorry, I should have had him come to the casting yesterday. Wasn't the description accurate enough?"

"Oh, no, I thought it would be a great idea. A beautiful, sexy cherub. But your guy just doesn't quite square with my idea of sensuality."

"He squares with mine – or at least with that of my 'almost' husband," snapped Sydney, an angry spark flickering in her eyes. "He has the same kind of animal charm that asshole Trevor had!"

"Maybe we could call the model agency and get them to us send one of the guys that we turned down."

Sydney turned back to Liberty, an apologetic expression on her face. "I'm sorry to be causing all these problems."

"Not at all – the calendar is a gift for you and it should be completely to your taste," replied Liberty reassuringly.

Brooke's gaze was drawn towards Eric, who was still crouched under the table, and a devilish smile appeared on her face. "Syd, honey, I think that I might just have found you a perfect Cupid."

Zoe followed the actress's eyes and nearly burst out laughing. "Oh, Brooke, I don't think…"

"Look at that cute ass," the woman continued, giving Sydney a nudge with her elbow. The model looked at Eric's backside, which was quite evident in that position, and raised her eyebrows.

"Not bad. But what about the rest of him?"

"Gorgeous!" Brooke assured her. "I've already met him."

"But Sydney hasn't," said Liberty with a sadistic smile, as she anticipated the scene that was unfolding. "Eric, can you can come out from under there for a moment?"

Zoe saw Eric back out on all fours and crack his head against the edge of the table as he tried to get to his feet. "Damn," she heard him mutter, rubbing his brown curls.

She smiled in amusement. Eric was the only guy she knew who could be polite and refined even when he swore.

The knock had sent his glasses flying, so Eric 's face was dishevelled but unadorned when he turned to face them. Sydney looked him up and down from head to foot, then nodded.

"I like him!"

Eric put his glasses back on and then stared in puzzlement at the female faces around him. "Did I miss something?"

"You are about to become a model," said Liberty. "Brooke and Sydney think you would be perfect for the role of Cupid."

Zoe put her hand to her mouth to try and stop herself from laughing out loud. The shocked expression on Eric's face was priceless.

"What?! No way! I'm not posing for a photo shoot!" he protested, looking over at her for support. "Tell them I'm not photogenic!"

"Well," Zoe hesitated, "he is actually is a bit wooden. I think he's really too shy for this sort of thing."

"Nonsense, we're amongst friends here," said Brooke, dismissing their excuses with a wave of her hand. She grabbed Eric's arm and dragged him towards them so that she could get a better look at him. "He's slender rather than muscular, but he's tall and has a beautiful face. He looks very sweet, and that's good, seeing as he will be representing the god of love. In Latin mythology, Cupid was described as young and clumsy and that sounds about right too. Okay, his hair isn't really blond, but it isn't in Caravaggio's paintings either, so…"

"You're right, he's perfect," said Sydney with an approving smile.

"So, Eric, if you want to go and change… You're second in order of appearance," said Liberty, immediately handling the practical side of the matter. But Eric kept shaking his head vigorously.

"Wait a minute, don't I get a say in this? *I'm not a model*!"

Liberty's expression began to grow more and more threatening and Brooke and Sydney looked at him in a puzzled way. Zoe took him by the arm, but Eric pulled away and began to leave the room.

"Leave him to me, give me five minutes," she said, before setting off after him.

She intercepted him at the other side of the door and grabbed him. "Eric, wait!"

"I'm not doing it," he hissed, giving her a glare.

Zoe dragged him into Liberty's office and closed the door. "There'll only be a couple of shots! I promise that I'll be quick, I already know exactly what I want to do, so it won't take long."

"But did you see how that clown was dressed?!"

121

"Oh, come on, make an effort!" Zoe said. "Aren't you pleased to know that two beautiful A-listers prefer you to Evan? Think of the satisfaction when you go back out there and steal his bow and wings!"

Eric mumbled something incomprehensible and Zoe moved closer to him. "Do it for Sydney. She's just been brutally dumped by a guy who looks just like Evan."

"Well maybe that'll teach her to prefer brains over muscles."

"Then do it for yourself and for Liberty. If you upset Brooke by refusing to co-operate, Lib might cut your wages!"

"A fine friend she is! She didn't even ask me for my opinion, she just immediately sacrificed me for the cause!"

"Okay, do it for me then." Zoe put her hand on his chest, fluttering her eyelashes as she often did in order to obtain favors from her prey. "You don't want to make me look bad in front of two women as important as them, right?"

"Are you flirting with me?" Eric blurted out, staring at her.

"Is it working?" she giggled.

"Why?"

"To get you to accept the role of Cupid?"

"Then no."

Was there another reason that have made a difference? Zoe wondered briefly. But she dismissed the thought and sighed.

"Listen, we'd also be running the risk of giving Cade some bad publicity. He was the one who recommended us to Brooke, remember? If we piss her off she might mention it to some journalist and poor Clover would end up in the middle of it all…"

"You sure know how to get someone in a corner," said Eric, and then he took a deep breath. "Ten minutes in all – and *don't* make me look an idiot!"

"I'll make you look like a god, I promise!" said Zoe, clapping her hands happily. "Go and get ready. Clo and the seamstresses will tell you what to do. I'll go and reassure the others."

She left before he could change his mind and joined Brooke, Sydney and Liberty.

"Everything okay? I didn't mean to upset him," began the model, sounding confused.

"He isn't angry, he's just terrified," explained Zoe. "But I've calmed him down and promised that it won't take more than ten minutes'

"I'll go and get him a beer, maybe that'll help him relax," said Liberty, leaving the room.

Brooke looked at Zoe, almost incredulously. "I've never seen a man get so anxious at the thought of showing off in front of a group of women!"

"Eric just isn't like other men," she smiled. "He's a nice guy who wants to get himself noticed for his other qualities."

"Well he certainly manages it. He's such a sweet guy that I'd gladly ask him out on a date!" laughed Sydney.

"Sorry, but he's already taken," replied Zoe in a tone of voice that was the opposite of Sydney's.

"Oh, I'm sorry. I didn't think the two of you... I thought you were with the soccer player?"

Zoe looked at her in surprise. "Oh, no! I mean, yes, I'm dating... I mean, I *was* dating Evan. Eric and I are just friends. But he has a girlfriend, that's what I meant"

"You said it so seriously that for a moment I thought you must be jealous!"

Brooke chuckled. "Maybe she's regretting letting him get away!"

"I'm going to tell Evan what's going on," Zoe said, ignoring their comments. She didn't understand why, but what they'd said made her feel uneasy.

Evan didn't take the news very well at all. He looked around angrily for his replacement, but Zoe said that the new model had already gone to get changed and that he would have to return the wings and bow. With an angry gesture Evan handed them over and then rushed off to get changed. He left without even saying 'goodbye' and Zoe knew that she wouldn't be seeing him again.

Twenty minutes later, the sound of voices had started to get really loud. Everyone had been in the room for over an hour, the first shots had been successfully taken and the remaining ten models were eager to get into their poses. Sydney was ready, wearing the dress chosen for the photo for February… but there was still no sign of Eric.

Seeing the impatient look on Brooke's face as she was being entertained by Clover and Liberty, Zoe headed off towards the small dressing room she had seen her friend enter.

He'd been in there quite a while. Had he changed his mind? Brooke would be really angry, to say nothing of Liberty…

She walked confidently over to the dressing room and stopped outside, ready to flatter him again if necessary. "Eric, you're taking too long," she began, drawing aside the curtain unceremoniously. Their relationship was such that they didn't have any inhibitions in situations like this. "I've already done January's model, now it's your turn and I need you out there as…"

At the sight of the spectacle before her, the words died in her mouth.

In the small, dimly lit cubicle, Eric was completely naked, offering her a perfect view of his smooth, well-proportioned back, broad shoulders and muscles that were well-defined and hard without being too big.

And an ass to die for. Firm, well-shaped…

"My God," she whispered as she stared and clung tightly to the dark curtain.

Eric turned abruptly, giving her a full-on view of his well-defined chest and the rest of his anatomy, just before he grabbed a sweatshirt to cover his modesty, his face turning a bright beetroot-red.

"Zoe! Damn you, couldn't you knock?!" he exclaimed, sounding embarrassed.

"Erm," Zoe cleared her throat, still unable to remove her eyes from his lean physique, "because… it's not easy to knock on a curtain?" she stammered. "For Christ's sake, Eric… why the hell are you naked?!"

"I'm supposed to be dressed up as Cupid, aren't I? If you'd prefer me to put my clothes back on…"

"No, no!" she interrupted, hurriedly, adding, "You go right ahead," before quickly closing the curtain.

God…

Her heart pounded in dull thuds in her chest. She had never been so shocked in her life!

What the hell had he been doing standing there as naked as the day he was born? She would have imagined anything except seeing him like that.

Incredulously, she drew back the curtain again, as though to make sure she wasn't hallucinating. But Eric was still there, now wearing the white cotton skirt. Although his nakedness was no longer on display, Zoe still felt an equally hot flush at the sight of the rest of that amazing physique.

She wasn't used to seeing him without his clothes on. She couldn't remember ever having seen more than Eric's calf or his bare arm in ten years of friendship.

Jesus, and to think that she had almost been convinced that he didn't actually have a body at all!

"Why the hell do you always cover yourself up?" she said, suddenly inexplicably annoyed.

Eric jumped, quickly pulling on one of the robes that the models had provided for him. "Are you still here?"

"I've come to tell you to hurry up and you keep wasting time," said Zoe, looking straight at him. His hair looked unkempt as if he had been repeatedly running his hands through it and there was some slight stubble on his face that made him look even more charming. He was looking for his glasses, which were on top of a pile of his clothes and she instinctively stepped forward to stop him. "Don't put those damn glasses on!"

"I can't see anything without them."

"You're not blind." She looked him up and down then, mystified, shook her head. "Why?" She asked him.

"Why what?"

"Why did you take all your clothes off?"

"I don't know, maybe because I still haven't learned this trick of getting changed without taking off all my clothes first, but I promise that I'll learn to master the technique as soon as possible," snapped Eric sarcastically. "If it annoys you so much, I can just get dressed again right now. I didn't even want to *do* this damn photo shoot!"

"I just didn't expect to see you completely naked. I thought… well, I thought that you would get undressed like all the other prudes, one piece at a time!"

"All I'm supposed to be wearing is this ridiculous skirt!"

Zoe sighed. "Okay, okay. But why do you always have to dress like such a loser when you could be showing off that physique of yours?"

"I'm sorry to hear that you don't like my clothes, but they are comfortable and I like them. I'm not a model, Zoe, nor do I aspire to become one."

"But…" Zoe continued to shake her head, trying to dispel the image of his naked body from her mind. "Whatever, never mind. Get yourself oiled up, we're all waiting for you"

"*Oil*?"

"Yes, oil, to highlight those muscles that I didn't know you possessed!" she snapped, leaving the cubicle. "You damn… *cheat*!" she muttered as she strode away.

Clover stopped her. "Is something wrong? Don't tell me that he's changed his mind…"

"Oh, no, not at all! He's really enjoying himself, standing there stark naked, gazing at the muscles he's kept hidden from us all this time!"

"Eric has *muscles*?" her friend teased her, running after her. "Are you sure?"

"He also has a nice ass," Zoe muttered. "And that's not all!"

Clover stared at her. "Zoe! How much did you *see*?!"

"I saw everything!" she replied, running her hands over her face and rubbing her eyes. "God… I won't forget that in a hurry!"

Clover laughed. "Was it *that* amazing? So why are you angry, then?"

"It's Eric! I wasn't prepared… I mean, he could have let me know!"

"Let you know what? That he's well-equipped and has a pretty nice body under those clothes of his?"

"Under those nerdy clothes that do absolutely nothing for him at all! Heck, with a pair of contact lenses, a sexy shirt instead of those awful sweaters he wears and a tighter pair of jeans he would look totally different!"

"Yeah, but would it matter? He would still be Eric – pedantic, sarcastic, fussy old Eric," smiled Clover, looking at her with a strange expression on her face.

Zoe ran her fingers through her hair. "Yeah, you're right," she said, sounding unconvinced. But she continued to feel as though she had been cheated out of something.

"Eric, it's your turn," said Clover, catching up with him as he came out of the cabin.

He nodded, taking hold of the flaps of robe with both hands. "You owe me a favor. A *big* favor!" he snapped, glaring at her.

"Why, what have I done wrong!?"

"Your friend Zoe talked me into doing this by telling me how much you would suffer if the news of an irritated Brooke Samuels made it into the gossip mags, seeing as it was Cade who introduced you to her."

"I see. And what about Liberty?"

"She was all set to scalp me when I said I didn't want to do it!"

"And Zoe?"

"Oh, I'll make her pay," he growled threateningly, "I'll make her pay more than anyone else." Clover chuckled. "By the way, I gather I owe you a compliment, but I'll keep it for later."

"What are you talking about?"

"I've never seen Zoe so upset at the sight of a naked man!" Clover looked around her, then leaned toward him. "She's in shock! She could hardly string two words together when she came out of your dressing room. That piqued my curiosity, so I can't wait to see you on that set now."

Eric felt his heart beating more and more rapidly. When Zoe had marched into that cubicle whilst he was getting changed, he had almost passed out. It had been the thought of posing half-naked in front of her that terrified him more than anything else. He knew his body was average – he was agile and slim, but considering Zoe's tastes, which were oriented towards roided up athletes, he felt unattractive and puny. But she had actually seemed quite flustered, and Clover's words had confirmed his impression.

His friend seemed to be reading his thoughts. "Just keep your head up and enjoy yourself. You've got everything these other guys have got and I'm sure it'll go great. Didn't you know that the wiry look is terribly fashionable nowadays?"

"Fashionable or not, I just hope I don't look ridiculous"

"You certainly won't look any more ridiculous than the model playing May!" laughed Clover. "He's wearing a thong with a fig leaf on the front and a garland of flowers on his head!"

"I've been lucky, then."

Before he could get closer to the brightly lit set, Clover took him by the arm. "Can you do me a favor?"

"Another one?"

"This one is for both of us," she said, mysteriously. "Imagine you're an Adonis – a man who can get anything he wants. Then think about Zoe and what you would say to her, do with her, how you would like her to feel about you – and when you've gotten properly into your role, lift your head up and look at her."

"Are you trying to ruin me?"

"I just want to do an experiment, that's all. I'll explain later." Clover began to walk away, but then turned back and grabbed hold of him so that her lips were almost touching his ear. "And hey – when you think about her, don't go into too much detail. Remember you're only wearing a skirt!"

Eric suppressed a giggle at her rude joke as he watched her walk away.

One of the seamstresses approached him, holding out her hand for his towelling robe, and his desire to laugh disappeared, immediately replaced by a heightened sense of anxiety. Undressing in front of all those beautiful women and those perfect professional models made him nervous. He took a chance and glanced over in Zoe's direction, but she seemed to be totally focused on her camera, so he took a deep breath and relinquished the robe. Immediately, one of the makeup people came over to cover him with oil, which made him grimace with disgust.

Sydney, who was sheathed in a fiery red evening gown, walked towards him. She was beautiful, her loose black hair falling onto her shoulders in perfectly formed curls. She looked at him with frank admiration.

"Wow, what a stud! You're even better than I thought."

"Well that's very kind of you, but I don't believe it for a minute!"

"Well I'm sorry but you're mistaken. It's a shame that you're already taken, you know?" She winked at him, then waited for her orders from Zoe, who was at that moment walking towards them.

"Is everything OK?" she asked while Eric slipped the white angel wings on.

"Remember your promise. No more than ten minutes," he said, staring at her.

"You'll like it, trust me!" smiled Brooke, who was standing nearby. "You just have to think about how beautiful you are and how beautiful Syd is, and the rest will come naturally."

Zoe cleared her throat to attract his attention. "Sydney already knows what to do. As for you, you need to wield your bow as if you were about to fire an arrow at her, with your legs planted firmly apart planted on the ground and I want you to look at her as if she is the thing that you want most in the world."

Eric grimaced but didn't answer her. He just raised his bow, holding it awkwardly as though it were red hot. "Which way round does this thing go again?"

Rolling her eyes, Zoe positioned his hands and arms, then she bent down to push his legs apart. Eric held his breath at the touch of those warm, slender fingers. "There, you're perfect," she murmured, passing a finger over the quadriceps that the stance he was holding made stand out proudly. Eric focused on all the unpleasant things he could think of to stop himself from getting excited.

Zoe got up quickly, took a step back and bumped into Brooke. "Oops, sorry!" she stammered. Then she spun round and went back to her position behind the camera. "Ok, let's get a move on. If you can give me the right pose straight away, it'll only take about ten minutes."

Sydney sensed the tension in his body and smiled, placing a hand on his back. "Just relax, Eric. You're not doing anything illegal."

"I'll try."

"Sydney, can you mess up his hair a little?" asked Brooke, who was now standing next to Zoe. "Let's make this handsome devil look a little more evil!"

"Aren't I supposed to be the god of love? What's evil got to do with anything?"

"Knowing Brooke's taste in men, it's got everything to do with it all right," chuckled Sydney, running her fingers through his hair.

"That's enough," shouted Zoe. "I don't want him to look too unnatural."

To Eric's ears, those words sounded like the greatest of compliments.

He started posing and looked at Sydney, trying to feel like a fierce, sexy archer, which was surely just how Evan Lewis would have felt in his place. The satisfaction of having been judged better than that hulk made him feel bolder and his self-confidence showed in his posture, which was much straighter than usual. Sydney smiled encouragingly and, just as Clover had suggested, Eric imagined for a moment that he was a confident, attractive man who was able to get what he wanted with ease.

"Put some more passion into it and it's perfect," said Zoe, clicking away like a mad thing from all angles. Eric closed his eyes for a moment, imagining that it was her he was aiming his arrow at instead of the model, and his heart skipped a beat. Wearing that dress, Zoe would have looked like a fairy tale come to life…

His eyes turned automatically to the object of his desire, his eyes filled with emotion. Zoe remained transfixed, her eyes on his, and time seemed to stop… at least until her fingers lost their grip on the camera with its telephoto lens and it ended up crashing to the ground with a thud.

In the anxious silence that followed, a female giggle was distinctly heard in the room and Eric knew, with certainty, that it was Clover.

"Shit!" Zoe snapped, picking up her camera quickly.

"Is it broken?" asked Brooke, sounding worried. "No, no… it's all right."

Eric looked around, catching Clover's eye and raised his eyebrows. In response, she gave him the thumbs up.

"Ok, I think that'll be enough. You can go," muttered Zoe, walking rapidly away.

Eric didn't need to be told twice. Breathing a sigh of relief, he gave his wings and bow to one of the assistants and then he turned to Sydney and took hold of her hand. "It was a pleasure," he said, bending down to place a kiss on it. He was feeling playful now that he was free to leave the set.

"It was for me too!" she said with a smile. "And if you are ever single, call me!" she added with a giggle, as he walked away.

Eric didn't answer and left the circle of lights. Passing near to Zoe he couldn't resist the urge to place his hand on her shoulder, and he felt her stiffen under his fingers. "Was I ok?"

"Yeah, you were fine!" she nodded, avoiding his eyes.

"Thank you for making it quick," he murmured, winking at her.

"Go and get dressed, for God's sake," she muttered, staring at him.

Although he wasn't sure what was going on in Zoe's mind at that moment, as he walked out of the room, Eric felt a kind of euphoria the like of which he had only experienced a few other times in his life.

*

She couldn't take her eyes off the computer screen. Eric's face was so intense, so beautiful... she still couldn't get her head around how good-looking he was, but most of all she still couldn't understand why it had taken her so long to notice.

Giving in to an impulse she ran her fingers along his features, going down his neck and along his clavicle, running them as far down his chest as the shot allowed. After years of friendship she knew the texture of his skin, she knew it was warm, smelling of shower gel and a subtle masculine scent the name of which escaped her but which she had always associated only with him. But he had never, until now, aroused in her this uncontrollable desire to feel her body against his.

The photos from that afternoon had left her feeling full of overwhelming desire, not simply because the theme of the shoot had been passion, but because they were of Eric, that shy and bashful boy for whom she had always felt only an almost fraternal affection.

When he had stared at her in that way, full of vibrant passion, she'd felt an intense heat wash over her. In a flash she had seen herself in the model's place, wearing that wonderful dress, with that semi-naked man, a man who represented love in every way, intent on possessing her...

She jumped up from her chair, fanning herself with her hand. Maybe it would be better if she waited a few days before going through the photos she had taken that afternoon. She still needed to recover from the surprise of seeing her best friend naked – and of having ardently desired him.

The phone rang, vibrating on the desk. She grabbed it without looking at the display, silently thanking whoever it was for the distraction.

"Hello?"

"Am I disturbing you?"

An unmistakable voice which until a few hours ago would have brought a smile of genuine happiness to her face but which now only made the blood rush to her already flushed face.

"Eric …"

"I need to talk. As soon as possible."

"Okay. What about?"

"Me… you. I mean, us."

Us? Now she understood why cardiologists were paid so much. This type of emotion created imbalances in the life of a human being, making the need for medical intervention more than likely.

"Yes." she stammered, as she tried to slow down the accelerated beating of her heart by taking a deep breath.

"Are you sure you want to hear this? Because once it's out of the box, nothing will ever be the same again."

Eric's voice was deep, full of barely contained emotions. In a flash, she knew that she wanted at all costs to hear what he had to say.

"You can tell me anything you want," she whispered.

"I'd rather tell you face to face."

"Then come round… or do you want me to come over to your place?"

The sound of the doorbell almost made her trembling legs give way.

Lifting the hem of the red dress that she'd forgotten she was still wearing, she ran to the door and flung it open. There he was, his phone still up against his ear, wearing a shirt that she'd never seen before. His hair was messy, there was a trace of stubble on his face and he was wearing his faithful glasses. He really was gorgeous…

She continued talking to him on the phone despite the fact that he was now standing in front of her. "What did you want to tell me?"

"You look beautiful."

"It's the dress…"

"No, you are, you always have been and I can't look at you any more without wanting you."

Letting the phone fall to the ground, she ran into his arms. She had no idea why this was happening right now, she hadn't expected it or ever imagined it but suddenly it seemed absolutely right, exciting, and perfect.

She couldn't wait to savor the delights of his kisses.

She closed her eyes and, breaking away from her embrace, Eric took her face in his hands and lowered his head.

"Stephanie, I love you…"

Stephanie?

"No!" she shouted, her heart sinking in her chest. "You want *me* –only me!"

"And why would I want you?" asked Eric, sounding deadly serious.

A sob escaped her lips, and the sound echoed round the empty room…

Feeling her heart beating wildly, Zoe emerged from sleep with a small groan of despair. She put her hand to her chest in an attempt to calm herself down and sat up. In the darkness of the room, the faint light of the clock radio showed that it was a little past three in the morning and that she hadn't been asleep for more than a couple of hours.

The images of her dream still filled her mind like some kind of out of control music video, making her shake her head in disbelief.

With trembling legs she got out of bed and walked to the window, which offered a spectacular view of the Empire State Building lit up in red for the forthcoming celebrations for people in love.

What the hell was going on? Was it just the desire to have someone by her side that had provoked those strange dreams, or the fear of someone taking away her best friend? Or was it that, after what had happened that afternoon at the photo shoot, she had really started to see Eric in a different light?

"You've already dreamed about kissing him, remember? And you hadn't even seen him naked at that point…"

Maybe it was time to talk to someone about these confusing thoughts that were swirling around in her head and get some dispassionate advice from someone who saw the whole thing from a different perspective.

Are you sure you want to hear this? Once this is set in motion, nothing will ever be the same…

The words that Eric had said in the dream echoed in her head, making her stomach churn. Was her subconscious trying to tell her something?

"Ok, it's official, these celebrations are having a strange effect on me," she murmured to the empty room, resting her forehead against the cold window pane.

Chapter 8

She felt tired and drained of energy. Maybe it was just because of how stressful things had been over the last few months, the freezing weather or all the chaos that there had been at work recently.

Actually, that morning she'd only had a couple of relatively simple photo shoots to do, after which she had dedicated herself to selecting, photo-shopping and printing off the photos for Sydney's calendar.

They had come out really well. All the models were handsome and credible in the roles they were playing, and Syd was just gorgeous. What really stood out, though, was how much she had obviously genuinely enjoyed posing for those photos, and that had really pleased Brooke Samuels. The idea had begun as a way of bringing a smile back to her friend's face and it could confidently be stated that she had achieved her objective.

It was five days until Valentine's Day and the calendar was almost ready. She would send the photos to Brooke for approval before sending everything off to the printers, but Zoe was sure Brooke wouldn't find anything wrong with them. The shoot had been a real success.

A success that, after dismantling the set and returning to her apartment, had left her with a splitting headache which was still throbbing annoyingly at her temples after an almost sleepless night and two aspirin.

Especially after the strange dream she'd had about Eric.

Again.

"It's just because Valentine's Day is getting nearer and it has this effect on you," she repeated to herself for the umpteenth time, rubbing her forehead. All that love in the air could go to your head.

But when Eric loomed into view, her justification crumbled before her eyes like a sand castle.

Damn it, she just couldn't look at him any more without seeing him naked! Beneath his striped sweater, his unpretentious jeans and the inevitable spectacles on his nose, all she could see now was that toned, wiry physique that had left her breathless.

She had seen a multitude of men undress in her life, both for work and for pleasure, and she had usually found herself being attracted to the macho, muscular types, so she was struggling to understand her reaction to Eric's more subtle beauty. Yet even fully clothed it was easy to make out from the breadth of his shoulders, his exciting athletic physique and his height. How come she hadn't noticed how potentially sexy he was before?

It was her *job*, damn it! To grasp the nuances, the personality behind a face, the harmony of a body, it was all part of her success as a photographer. Instead, after ten years of friendship, she'd never managed to see the young man's exciting qualities – she had been blinded by his nondescript appearance, by his unassuming way of going about things and by that shyness of his that seemed to be always holding him back from doing what he really wanted to…

Sexy? Exciting?

Why had she suddenly started thinking about Eric that way? Seeing him naked certainly hadn't changed things. Clover was right, he was still the clever know-it-all that they all knew, and the fact that he was suddenly able to make her drool simply by wearing a skimpy cotton skirt and a layer of baby oil to highlight his muscles or by wearing a pair of wings and holding a bow and arrow shouldn't really change anything.

"You okay?"

The voice, as warm as the hand that rested gently on her back, surprised her, and Zoe sat up suddenly and turned round.

"Yup!" she exclaimed hastily. The idea that Eric might be able to read her thoughts by looking into her eyes made her turn her face away immediately.

Eric looked puzzled. "It looked as though your head was about to hit the counter."

"It was kind of you to worry."

"It wasn't kindness, it's my job. We need that counter, I can't let your head collide with it. It might get broken," he joked.

Relaxing slightly, Zoe pulled a face. Now she recognized her lifelong friend.

"Ha-ha-ha. How hilarious."

"Hey, what can you do. I've discovered new opportunities that previously weren't accessible to me. After my recent experience as a sex symbol, I might almost even consider taking up stand-up comedy."

"A man of many hidden talents, no doubt about it."

Zoe watched him place a huge, fluffy heart in the window and found herself craning her neck to get a better view.

Good God, she was looking at his butt!

Pulling herself together she got up quickly, covering her eyes with her hands.

"What are you doing?" asked Eric, walking back over to stand next to her.

"I've got a headache."

"Go and take a rest, I'll take care of things here."

"No, I need some distraction. You have to edit Brooke's video. I haven't got anything to do until four and with this weather I doubt many people are likely to come by. I can manage."

Eric stopped in front of her, his green-blue eyes looking anxious behind his lenses.

"You sure? I can do the video tonight."

"Haven't you got anything better to do than taking work home with you?"

"No, actually, I haven't," he replied without hesitation.

Zoe stared at him. "And what about Stephanie?"

Eric hid his slight embarrassment behind a careless gesture.

"I didn't mean it like that. But she has another commitment tonight, so I'm free." He went back to staring at her attentively, and Zoe felt herself getting agitated. "Is that invitation for a pizza still going? I mean, I still haven't forgiven you."

"Err… I don't know" she hesitated uneasily, something she had never done before. What the hell was happening?

"You're right, sorry. You don't feel very well, and then there's all this snow. Forget I asked." Eric gave her a pat on the back and disappeared into his office without giving her time to answer. Moreover, it would have taken her several minutes to put together a meaningful sentence, since her tongue was stuck to the roof of her mouth.

With a groan, she lay her head on the cold counter.

The door opened letting a soaked but smiling Clover in as Liberty came down the stairs.

Zoe sighed.

"Look at her, Lib. She's been out in this awful weather and yet she still manages to smile!"

"The power of love!" Clover sighed, and put her hands to her chest. "Cade came back last night."

Zoe turned to her boss. "Can I kill her now or do you need her for anything?"

"Ask me again after Valentine's Day – right now she's almost indispensable," said Liberty, turning towards the coffee machine that was in a niche behind the counter.

Clover moved towards the counter and waved a paper bag under Zoe's nose. "If I offer you a frosted donut will you forgive me for being so happy?"

Zoe took it.

"Only if I can have all of them. I'm going to need a *lot* of sugar to fight off this pervasive sadness."

"*Sadness?* Everyone's so damn sickly-sweet at the moment I'm starting to worry about getting tooth decay," muttered Liberty, warming her hands on her cup of coffee.

Zoe looked at her in surprise. "You too, Lib?"

"Me too, what?"

"I thought I was the only bitter, jealous one in here. I mean, it would be normal – I'm the only one who's single."

"I'm not jealous," smiled the blonde. "Have you ever seen me sighing dreamily or going into raptures over romantic drivel?"

"No, actually."

"A little sweetness would do you good, Lib," said Clover, offering her boss the bag of donuts. "Have one."

Liberty stepped backwards as if she'd been confronted by the devil. "No thanks!"

Clover raised her eyebrows. "What have you got against sweet things? You always react to them like you're being offered rat poison."

"Hey, it took me years to get into a size forty, I'm not going to let a handful of carbohydrates ruin everything again," she snapped, turning on her heel and marching off to her office.

Zoe and Clover looked at each other in amazement, then launched into their donuts.

"How's it going?"

Zoe shrugged. "Aside from the headache, business as usual."

"Eric?" Clover asked, holding back a laugh as she saw her raise her head sharply.

"If you want to know how Eric is, ask him," she huffed, trying to make light of the situation. Clover had been watching her suspiciously since the day before, she knew something was up. Moreover, after her weird reaction to seeing Eric naked, it was hardly surprising. "Stop looking at me like that," she said threateningly.

"Zoe, when you dropped your camera, I thought I was going to die with laughter!" chuckled Clover. "If I were going to draw that expression of yours from yesterday in a cartoon, you'd have your mouth wide open and drooling, your eyes bulging out of their sockets and your heart pounding visibly under your blouse! I could ask Lib to do us a sketch…"

"What the hell are you talking about?" Zoe sank her teeth deeper into her donut. "I dropped the camera because I was distracted."

"Oh, yes! We all noticed."

"Give it a rest, it's not what you think," Zoe repeated to Clover and to herself, hoping that she sounded convincing. Thinking back to that awkward moment and her subsequent dreams, the alternative was to admit that she had been disturbed by that magnetic gaze and by all the desire that Eric had communicated to her in that particular moment. But it was just coincidence, obviously. It had been her who had told him to put more passion into it while he was posing for the calendar pictures. Eric had just carried out her orders.

Perfectly.

"I must admit he did look really good dressed as Cupid," Clover continued, undeterred. "I wasn't expecting that."

"Exactly. So you can understand my surprise."

"Yeah, but I didn't stand there with my mouth hanging open like someone starving to death at the sight of a table set for a Fourth of July picnic! Though it's true that I didn't get to see what was under his skirt…"

Zoe nearly choked on her last mouthful of donut and coughed loudly, much to the amusement of Clover, who added, "It's a pity that he has a girlfriend now."

Recovering slowly, Zoe brushed the crumbs from her hands. "It wouldn't change anything. We've been friends for a long time, and yet we seem to spend half of our time bickering over nothing. Us two being together would be a disaster, it would ruin everything. I'm too complicated for a straightforward guy like Eric. I'd make him miserable."

The triumphant look on Clover's face made her realize that she had fallen into a carefully prepared trap. And suddenly she understood.

Her words had highlighted an accurate analysis of the situation: she had practically admitted that she had seriously considered the hypothesis of a relationship between her and Eric.

She hastened to rectify the situation. "Well, this conversation is neither here nor there, anyway. Feeling embarrassed about seeing a friend completely naked doesn't mean anything."

"I wasn't suggesting anything – you did that all by yourself," smiled Clover, picking up the now empty donut bag. "I'm going to call my next customer. If I can finish soon, I can go home early and see Cade. The snow does have some good points, after all. Among other things, it discourages people from wasting time shopping and it creates a very romantic atmosphere!"

Zoe saw her go into the office she shared with Eric, and sighed for the umpteenth time that day.

She would have preferred not to have to deal with people who were in love until Valentine's Day was over and done with – and perhaps not even afterwards. Instead all she seemed to do was meet dreamy-eyed women, and men intent on surprising their partners with special gifts.

And speaking of the devil… The door opened again, and in came Stephanie. Zoe felt a small flicker of irritation. It wasn't unusual to see her in Giftland, and she knew that the relationship between her and Eric had become more serious after that disastrous evening when the four of them had been out together. But she wasn't expecting to see her that particular day. Eric had said that they weren't seeing each other.

"Hello Zoe," Steffy smiled, brushing the snow off her jacket.

"I wasn't expecting you today. Not this early, anyway."

"I wasn't going to come, actually. But before going to my best friend's bridal shower, I decided to pop in and surprise Eric." The blonde shrugged, her face glowing with happiness. "I'd be sorry to miss even a moment that I could spend with him."

"I see," Zoe deftly changed the subject. "Your friend is getting married, then?"

"Yes, on Valentine's Day and luckily the wedding is at the Plaza, so at least we'll be dry. They're forecasting a blizzard for that night."

"Well I'm glad I'll be spending it in the warmth of my apartment, then," Zoe smiled, lying through her teeth.

"You and your boyfriend are celebrating at home?" asked Stephanie candidly.

Zoe felt a sudden and irresistible urge to strangle her.

Fortunately, she didn't need to reply because Steffy continued thoughtfully. "I don't know what will happen. I mean, Eric and I are going out together, it's true, but I don't know if we can really call ourselves a couple yet. So I don't know whether to ask him to come to Nicole's wedding with me or not."

"You haven't been together long enough to figure out what direction your relationship will take yet?"

"But I would still like to give him a little present." Stephanie lowered her voice. "What do you suggest? You know Eric much better than I do."

"Oh," Zoe looked around, taken aback. "I know what he likes, that's true, but I can't choose something for Valentine's Day. It's not the same as getting him a birthday present or a Christmas present."

"I don't want to just get him the usual chocolates, or some tacky card." The girl began to wander round the stands full of overflowing hearts, cards with hearts on, dolls that held hearts, hearts in various sizes and textures, all strictly bright red. "I would like to give him something simple, something that's not going to frighten him, but something that's sweet enough for the occasion and original enough to elicit a smile."

"Ok, let's see." Zoe followed her, scanning the merchandise.

"How about this?" Steffy asked, grabbing a key ring in the shape of the Statue of Liberty holding a sceptre in the shape of a heart. Zoe shook her head.

"Eric doesn't particularly like key rings. He's kept the same one he's always had for years and apparently has no intention of changing it, even if he does actually need to."

Now she thought about it, it had been her who had given it to him, shortly after his graduation.

"Oh, you mean the one of the Empire State Building? You're right, it's completely worn out." Stephanie shook her head. "Maybe it holds some sentimental value for him. No key ring then. I don't want to risk giving him something that he wouldn't appreciate. Please help me! Put yourself in my shoes and tell me what I could possibly give him after being with him for such a short time."

Put yourself in my shoes…

Zoe tried to imagine herself as 'Eric's girl'. She saw herself being surrounded by his attentiveness, constantly looking into those bluey-green eyes as they peered out over the upper edge of his glasses, being comforted by his gentle voice…

And close to that body that she had thought was almost scrawny but was actually strong and sexy, and…

"Here we go again!"

She shook the disturbing images that filled her head away and began to think seriously about what could possibly be a romantic but fun gift for someone like Eric. After a few minutes of looking around her, her eyes fell upon one of the many cuddly toys that she had put out on display that very morning: a teddy bear clad in pyjamas, wearing slippers and glasses. A small, hidden button, when pushed, made it play the chorus of Rod Stewart's 'Da Ya Think I'm Sexy ?' while the bear gyrated his hips gently. Under the pyjamas, which were

147

fastened by a zip, the bear was wearing a red shirt that said, 'I like you. Do you like me?'

"I'd get him this," she smiled, taking it off the stand. "It's perfect for him."

Stephanie pressed the button, chuckling to herself, then turned it off. "It's really cute, just like him! And especially because – and this is just between me and you – beneath all that good-guy stuff, Eric is… well, wow!"

And judging by the twinkle in her eyes, Steffy was not just referring to Eric's physical appearance. Zoe began to suspect that her friend might have several other cards up his sleeve of whose existence she was completely unaware.

Refusing categorically to imagine sleeping with him, she grabbed the bear and took it over to the counter. "I'll wrap it up before he sees it."

She had just finished tightening the red bow when Eric emerged from his office, rubbing his eyes under his glasses. Seeing Stephanie he paused, looking surprised.

"Hello. What are you doing here?"

"I just came by to say 'hello', as we're not going to be seeing each other tonight."

Zoe saw her approach him, rise up on tiptoe and kiss him on the lips. She looked away. "Just to let them have a bit of privacy," she said to herself.

But the slight flutter in her stomach didn't really convince her at all.

She busied herself filling the space left by the teddy bear on the stand, so that Eric wouldn't notice it was missing, and waited for the two of them to say 'goodbye' to each other. Fortunately, Stephanie left without further ado, leaving her free to return to the counter.

"Tell me, Steffy had a romantic gift for me in her hand, didn't she?" asked Eric, looking at her out of the corner of his eye.

"Don't you want to get a present from your girlfriend?"

"We've only just started dating…"

Zoe dismissed his excuse with a shrug of her shoulders. "It's nearly Valentine's Day, it's natural that she wants to get a gift for the person she's sleeping with. Even if it's still early days, I'm guessing both parties are interested in continuing this relationship. Or am I wrong?"

Eric froze. "Did she tell you that we…?"

"My dear, I don't need anyone to explain certain things to me, I'm old enough to know the ways of the world," joked Zoe, giving him a pat on his nose. "Anyway, your girlfriend looked really happy. So… well, *bravo!*"

Eric's ears began to turn a slight shade of red. "You women really can't help talking about these kind of things, can you?"

"You men are even worse. Drawing up charts of all your sexual conquests, giving women marks on their physical attributes as though they were horses for sale – and going into *very* specific details."

"I don't do that."

Yeah, not him. Not the sweet, polite guy standing in front of her.

Zoe smiled, softening. "There should be more Eric Morgans in the world. If that were the case, I might even decide to keep one for myself," she added, winking at him. She had deliberately said it jokingly, but she was taken aback by how heartfelt her words had sounded.

Was it possible that her feelings for Eric had changed so suddenly? Surely it couldn't have been just the fact of seeing him naked that had this weird effect, could it?

149

"I suppose I should think about a present too," he said, distracting her. "For Stephanie."

"Tell me what would you like to give her and I'll give you the benefit of my female insight."

"I've no idea. What could a girl who has only been out with me a few times without us having anything approaching a serious conversation possibly want?"

"If you want something deeper with her than just a regular appointment between the sheets but you're still not quite sure about how all of this is going to turn out, choose something classic. We women are quite easy to please – flowers, chocolates, a few sweet words and a bit of originality in the way you wrap the whole thing up and there you have it, we melt like snow in the sun."

"A bit of originality in the way I wrap the whole thing up..." murmured Eric thoughtfully. Then he nodded. "I'll think about it."

I don't care, I don't care...

Zoe repeated the words to herself as she stared at the shop window without even really seeing it.

But it did bother her – it bothered her plenty.

Giving romantic advice to men, advice that they would then use on other women, was really depressing.

*

Something classic, wrapped up in an original way...

Eric kept mulling over those words and wondering what exactly he should do.

Every year on Valentine's Day, completely anonymously, he gave Zoe a small present, and every year, without fail, his gift ended up in the pile of flowers, cards and chocolates that Zoe received from her many admirers.

He knew he couldn't really expect otherwise, given the situation. It was cowardly of him, but he deliberately chose that day to give her a little sign of his love, aware that it would pass almost unnoticed. The first few years, Zoe had been intrigued by the nameless little packet that was amongst the others, but then she had gradually got used to its silent presence.

Just as she had got used to him.

But Eric didn't want to pass unnoticed, or to be just something she was used to. It was time to change their relationship.

He had noticed a subtle change in the way Zoe had been behaving since he had posed for that stupid calendar. Maybe it was just his impression, but she seemed a bit less relaxed in his company, almost as though she felt uncomfortable. There was still camaraderie and affection, of course, but sometimes the strange light he glimpsed in those curiously beautiful cat's eyes of hers surprised him, and the idea that there could be something between them that wasn't just friendship made him tremble like a kid in front of a candy store.

He would never just be able to declare the feelings he had been hiding for years out of the blue like that. He needed a gimmick to help him do it, and a Valentine's gift that was sweet, romantic and original could be a good way to start.

He glanced at Zoe, leaning against the counter looking thoughtful. She looked more and more beautiful every day. Those delicate features, her slightly almond-shaped eyes, her porcelain skin... Nature had really created a work of art when it had sculpted her face, never mind the rest of her!

With those tight jeans, her red v-necked sweater and her hair pulled back to reveal the long white curve of her neck, she was irresistible. Her slender fingers fiddled with a heart-shaped pendant that he himself had given her, in secret, one Valentine's Day in the past, and it drew his eye to her pert, firm breasts which were highlighted by the fabric of her sweater. Over the last few days she had relinquished the role of stiletto wearing man-eater, but that didn't mean she was any less sexy. Her sensuality was innate, like a second skin. It was still there even when she was wearing pyjamas.

It was inconceivable to him to think of her being single. None of the guys who had been lucky enough to get her attention had understood a damn thing – that was obvious from the ease with which they had let her slip away.

Some customers came into the shop, disturbing them both from their silent reflections. Eric was about to assist the newcomers when, out of the corner of his eye, he saw Zoe stiffen at the sight of a guy in a suit approaching the counter. Intrigued, he stayed where he was.

"Zoe? Is that you?" exclaimed the man, sounding surprised.

"Stuart," she replied, her face expressionless.

Eric pulled himself up to his full six feet, every nerve in his body at the ready.

It was Stuart Harris, Zoe's ex-boyfriend. That bastard, the one who had betrayed her in the worst possible way and the only one she had really suffered over, was rapidly walking towards them. He had only seen Stuart briefly a couple of times four years earlier. Not enough to remember that stupid face of his. Dark hair, blue eyes, and an intense look about him. He wasn't a gym bunny but he was tall and elegant – a fairly ordinary type who somehow had managed to conquer Zoe's heart like nobody else.

He had hated him then and he hated him now.

"What a surprise. I knew you had changed jobs, but I didn't expect to see you here," said Stuart with a smile as he leant on the counter like an old friend.

What a nerve!

"Me neither," Zoe said, folding her arms over her chest. Eric saw Stuart slyly glance at Zoe's breasts, which were now emphasised by her posture, and felt a sudden, almost physical, desire to break his nose.

"Oh Zoe, you still have that wild temper I remember so well," he chuckled, shaking his head.

"What do you want, Stu?"

"I saw you through the shop window and came in to say 'hello'."

Stuart looked at her almost tenderly, but Eric didn't believe a word of it, not even for a moment. "I know you'll find it hard to believe, but I am really pleased to see you."

"Well yeah, actually, I *do* find it pretty hard to believe," sighed Zoe as she he stepped back. "Thanks for coming in to say 'hello', but, as you can see, I'm busy."

"Why don't we get together one of these nights?" said Stuart with a serious expression. "I would really like to have a chat with you."

Zoe pulled an incredulous face. "Are you kidding me? Why would I want to talk to you?"

"There was something very strong between us, don't you remember? We were together for two years."

"Of course I remember, just like I remember how you went to bed with Miranda!" she snapped, shaking her head. "You are disgusting, coming in here and asking me out like nothing ever happened."

"You never let me explain what really happened," he protested, walking round the counter when he saw her moving away. "Even if you're not in love with me any more, just let me explain so at least you have one good thing to remember about what there was between us."

"Explain? Explain what? You had been screwing my best friend for a month when I found out. She told me everything."

"Miranda was envious of you. She told you a pack of lies."

Eric saw Zoe's eyes darken and she looked distant and confused. He felt himself starting to panic.

She wasn't going to fall for all that nonsense, right?

He stepped forward and took her hand, intending to comfort her with his presence. He felt her relax instantly and cling to his side. He was ready to do anything to stop that idiot from messing with her head any more.

Stuart noticed the gesture and raised his eyebrows.

"Are you two together?" he asked cautiously.

Eric didn't answer. Zoe gave him a quick glance before turning her eyes back upon her former boyfriend.

"That's none of your business."

"Look, I'm in town for work and I'm going to be staying here locally for a while, Zoe," said Stuart, adjusting his jacket. "It doesn't matter whether you're seeing someone or not, I'd still like to talk to you about what happened and try and clear things up once and for all. I don't want you to think ill of me, I have really happy memories of the two years we spent together."

He looked at them both, pausing for a moment to look at Eric, then moved to leave.

"Think about it. I'll be in touch."

When he left the store, Zoe fell back against Eric's chest, her fingers still intertwined with his. Eric put his arm around her, resting his chin on her soft hair.

"You're not actually going to believe all that nonsense, are you?" he murmured, terrified at the thought. He had watched her put up with Stuart Harris's ridiculous behavior rather than lose his 'love' so many times while they had been together. The guy had always had a powerful influence over her – was it possible that he still did, even all these years after they had split up?

"Of course not," said Zoe with a sigh. "But seeing him has shaken me up all the same. He had the exact same look in his eyes that he had all those years ago, that look that always confused me."

"Yeah, and he had the same idea in his head while he was staring at your tits too," mumbled Eric, squeezing her hand tightly.

Zoe giggled. "Why do you think that no guy ever looks me in the eye when he's talking to me?"

"Try wearing a sack if you want them to look at your face. But it'll need to go right down to your feet and be wide enough to hide all your curves – and I'm *still* not sure you'd get the desired effect."

"You're sweet," murmured Zoe, giving him a hug. "Do you think I'll ever find someone who wants me for more than my looks?"

You've already found him, thought Eric. But he kept the thought to himself, merely planting a kiss on her forehead. "I'm going to serve those customers. If you need me, give me a shout."

Turning away, his only thought was that he had to somehow do something about this situation between them as soon as possible. But first, there was another prickly issue that he needed to sort out... He felt a pang of guilt as he realized that he had been thinking about how to win Zoe over without worrying in the slightest about Stephanie and what she felt for him.

He was a lowlife. He had taken advantage of that girl's sweetness to try – completely pointlessly – to drive Zoe from his mind, and now he had no idea what to do or how to behave.

But he couldn't be with Steffy if he didn't love her, no woman deserved that. Better to end the affair immediately before the girl got strange ideas. He would tell her the truth – being honest was better than giving her some feeble excuse, of that he was sure.

*

He felt a bit less sure of himself later that evening when he found himself at the door of Stephanie's small apartment in Little Italy. How could he tell one girl that he was madly in love with another? Would Steffy, like all his other exes, understand right away who the woman in question was? Would she make a scene or just burst into tears?

God, he never knew how to behave in front of a woman in tears. He preferred being yelled at, or something thrown at him...

When he got to the fourth floor of the brightly-colored building he paused in front of the door. Now that he came to think of it, he wasn't that crazy about the idea of being hit in the head by some blunt flying object either.

Stephanie opened the door wrapped in a pink towel, her hair wet from the shower. "Eric, hello!" She smiled, surprised to see him. She stood aside to let him pass and bit her lower lip as he noticed what a mess the room was. "Erm, I'm sorry about this, but I was in the process of getting ready for this evening and wasn't expecting anyone…"

"Don't worry. It should be me apologizing, I'm the one turning up here without warning," Eric sighed, feeling increasingly more uncomfortable.

"Is something wrong?" she asked, staring at him.

Eric looked up at her, his face serious and sad.

"I need to talk to you and I'm sorry to have to do it at the start of what should be a fun night out, but I can't wait any longer. It wouldn't be right."

Alarmed, Steffy took a step backwards.

"Maybe it would be better if I put some clothes on," she said in a quiet voice, before rushing off into the bathroom.

Left alone, Eric looked around him. He had been in her apartment before, of course, and thought it was it lovely – small but cheerful, just like its owner. The vanilla colored walls and exposed brickwork gave it an air of intimacy and individuality, and the brightly colored furniture gave it a fun atmosphere. In another universe – one where Zoe didn't exist – Eric would have taken real pleasure in spending his time somewhere like this with a girl like Stephanie. The few days he had spent with her had been nice… but there was no point continuing to lead her – and himself – on. As adorable as Steffy was, he'd just go on comparing her to Zoe and now it was more certain than ever that he could not break free from that obsession.

She returned, wearing a t-shirt and a pair of leggings, her hair in a ponytail. She was holding a red bag with a pretty bow,

Eric instantly recognized it as the Valentine's Day gift she had bought from Giftland that very afternoon.

"Before you say anything… this is for you. I got it today when I came to say 'hello' to you in the store. It's just a little something that Zoe helped me pick out."

Eric took the bag, feeling cowardly. He was tempted not to open it, but one look at Stephanie's bright eyes dissuaded him. It was as if she already knew. He pulled the teddy bear out of the bag and smiled sadly.

"I'm really sorry, Steffy, believe me," he muttered.

"Did I do something wrong? Was I too clingy, or did I try and move too fast?"

"No, you didn't do anything wrong. The problem is me."

She shook her head, a bitter smile on her lips. "Yeah. That's what they all say."

Eric put the bear on the floor and took a step forward, taking hold of her hands.

"In my case it's true, things always go the same way. I start out with the best intentions, convinced that this time I can carry on with a relationship and instead I find I have to resign myself to the facts." At the sight of her confused expression, Eric took a deep breath. "See, I… I have a serious problem. In spite of all the beautiful girls I meet, and who incredibly seem to want to take an interest in me, I just can't seem to fall in love with any of them."

"Why not?"

"Because my heart is already taken."

He was able to sense the exact moment Stephanie understood. He'd had a lot of practice, because he'd given this speech many times. But it was also true that women seemed to have a sixth sense when it came to dangerous rivals, and

Stephanie was no exception. She, like his exes, immediately understood the truth, long before he had even confessed.

Steffy untangled her hands from his. "I should have realized earlier," she snapped bitterly. Then she looked at him, her green eyes filled with rage. "So what have I been for you? Just someone to pass the time with? Someone you dated while you were waiting?"

"No, nothing like that. You're a beautiful woman and I really wanted to spend time with you. My situation is hopeless, but sometimes I try to do something about it. I was hoping that you… that we…"

"Does she know?" Stephanie asked, disappointment etched on every inch of her face.

Eric shook his head. "No. She's never realized. I've always been very careful not to let her guess my true feelings."

"Well, I think she does know and that she's taking advantage of the situation," she huffed, running a hand over her face. "She's the kind of woman who wants to have everyone at her beck and call and she just strings men like you along. The saddest thing is that you let her… I thought you were smarter than that."

Eric stiffened, split between his wounded pride, his doubts and that strong instinct of his to defend Zoe. But there was no point him trying to explain the situation to the girl he was dumping.

Stephanie furtively wiped away a tear and tried to compose herself. "It doesn't matter. Anyway, if you don't mind, I have to get ready for Nicole's bridal shower."

"Forgive me if you can. I really didn't mean to hurt you," Eric said, looking genuinely contrite. "Zoe will probably never know about any of this, and even if she did it wouldn't change anything. I could have stayed with you forever, enjoying your sweetness and your happiness, but I don't like leading people on. I've been doing it to myself for years, and it's not a nice feeling. I hope you can tell that I'm speaking from the heart."

"Well maybe you should have come out with it a bit sooner," said Stephanie. She stared at him in silence, presumably waiting for him to go, and Eric had no choice but to turn around and leave.

Once on the stairs, he took a deep breath, feeling both relieved and sad at the same time. Steffy Parker was a sweet girl and by accepting the situation without getting too upset with him she had behaved like a grown-up. She had certainly earned all his respect, if not his love. Surely she would find someone better who would really appreciate her.

But as he started walking away down the street, a window opened...

"And give this to your friend, asshole!"

At the sound of Stephanie's angry voice he turned around and at that precise moment an object hit him directly on his chest making him yell in shock, before ending up on the ground among the feet of the curious passers-by who gave him amused or dirty looks.

Ok, perhaps she hadn't taken so well after all... He picked up the dancing bear from the ground and left quickly, feeling as embarrassed as hell. Only when he was a long way away from Little Italy did he allow himself to think about what he was going to do.

Now he had no more excuses. There was nothing preventing him from resolving this issue with Zoe. As he had said to Stephanie, maybe confessing his feelings wouldn't change anything, but he was no longer able to endure this situation without trying to do something to sort it out.

He felt his brain racing through each of Zoe's hypothetical reactions, from the most romantic to the worst, and forced himself to stop letting his imagination get the better of him.

He must act, and act now. Thinking too much about it would only make him lose the little courage he had.

Chapter 9

"Hey guys!" cried Zoe with a puzzled smile as she threw open her front door to let Clover and Liberty into her apartment. "What are you two doing here?"

"You seemed a bit down today," said Liberty, holding out a bottle of expensive French wine, "so we just wanted to make sure you were okay."

Clover handed her a paper covered tray from under which a delicious sweet aroma emerged.

"We were thinking about having a girls' night in! What do you say? We can chat, eat unhealthy crap…"

"*You* can eat unhealthy crap…" muttered Liberty, pulling off her stylish coat.

"God, you're so boring!" joked Clover, giving her a dirty look. "What is it you're afraid of? You're as thin as a rake!"

"I know, and that's precisely *because* I refuse to eat unhealthy crap."

"Nothing's going to happen if you let yourself have a food orgy for one night."

"I'd just rather not to take the risk, thank you very much."

"Does that mean you're going to spend all evening sitting watching us pig out?"

"So I have to eat even if I don't want to?" Liberty snapped angrily.

Zoe held up her hands to calm things down. "Please, don't argue. I'm so depressed that I'm pretty sure I'll be able to eat whatever you've brought with you all by myself… and I could down that whole bottle of wine too, so – problem solved."

"Incidentally, Lib, wine is as fattening as a dessert, did you know that?" muttered Clover, bending over her friend.

Liberty quickly handed the bottle to Zoe. "It's for her."

"Well, after knowing you for three years, I've finally found something that breaks through that unruffled surface of yours," said Clover, walking into the kitchen with a satisfied expression on her face. "That's good to know."

"Why would seeing me so irritated make you happy?" sighed Liberty as she followed her.

"Because you usually border on perfection, which is more than a little disturbing. So obviously I am pleased to discover that you're human after all!" laughed Clover. "I'm a naïve ingénue and Zoe is a perpetually horny bellyacher – all that's missing is a hysterical control freak to make the three of us officially and humanly insane!"

Zoe followed them into the kitchen, already feeling better now that she had company. "Hey, I'm not crazy about way you just described me, red…"

"You mean you're saying that you're *not* perpetually horny?" asked Clover, raising her eyebrows.

"Absolutely not," laughed Zoe, "I'm just saying that I'm not a bellyacher!"

Liberty let out a small giggle then turned her deep green eyes to face her friend. "If that's not the case then tell us why you've been mooching around with such a long face recently."

Zoe sighed while she got on with laying the table.

"Maybe I'm just getting old. I'm almost thirty and if I'm honest, I'm not satisfied with my life."

"Being dissatisfied has nothing to do with age. I'm thirty and I'm perfectly satisfied with my life."

"Yeah, but you share your life with someone."

"I don't share anything with anyone," Liberty said, sitting down at the table. "Personal satisfaction should never be dependent on another person."

Clover smiled sweetly at Zoe. "You have a job you love, good friends, you're beautiful, intelligent and you know how to enjoy life – you can't be dissatisfied! Your problem is something else – you haven't got a man and it's turning into an obsession that's making you lose sight of everything you've always loved doing."

Zoe sighed as she bit into one of the frosted cupcakes Clover had arranged on a plate.

"You're right. I'm tired of being alone."

"And has this sudden desperation got anything to do with the return of your ex?" asked Liberty, pouring herself a small glass of wine.

"No… well, maybe."

Clover sat down, a concerned expression on her face. "Please don't tell me you still have feelings for that guy!"

"Of course not, that would be stupid. But seeing him reminded me again of what it was like to be infatuated with someone, to be part of a couple – to be with someone who makes your heart beat wildly. I was only twenty-three years old when I fell for him, too young to understand that he wasn't the right kind of guy for me. But the emotions that I felt were real. And I haven't felt that kind of emotional intensity – that desire to be with someone every day, even without doing anything – since." Zoe raised her grey eyes and looked at her friends. "He was my first love. You remember how you feel when you're really in love for the first time?"

"Well really, I don't think I can say that Simon Wesley was really my 'first love'," said Clover, with a grimace. "It was more like an obsession that lasted six months. He certainly

164

made me sigh, and I used to spend hours in front of the mirror making myself pretty for him, daydreaming about romantic declarations that were actually never made and glaring at anyone who approached him. But I certainly wasn't actually in *love*. Cade is my first true love. What I feel for him is something deep, something unlike anything I've known before."

Zoe looked at Liberty. "And what about you? Do you remember your first love?"

"Personally, I think the word 'love' is over-used," said Liberty, staring at the wine glass she was cradling in her hands.

"Hmm, I think there might be a lecture on the way," joked Zoe, pouring herself a generous amount of wine. "Maybe I should let you speak, because all this over the top happiness of Clover's is really getting to me... But, hell – to be honest, tonight I need to believe that actually there is such a thing as a happy ending."

"And there is, but I just don't think that every single romance has to be all magic, beating hearts and starry eyes. Love means compromises and sacrifices too," said Liberty, shrugging her shoulders. "Prince Charming doesn't exist and fairy tales are for children."

"I don't agree," protested Clover, "I firmly believe that everyone has a soulmate. I mean, look at me and Cade. Who would have imagined that a man like him could fall in love with someone like me? I mean, I'm like some kind of clumsy elf with my head in the clouds and he is surrounded by beautiful women every day. In theory, he shouldn't have even noticed me, but... Things like that don't come along every day, but maybe we were just destined to meet. Our whole relationship is a fairy tale."

"Ok, but you two haven't been together all that long..."

"What does that mean? That in a few months he might get bored and dump me?" snapped Clover.

"You might be the one to get bored of him."

Zoe leaned towards Clover. "If you get rid of him, can I give him a go?" she joked.

Clover glared at her, then began wolfing down a brownie. "Ok, now I'm the one who's depressed."

Liberty reached out to touch her friend's hand, a hint of a smile on her generous lips. "Honey, I didn't mean to scare you. You and Cade are a wonderful couple, absolutely perfect for each other. You are the exception to the rule, the reason why people still hope that they'll be able to live a fairy tale."

"And why don't you believe in them, then? Why shouldn't everyone get to meet their soul mate? I can't believe that I'm the only lucky girl on the face of the earth!"

"You know, Lib, the way you're talking, you sound like someone who's been hurt," said Zoe softly, looking over at her.

Clover sat up, becoming more attentive. "Oh my God! Is it Justin? He hasn't been unfaithful to you, has he? I always suspected that there was something strange about him... He never convinced me at all!"

"Hey, don't go jumping in at the deep end like you usually do!" said Liberty, rolling her eyes. "Justin's a good guy. He hasn't been unfaithful and he gives me everything I need. He's perfect for me."

"If he's so perfect, why do you have such a bleak idea of love, then? Was there a man in the past who broke your heart?"

Looking uncomfortable, Liberty shifted in her chair. She didn't look up from her glass, but shook her head. "Don't get carried away with your imagination. I just love differently to the way you do. I don't believe in fairy tales because I'm not a little girl any more. I don't *want* to have butterflies in my stomach, or to feel empty or depressed if he's not there, never mind walking around with a stupid grin plastered on my face, writing nonsense in a diary and daydreaming. I want to be with someone who appreciates me, who understands my needs and who looks beyond my physical appearance, someone with their feet on the ground, someone mature who can be with me as long as we both feel the need. A friend I can share my achievements and my problems with."

"A friend?" Zoe stared at her glass. "OK, but there is a subtle difference between a friend and a partner for life, right? There has to be something more… Otherwise, I might as well just go off and marry Eric!"

"Hmm, this is getting interesting," murmured Clover, settling herself into her chair.

Zoe gave her a funny look. "Don't start."

"You're the one who started it, not me!" said Clover with a wink, resting her chin on her hand and smiling. "Carry on, I'm all ears!"

"All I meant was that if you take into consideration what Liberty has just said, the perfect man for me ought to be Eric. He's sweet, caring, funny… He's always been there for me, he understands me in a flash, if I need him he's always there for me. He's the only man who's been able to look beneath the surface without running away afterwards, he puts up with my insecurities, my caprices. When he pretended to be my boyfriend on New Year's Day, he behaved exactly like the person I would like to be with."

Zoe saw Clover smile and sighed.

"But he's never been attracted to me, nor I to him. That's what I mean – if there's no sex, that's not a loving relationship... right? That's what makes a friend different from a boyfriend."

"Sex is fine at first, but friendship and complicity are still there even when the passion fades," Liberty said.

"I agree with Lib... But not altogether with you, Zoe."

"Why not?"

"You're telling me that you're really not physically attracted to Eric?"

Clover was observing her carefully and it made her feel uncomfortable.

"No!" She lied. She felt her face burning up as she remembered Eric's naked body and that passionate kiss in that damn dream. She looked away from Clover's skeptical face and waved her hand, dismissing the subject. "He's a nice guy, but... well, this is *Eric* we're talking about! If we *were* 'destined' to be together the way you say, it would already have happened..." An image of herself and Eric entwined around one another in bed leapt into her mind and she shook her head to dispel it. "I mean we would be *together*!"

"Maybe you were afraid of ruining a friendship," suggested Liberty. Clover nodded in agreement.

Zoe got up from her chair, feeling more and more uncomfortable. "Oh, come on, it's pointless talking about this stuff. I feel lonely, ok, but that doesn't mean you two need to push me into the arms of the first available man that comes to mind! Have you ever had this conversation with him?!"

For a moment she was afraid of hearing their answer.

Liberty shook her head, but Clover smiled mischievously.

"I'm quite willing to, at any time."

"You do that and I'll kill you!" threatened Zoe. "I already feel depressed and confused enough as it is, I don't want to risk creating embarrassing situations with my best friend. He's shy and it might scare him off if he knew that I thought he was attractive!"

"So you *do* admit that you like him from a physical point of view, then… Hmmm, very interesting. His personality is perfect for you, temperamentally that is, you've worshipped him for ten years and you're attracted to him. But you don't think it would work. I don't understand why not." Clover shook her head, sighing.

You know, it actually might work, thought Zoe, but she paused before saying it out loud. She didn't even know herself where the hell that thought had come from.

She reflected for a moment in silence, wondering if it was really possible for there to be romance between her and Eric, then she remembered why it wasn't feasible.

"There must be a reason why nothing has ever happened in these ten years, despite all the time we've spent together," she sighed, trying to look bored and indifferent. "And the most important reason of them all has long blonde hair and big green eyes," she said, looking over at Clover. "Stephanie Parker has been his impossible first love since he was back in college, and now they're back together."

"Young love can be forgotten…" said Clover, and Liberty nodded emphatically.

"You're not mature enough when you're that age. It's a mistake to idealize those moments."

"Eric wasn't a teenager then, maybe he never was! If he fell in love with her when he was twenty and then preserved the memory in his heart, it's because she was really important to him – and now she has come back for him. End of story."

Clover and Liberty didn't say anything and Zoe quickly took the opportunity to change the subject.

But when, a couple of hours later, her friends went home, leaving her alone again, she began thinking again about what Clover had said and what she herself had started to think, and her confusion mounted.

"This is *all* I need," she thought, dropping onto her bed and burying her face in the pillow. Starting to think about Eric differently and not just as a friend was more than dangerous, it was potentially lethal. He was her rock, because no feelings of love or lust had never gotten in the way of their relationship.

Now, however, she could no longer help but wonder what it would be like to be in his arms…

"I have to find myself a guy as soon as possible," she snapped to no one in particular.

The phone rang. Reaching out blindly towards the table, she grabbed it.

"Hello?"

"Hello, Zoe."

Stuart's voice made her jump, she was instantly alert. "How did you get my number?"

"You never changed it, honey."

"You're right, I didn't. I should have done," she retorted aggressively. Stuart laughed softly, a husky laugh that once upon a time would have made her tremble but which at that moment in time only made her more irritable.

"What is it you want, Stu?"

"I want to see you. Come out for dinner with me one of these nights."

"I don't see why I should."

"For old times' sake. We were good together, we were a well-matched pair. You let yourself get taken in by malicious rumours in a difficult period, and it wasn't fair on either of us. I would like to explain to you exactly what happened four years ago, and if after that you still want to leave things as they are, I'll understand. But I would at least like to try."

That man's calm and persuasive voice still knew how to hypnotize her, and Zoe fought against the desire to rekindle that old feeling. Her loneliness was a weakness that wasn't playing in her favor. She had to be careful.

"I don't know, Stuart. I don't want to re-open Pandora's box after all these years. What has happened has happened, so let's just leave it at that."

"That's easy for you, but it isn't for me. Seeing you again reminded me of how perfect we were together. Maybe our time has passed, but at least have dinner with me and let's talk. A chat, a smile and a handshake to clear up bad memories, that's all I ask."

What did she have she to lose?

She felt torn between her desires.

A part of her knew that Stuart was lying, that he had really been to bed with her best friend even though, in the absence of hard evidence, she couldn't be absolutely certain. But four years earlier Zoe had believed Miranda without a moment's hesitation, and that had thrown any trust she might have had in him back then out of the window. What sense could there be in re-opening an old chapter of her life – a chapter that, in retrospect, wasn't as perfect as she had once believed? As she had matured, she had realized that Stuart Harris was not the kind of person you would want to share your life with, and he certainly wouldn't have changed in the meantime.

Another part of her – the insecure, lonely part – yearned to be told that in fact she hadn't been betrayed, that what was between them was important, that the feelings she had felt for him hadn't been wasted. From the moment she had discovered his betrayal she hadn't been the same again – she had closed herself off from love, throwing herself into squalid, meaningless sex, and she wasn't proud of her behavior. Discovering now that she had been wrong not to believe Stuart's words wouldn't cancel the years that had passed, but maybe – just maybe – they could restore her confidence.

And then there was that little angry part of her that wanted revenge. Thanks to the confidence and experience she had acquired over the years, she felt that she would be able to do whatever she wanted with Stuart without even having to work too hard.

She could use him and then throw him away like a dirty sock, just the way he had done with her.

But what satisfaction would that give her?

"Look, I just don't feel like talking to you," she said, coldly.

"I won't give up. I'll make you change your mind," promised Stuart.

Zoe hung up and stared at the phone.

She should have told Stuart to go to hell and be done with him, and she was well aware of the fact, but at that moment in time she wasn't in the mood for making decisions. She just wanted to sleep and turn off her brain for a few hours.

Hoping that she wouldn't dream anything untoward.

*

"We need to talk!"

Eric turned to look at Clover who was zooming towards the counter like a tornado. She took him by the arm and dragged him off into the office they shared, closing the door behind her.

"What's the matter?" he asked, a puzzled expression on his face.

"You've got to do something! She's ready, I can feel that the time is right, but you're going to have to be strong and work with me, otherwise you're going to regret it!"

Eric didn't ask any questions. There was no need for Clover to explain what she was talking about – he knew all too well. Moreover, he thought the same thing, even though he was less confident about the outcome than his friend.

He sat down at his desk and ran his hands through his hair. "Ok," he said, his heart pounding.

Clover brightened up. "Finally!"

"But why are you so sure that it's going to work?"

"We were at her place last night and we talked a bit. The things that she said made me even more certain than I already was."

He was so agitated that it felt to him that there wasn't enough air in the room – maybe he was actually having a panic attack. He forced himself to breathe more deeply. "She said she would like to go out with me?"

Clover shrugged. "Not in so many words, but from the way she spoke, I definitely wouldn't exclude it."

"You wouldn't *exclude* it!" Eric sighed, feeling his euphoria start to fade. Clover was too optimistic and romantic and he wasn't entirely sure he could trust her instincts as Cupid.

"Oh, really! What did you think she would do, just come out and *say* something like that without batting an eyelid? She knows we're friends and that I wouldn't be able to resist the temptation of trying to get you two together, so she kept quiet! And since I couldn't tell her that you've been in love with her since the first time you saw her because I swore that stupid oath you made me take years ago, I couldn't push too far with my questions. But if I was practically certain before, now I'm absolutely convinced. You two are already united by a deep bond, and now she finds you attractive as well... And what's more, she has this mad desire to fall in love."

"I don't want her to throw herself at me just because she has nobody else."

Clover sighed loudly, dropping into the swivel chair at her desk. "Eric, have you ever thought that if Zoe can't find a man worthy of her, perhaps it's because no one gives her what you give her? What does she need another man for when she already has you? Apart from sex, of course."

Eric gritted his teeth and Clover chuckled.

"That was precisely what last night's conversation was about – Liberty said she was convinced that a loving relationship should be based on a deep complicity, like the complicity there is between two friends. And Zoe said that in that case she ought to marry you! But that there also needs to be sexual attraction in a relationship... Don't you understand? You're halfway there! Show her your passion as well as your heart and she'll be yours forever!"

Eager to believe what she was saying, Eric couldn't find any reason to contradict her. After all, what did he have to lose?

How about a beautiful friendship? suggested his fear.

Yeah, well someone who was just a friend wouldn't keep dreaming about seeing her naked, said reason.

"Okay," he muttered. "In any case, I can't take any more of her messed-up relationships, so our friendship is already hanging by a thread as it is."

"Perfect. Now we need a plan of attack." Clover drew her chair nearer to him and smiled, her eyes shining. "And I already have a great idea... but you're going to have to collaborate."

Clover's plan was simple but effective. It consisted of a bit of resolute but anonymous courtship aimed at stimulating Zoe's curiosity which would culminate with a full-blown declaration of love on the evening of Valentine's Day.

And as there were only four days left to Valentine's Day, Eric didn't have much time, so they planned all the details in a few minutes and began work that very afternoon.

Shortly before closing, one of the delivery boys arrived at Giftland with a white package tied with a big red bow and handed it to Zoe.

"For you."

Gratified, Zoe smiled at the boy.

"You brought me a present, Jimmy? How sweet you are!" she cooed, taking the box. From his quiet corner, Eric glared at the boy, who was just eighteen and made deliveries for the best bakery in the area, ready to jump at his throat if he dared take the credit for that gift. But the boy, as bashful as he always was in the face of Zoe's beauty, just shook his mop of brown hair.

"Unfortunately, I don't think you'd ever look twice at a kid like me even if I brought you a gift every day."

"Never say never, honey. Nowadays it's not so strange to see a woman with a younger boyfriend. Ms Ciccone has been a good teacher, right?" joked Zoe, being her flirtatious self as usual and giving the boy a wink. Then she went back to the box. "Who sent it?"

"I don't know. We received an anonymous order that just said where and to whom we were supposed to deliver the box."

"A mysterious admirer, eh? Well, thanks Jimmy."

Eric waited for the delivery boy to leave, then walked over to the counter. Zoe was still staring at the box with attentive eyes and a slight smile on her lips.

"What's going on?" He asked, pretending to be disinterested.

"A gift from someone who doesn't want to reveal himself," Zoe said, shrugging.

"What is it?"

Zoe untied the red ribbon and opened the box. Immediately the appetizing aroma of a cake filled the room.

"An entire Red Velvet!" she exclaimed, her eyes suddenly alight with pleasure. "That is my *absolute* favorite dessert!"

You don't say… thought Eric, mentally giving himself a pat on the back.

The first time Zoe had sat down at his table in the university cafeteria, Eric had offered her a slice of that very cake. In quite an embarrassing way…

"You are officially our best customer, did you know that?" she said as she stopped in front of his table.

Eric almost choked on the mouthful of coffee that he had just drunk. He didn't actually even like the stuff, but if you wanted to sit in the café you had to order something. He could have ordered something else, of course, but the previous week he had foolishly told the manager of the cafeteria that he spent hours in that place because of the 'exquisite' coffee, and now he felt compelled to stick to his guns.

He couldn't confirm the man's suspicions that he spent entire afternoons in there just to see her.

He knew her name: Zoe. Even those three simple letters, arranged in that particular order, were wonderful.

He had never seen a more beautiful girl. Maybe it was because of her perfect oval face, or because of her winning smile, or her slightly almond-shaped eyes – a shade of grey so unique that it suggested molten silver… Without forgetting, of course, her fantastic body, tall and lithe but with incredible curves in all the right places.

Since they had taken her on, the place had become the main attraction on the campus. Dozens of guys would gather there every day with the most improbable excuses or just straight out admitting that they came just to catch a glimpse of her. The manager of the cafeteria had now realized that students lingered longer than necessary to admire the brunette beauty who served at the tables and he never missed an opportunity to tease them about it.

But Eric was too shy to admit to being totally and hopelessly infatuated with Zoe. The thought of openly declaring it was ridiculous – a girl like that would never have deigned to take one look at a dull nobody like him. She could have any guy that fell at her feet, she was spoilt for choice!

Yet, for some reason, that particular time she had stopped right in front of him, with a smile that could have melted ice…

He raised his face and adjusted his glasses on his nose, trying not to stutter. "Do I get some kind of prize for it?"

"You should! You come in here every day and order almost half a dozen cups of coffee every time! You're making that asshole Isaac rich – you deserve a commendation at the very least!"

"It's usually decaf," he said, then kicked himself mentally. *What kind of dumb thing to say was that? What the hell does she care what kind of coffee you drink?*

"I guess it must take a lot of concentration, as well as a lot of caffeine, to understand all those weird formulas that you're studying," said Zoe, leaning across the table and scanning the page of his physics book. Eric found himself breathing in her smell as well as ogling at her cleavage, which was revealed thanks to the top buttons of her white blouse being undone. He really hoped he wasn't blushing like an idiot.

"What are you studying?" she continued.

"Stri…" Eric muttered, hoarsely. Then he pulled himself together and cleared his throat. "String Theory," he improvised. Being a fan of The Big Bang Theory was always useful if you were a nerd.

Zoe stared at him with a puzzled expression. "I have no idea what that is, but something tells me that it has nothing to do with shoelaces, right?" she joked.

Eric smiled. He didn't give a damn that she didn't know anything about physics – he loved the wry way she joked about her own shortcomings. He had heard her talking to other students during the hours he spent sitting at that table and she had always seemed curious, never a know-it-all or wilfully ignorant.

"It's just a theory that tries to reconcile relativity and quantum mechanics." He didn't add anything else so as not to bore her. If there was one sure way of scaring away a girl, it was to start talking about science.

"And do you really like this stuff? I mean, I don't doubt that it can be fascinating, but it must be really difficult… at least judging by the time you spend on it. You need to have a large brain to be able to understand something like that."

"I suppose I should thank you," sighed Eric, looking miserable, "For suggesting that I have a large brain at least, although a terribly boring and nerdy one."

"Oh, no! Don't get me wrong!" she laughed. "I admire people like you. I often regret not having a brain like yours… Maybe if I had, I would be doing something a bit more worthwhile than waitressing."

"Serving people is an undervalued job. I mean, you hold got the success of a lot of people's lunch break in your hands every day. You need to be efficient, fast, friendly and nice… All things that you do very well," said Eric with a shrug, his eyes averted from her. *"And if we did a survey, I bet that most of the population would rather have your head than mine!"*

She didn't reply, forcing him to look up at her. Then he saw her smile and offer him her hand.

"My name is Zoe. Zoe Mathison."

"Eric Morgan," he said, hoping his palms weren't sweaty.

"I have a ten minute break. Do you mind if I sit here with you? We can chat – or I can help you study, if you prefer."

Am I dreaming? *thought Eric. Then he nodded quickly. "Sure, whatever you like… but only if I can get you something."*

Zoe glanced at the sweet counter. "If you insist… There is a slice of Red Velvet that feels like it's been calling out to me since this morning, but the rules of the cafeteria say that I can't consume anything that is on display – at least not until closing time."

"But no one can stop me from ordering that cake and feeding it to you!" said Eric. The very idea made him come out in a sweat and his ears started burning. Great – now he was definitely blushing, dammit!

He stood up abruptly and steadied himself. "Be right back," he said, as he walked over to the counter, taking deep breaths to calm himself down. But all the time he was aware of Zoe's eyes watching him.

Years had passed since that day and yet he still felt like that same nerdy, unattractive student whenever he was around her.

Clover says that Zoe finds you attractive, a voice in his head reminded him.

Well, that distant afternoon ten years ago, he'd thought that she liked him too. In short, the fairest of them all had stopped to chat to him – to *him*! Him, out of all the boys who were in the cafeteria every day. But the only thing he had ever received from her was sincere affection, nothing more.

He tried not to be discouraged by his usual doubts and saw Zoe extract a red envelope from the box. She opened it and read aloud the short message that Clover had dictated to him over the phone.

"To add a touch of sweetness to your day... And looking forward to being able to add some to your life. Wow!" She laughed, looking for a name that, of course, wasn't there. "Who can it be from?"

"One of your many admirers," said Eric. He wasn't lying, after all.

"They *usually* put their name on. Men are always eager to show their intentions towards a woman and to try to beat off the competition."

"Not all men are that vain. Maybe this one is just more of an original than the others," said Clover as she joined them. "I heard the message... how romantic!" From behind Zoe's back, Eric gestured for her to stop, but Clover ignored him. "Have you met someone new and interesting and not told us about him yet?"

"Absolutely not! The last guy I went out with was Evan..."

"Well *he* certainly doesn't have enough intelligence to write an entire, meaningful sentence," mumbled Eric, looking bored.

Zoe giggled. "He certainly doesn't..." Suddenly, she stared at the cake in the box with a pensive air, and her eyes darkened. "I just hope it's not who I think it is," she muttered.

Eric felt a chill. Who could she be talking about?

He wanted to ask, but lacked the courage to do so. Clover had the same question on her face too, but the arrival of a few customers in the store distracted them, and Zoe hastened to put her gift under the counter before walking over to the new arrivals.

"What if she's talking about me?" Eric whispered in Clover's ear.

"Don't be paranoid," she hissed, gritting her teeth, adding, "Maybe she thinks they're from Harris," before walking away.

Eric stiffened.

It would make sense. Harris could easily know that her favorite cake was a Red Velvet – they had been together for two years and Zoe had been shaken up by the return of her ex, so it was natural that she would think of him.

He clenched his fists and decided that in the remaining three days he would send her more specific gifts. Gifts that could only bring back memories related to their friendship – and not to that idiot of a doctor…

Chapter 10

"Well here we are. It's Valentine's Day," sighed Zoe, sitting herself down on the edge of Clover's desk. She held a basket containing several gift-wrapped packages and small bouquets of flowers, which she observed almost indifferently. "Don't you think there look to be less of them than there were other years?"

"You've always been the only one around here to get any Valentine's Day gifts, so how do you think Lib, Eric and me feel?"

"I'm also losing my charms as well as my admirers. Since Evan, no one has been in to ask me out on a date," said Zoe, opening a box of chocolates and popping a praline into her mouth. "I mean, unless you count Stuart, obviously."

"Stuart?" Clover arched an eyebrow and cast an anxious glance in the direction of Eric, who was staring grimly at his computer screen.

"He's been going all out to try and win me back," said Zoe, thoughtfully. "He seems to be really determined."

"Once they hit forty, some men are very eager to try and cleanse their karma of all the shitty stuff they've done in the past," muttered Eric, cuttingly.

Zoe bit into a chocolate covered strawberry which she had extracted from another be-ribboned package. "I honestly don't know what to think. He calls me practically every day now, and he really does seem to be remorseful. If he's lying, he deserves an Oscar for his performance."

"What, you mean you're starting to believe him?" asked Eric, suddenly attentive.

She shrugged. "I'm just hearing him out, for the moment."

"Well that's a good way to waste your time."

"Don't be so hard on him, you should always give people a chance to explain themselves," said Zoe, giving him a wistful smile. "If what he tells me is true, it was wrong of me to just walk out and dump all the blame on him back then."

Eric jumped to his feet, took off his glasses and ran his hand over his face. "I can't believe it, you're letting yourself fall for it again…"

"I'm just looking at the facts from a different perspective."

Clover shook her head. "I don't know what he's been telling you, but I don't think you should trust him. Hey, remember, unless he was drugged or under threat of death, he went to bed with Miranda of his own accord!"

"He says that they just kissed. And that he'd tried to tell me at the time that things weren't going the way they should have been between us, and that he was depressed about it and that Miranda consoled him. He was a bit tipsy, and she put the moves on him… I'd suspected for a long time that she was hot for him, but I couldn't be certain."

Eric pulled a disgusted face.

"This is bullshit. You were his devoted slave, it was ridiculous how desperate you were to do whatever he wanted, and he took advantage of the fact every way he could! So don't start telling me that you two were having problems and that he decided to turn to your best friend for consolation, because it's an insult to your and my intelligence!"

With an angry gesture, Zoe closed the box of chocolates. "There's no need for you to get your knickers in a twist."

"He's angry because he is worried that Stuart is going to make you suffer again," interjected Clover, giving a warning glance to Eric, who seemed on the verge of losing control. "And to be honest, I'm worried too."

"I'm an adult, I know what I'm doing. I was just filling you in on what happened, I'm not saying that I believe him."

"And did you tell him you're never going to forgive him and that he shouldn't try and get in touch with you again?"

The way Eric stared into her eyes was so threatening it made her feel uncomfortable. Swinging her leg, Zoe looked away.

"He keeps asking me to go out on a date with him. I told him that I didn't think it was a good idea, but he says he's going to try and convince me by any means possible."

Eric cursed and stomped out of the office, and Zoe looked over at Clover. "God, he's got such a quick temper."

"If you go out with Stuart again, Zoe, I think I'll cross you off my list of friends," the redhead muttered, standing up and following Eric.

"Thank you so much!" Zoe shouted after them, then turning to look in annoyance at the gifts that her 'admirers' – those few diehards who were still trying to get a date with her – had had delivered to the store.

No one understood how she felt at that moment. It was easy for Clover to be so sure of herself: she had a wonderful man by her side, who that afternoon would be putting her on a private plane to Paris! And Liberty would go out with Justin, as always. Even Eric had someone to be with, she imagined, even though it had been a few days since she had seen Stephanie in the store.

But she had no one. Just a dozen guys who were practically strangers and who were determined to get a date with her by showering her with gifts, and an ex-boyfriend who had suddenly decided he wanted them to get back together. She wasn't crazy about either of the options, but at least Stuart's back-pedalling was good for her self-esteem.

Reluctantly, she began to observe the gifts she'd received: romantic cards, soft toys, hearts, pendants…

And then a bouquet of flowers that was bigger than the others. Nine beautiful red roses tied together with a silk ribbon, to which was attached an anonymous envelope that caught her eye.

Another message from her secret admirer!

She opened it and pulled out the sober, heart-shaped note inside, upon which was written a few words:

I don't want to be just another name on a list any more, and my heart can no longer stay in a drawer.

At the top of the Empire State Building you will find my last gift to you.

Intrigued, Zoe put the rest of the gifts down on the desk and walked out of the office, her nose pressed into the soft rose petals.

"I got another one!" she exclaimed, attracting the attention of her colleagues. At that moment Liberty too was at the counter, and all present turned in her direction.

"You know, I think this time I want him to reveal his identity!"

She handed the envelope to Clover, who opened it.

"And you want him to do it right on Valentine's Day?" asked Liberty. "Romantic!"

"I'm dying to know who the hell it is," sighed Zoe, caressing the flowers.

Over the last three days she had received three anonymous gifts. After the Red Velvet and the first message, a fluffy hamster toy had arrived, holding between its paws the message: 'Love can have many faces... For me it has only one.' On the third day, she had received a beautiful bracelet with a star shaped pendant – a transparent, sparkling crystal upon which was engraved her name. The note that accompanied it said only: 'Will you ever shine only for me?'

And now these beautiful roses...

After reading the brief message, Clover looked at her.

"Whoever it is, he is disarmingly sweet. And it was really nice of him to organize all this."

Zoe nodded. "You're right... Unless he's a dangerous psychopath." Her face suddenly grew slightly dark as a thought flashed into her mind. "And what if it's Stuart?"

"Why," snapped Eric, "does he know how to write now?"

"Just because doctors have bad handwriting, that doesn't mean that they are illiterate," joked Liberty.

"Don't you think it's a really weird coincidence? He turns up again after four years, vowing that he's going to change my mind, and since then, every day I've received an anonymous gift. And now this..." Zoe reread the message, then closed the envelope. "It does seem pretty likely."

"I very much doubt it's the same person. What sense would it make to organize something romantic like anonymous messages, and then hassle you by phoning you every day to beg you for a date?" Clover looked at Eric. "What do you think? You've met him, you know what he's like. Do you think that's his style?"

"No."

186

"He may have honed his technique over the years," murmured Zoe.

Clover smiled. "The only way to find out is to go up there and see what this mystery man has left for you. Maybe there's a more precise clue!"

"Or why don't you just forget about it?" said Eric, finally raising his eyes to her. "The whole thing's stupid. Whoever sent those messages knows how to get in touch with you, he could show up here and say all this directly to your face instead of hiding behind anonymous notes. Perhaps he's just worried that you won't be pleased when you eventually find out his identity, and that's why he's playing the mystery card."

"Well at least he's been original," said Clover, between her teeth. "I think that you should go."

"It's still really sweet, even if he doesn't turn out to be Prince Charming, and he's made me curious." Zoe looked over at Liberty to get her permission, and her friend nodded.

"Go ahead."

"Thanks! I hope it won't take long," Zoe smiled as she grabbed her coat.

Clover gave a quick glance at the clock, then hugged her. "I won't be here when you get back. Cade is supposed to be arriving at any moment and then we're going straight to the airport. So call me tomorrow, okay? I want to know *everything*!"

"Have fun in Paris! And say 'hi' to Cade for me," said Zoe with a smile as she left Giftland.

As soon as Zoe and Liberty were out of sight, Clover nudged Eric.

"What's the matter with you, are you nuts? You tried to talk her out of going!"

"It was a bad, bad idea," snapped Eric, running a hand through his hair. "And I'm *really* starting to regret ever having listened to you."

"It's going to work, though, I can feel it," smiled Clover. "Zoe loves being surprised and wooed, and that touch of mystery was exactly what was needed to stop her from thinking about that idiot."

"What do you mean, stop her thinking about him?! He was the first guy she thought of!" Furiously, Eric squeezed his hand into a fist. "He just *had* come back before Valentine's Day, didn't he? Damn it, she'd agree to go out with the devil himself tonight if it meant she didn't have to feel alone!"

"But that's not going to happen because even if she does go to the restaurant expecting to find Stuart, she'll find you there instead."

"And what if he's made a date with her for this evening too? Maybe in the same place?"

"Eric, don't be so silly!" Clover squeezed his hand. "Harris has no chance with her – much less against you."

"But what if she's already worked it all out and decides not to show up? I can already see the scene, me sitting there in the restaurant all dressed up like a penguin, waiting in vain for someone who's never going to show."

Clover raised her eyes to the ceiling in frustration. "And they say that *women* are insecure in love!"

Eric glared at her and she gave him a kiss on the cheek.

"You're so cute! Zoe won't be able to resist you."

"Oh, *sure*! That's why I've been drooling over her for years and she's never even noticed!"

"You've always been close to her as a friend and hidden your real feelings in every way you could. How was she supposed to realize that you felt something for her? And even if she had realized, the fear of confusing you or of ruining your relationship would have stopped her from doing anything."

"Zoe's not as conscientious as you make out," protested Eric. "When she wants something, she takes it."

"Zoe takes things that are uncomplicated," Clover corrected him. "After Stuart, she was so scared of being betrayed again that she devoted her time to useless people. And you would be a serious commitment."

"A commitment that she doesn't want to make."

"God, you're such a pessimist!" snorted his friend. She admonished him with a wagging finger. "Now listen carefully: Zoe is ready to fall in love again, she said so herself. Seeing me so happy has infected her: she's tired of meaningless relationships and she's looking for a serious one. And even if she hasn't opened up much about, I am one hundred per cent sure that she has revised her ideas about you as a man, especially after your nude performance on the day of the photo shoot."

"I didn't do it on purpose!"

"That doesn't matter. She was shocked and almost offended about not having realized before that, under your boring clothes, you're super sexy! Combine that tantalizing discovery with the deep affection that there has always been between the two of you, stir in the romance of the River Café and the irresistible feeling of having been loved for ten years, and the result is pretty much guaranteed!"

Eric shook his head. "I'm not convinced. If nothing has ever happened between us, perhaps it's destiny."

"Or because until now you've always been a shy coward, and she's been blind and diffident. Maybe neither of you were ready: sometimes it takes the right moment to unlock a situation." Clover took him by the arm and looked into his eyes. "Don't give up now, Eric. What have you got to lose? You won't be able to save your friendship forever, you're already at the limit. If you give up the chance to win her over, sooner or later someone else will manage to do it in your place, and at that point you'll lose her. You won't be able to stand the fact of knowing that she's with someone else, and that will end up ruining your relationship anyway."

"Getting turned down will ruin our relationship anyway."

"Well it'd be better to get turned down after at least trying than just imaging it. It is always better to regret what you have done than what you haven't."

Eric did not answer. Until a few hours earlier, he had been sure that Clover was right and that it was high time to take the bull by the horns once and for all. If he had to suffer it was better at least to have a definite answer to his questions.

Yet now he was terrified of seeing a disappointed expression on Zoe's face as soon as she realized who was behind the anonymous notes she'd been receiving for the last four days.

"If she turns me down, I'm going back to Boston," he said quietly, putting his hands in his pockets.

Clover sighed. "Although I don't agree with you, I can understand. But I really hope it won't come to that."

*

The feeling at the top of the Empire State Building was always the same: power, unreality, confusion. With its dizzying height, the building gave you the feeling that you could challenge the sky, and at its summit you felt as though you'd entered a different world – it was like you'd taken a lift to another dimension.

Inside the mysterious envelope, Zoe had also found a pass which allowed her to skip the long lines of tourists who thronged the most famous skyscraper in the city, and go directly to the two hundredth floor.

It was the perfect time of day for the trip. The view of Manhattan from the top was always spectacular, but at sunset the view drew gasps of pure ecstasy.

It had been quite a while since the last time she had been up there, and she wanted to thank whoever it was who had arranged this surprise for her.

The first time she had climbed to top of the skyscraper, she had wept with joy. Eric had been with her that day, and could confirm it. Her dream had always been to live in Manhattan, and finally she had succeeded. And so, to celebrate, she and the freshly graduated Eric had eaten a pizza together and then decided to go up to the observatory. The queue for the tickets, security checks and elevators had provoked several irritable mutterings from Eric, but Zoe was as excited as a child. To repay the patience that her friend had shown in taking her up there, and to congratulate him again on graduating, Zoe had stopped at one of the many souvenir shops and bought the skyscraper-shaped key ring which he still treasured. It wasn't a great gift, she knew, but at the time she had been saving every penny to pay for the rent on her apartment, and anyway, Eric seemed to like it.

Her mouth hidden behind her scarf, she chuckled softly when the elevator began to shoot upwards. Eric had almost had a heart attack the first time at the feeling of being sent hurtling upwards at the speed of a rocket. She had teased him for days, reminding him of the greenish color his face had been for twenty minutes after they had got out.

They'd had such fun together! And Eric had always shown her so much affection, despite all her caprices.

Back at Giftland, though, he had seemed genuinely disappointed. The thought that she might be fooled a second time by Stuart had really made him lose his temper.

And could she blame him? She wasn't particularly proud of herself either. She should have been icy and indifferent towards her ex, telling him to go to hell and making it obvious that he didn't stand a chance with her. She deserved something more than a guy that she couldn't trust.

But she had loved Stuart. Of course, she'd been young and foolish at the time, and not really able to understand what true love was, but the emotions she had felt with him she had never felt since. Perhaps she hadn't thrown herself into the relationships that had followed with enough conviction after that setback, but finally she felt ready to overcome her fears and fall in love again. And Stuart had happened to re-appear in her life right at that moment, ready to grovel at her feet just the way she had so often dreamed of.

She wasn't sure that she wanted to believe him, but after his seemingly heartfelt words, a small part of her wondered if, now that she was an adult and more aware of her power, things might not go differently.

She recalled Stuart's face, and tried to focus on her reactions to that image. Those intense eyes, wiry body and cocky way of acting. As a young girl she had found him more charming than beautiful, and she had let herself be won over by his confidence and his elegant manners. After they had split up, she had always deliberately chosen rough, straight talking men, so as to always have before her eyes the harsh reality and not an attractive facade.

She remembered with a touch of melancholy the way she had always felt as if she was floating several feet above the ground when she was with Stuart, but maybe it was only the feeling that she was missing.

How could she go back to trusting someone like that? Any time he was a little late, any message he received on his phone, any unexpected commitment would make her suspicious. She would even start worrying about Liberty and Clover for the simple reason that she had already been betrayed by a friend. She was in serious danger of getting herself into trouble with her own two hands.

But what if Stuart really had changed? Was it right to reject him out of hand, without giving him a chance at redemption?

She was so tired of being alone, of not being courted, or desired, or loved by anyone…

"Would you really settle for something like that just so as not to be single any more?"

That thought kept going round constantly in her head, making her shiver. Could she, who had been so excited to see Clover and Cade get together, who dreamed of a love story like that of her parents, who at that time envied every couple she saw in the street, really settle for the first man who came along just so that she wouldn't have to be alone? It was a terrible thought.

Another love would come, sooner or later. She just had to be patient.

But patience had never been her strong point…

The gust of cold air that slammed into her as she walked out onto the roof terrace took her breath away. It wasn't snowing any more, but the temperature was still very low. And up there, over three hundred yards above the ground, it was pretty damn chilly.

The smell of approaching rain filled her lungs. The dark clouds and lightning had been gathering for hours, obscuring part of the pink sky. The forecast was for torrential rain that evening.

"Who cares? I'll be lying on the couch, buried under the covers, watching some tearjerker and stuffing my face with donuts, crying over the days when I used to spend Valentine's Day with a man."

She stuck her hands in her pockets and her fingers brushed the envelope, reminding her of why she had come to the top of the Empire State Building.

Summoning up a little fresh curiosity, she began to look around. It was hard to see anything through the crowd of people, so she took a wander round the terrace, keeping an eye open for anything unusual. After a few minutes, a flash of red in the corner of the viewing platform overlooking Central Park caught her eye.

Cast in shadow by the light of the pale setting sun, two heart-shaped balloons were fluttering in the icy air. Feeling a smile appear spontaneously on her face, she walked over, making her way through the curious crowd. One of the two balloons, which were both secured to the railing with a thick ribbon, had her name on it very clearly; on the other there were only three dots. At the bottom of the ribbon was a red rose tied to another envelope, this one bigger than the others.

When she reached the small secluded space she undid the red envelope and opened it, more curious than ever, hoping to find some useful clue which would reveal the identity of her mysterious suitor. But the note didn't bear any signature, just a few words printed on a white card:

Valentine's Day is just a day like any other. But I think of you every moment of my life.

Feeling her heart beat faster, she checked that there was nothing else, and only then did she notice a folded piece of cardboard: it was a copy of the menu from the River Café, one of the most romantic restaurants in all of New York. At the top on the right was written a time – ten o'clock that evening.

Zoe peered around her, hoping to identify a suspicious face in that sea of people. Lots of them were staring at her, curious about the balloons and the situation, but she couldn't see anyone that she knew, and that made her realize that the mysterious man only intended to reveal himself if she accepted his invitation for that evening.

Who could have organized all this? Could it really be the work of Stuart? Another way of trying to break down her resistance, or a sincere attempt to win her back?

Whoever it was, he had certainly succeeded in his goal of surprising her and capturing her imagination in a way that had rarely happened before in her life. That romantic gesture in those few, brief moments atop the Empire State Building had made her feel special. Even if it didn't end up having an interesting continuation, the originality of the whole thing had revived a St Valentine's Day which would otherwise have been lonely.

She undid the balloons, holding the ribbon and the rose between her fingers, put the card into her bag and walked slowly towards the furthest corner of the terrace, intent on reflecting on the day's events and enjoying the last minutes of the sunset.

It could have been anyone who had organized the surprise. A rejected admirer, a former boyfriend, Stuart… even some kind of psycho! Or it could have been those two crazy friends of hers, to distract her from the depression that she'd sunk into over the last few days. In that case, she wondered who they could have forced to wait for her at the restaurant that evening, since Clover was going to go to Paris with Cade and Liberty was going out to dinner with Justin.

Eric flashed into her thoughts, but she dismissed the idea forcefully. He wouldn't have let them involve him a stupid joke like that, and anyway, he would certainly be going out with Stephanie that night. He wouldn't have had time to have dinner with his pathetic single colleague.

All of them had something to do – except her. And keeping the appointment was the only alternative to solitude that was left.

*

The first drops of rain began to fall while Liberty was locking the door of the shop. Zoe looked up at the threatening sky and snorted.

"Typical. When you have an important occasion on your hands it always starts raining so that you end up having to spend hours in front of the wardrobe choosing a dress that can handle the cold and the damp while still managing to look hot. And that's without even mentioning the hair!"

"So have you decided to go to the appointment?" asked Eric, raising his head. Zoe had returned from the Empire State Building with her cheeks burning with enthusiasm, showing him and Liberty the balloons, the rose and the card, but saying that she was still unsure about what to do. Two hours later, though, she seemed to have changed her mind…

"Well I'm certainly not staying at home. The silence in my apartment would kill me."

"Do you still think that it's Harris who's behind it all?"

"I don't know. But whoever it is must have knocked themselves out to get a table at the River Café on Valentine's Day: that place is always full."

His heart pounding, Eric didn't answer. So the moment of truth had actually arrived. Perhaps that evening he would finally reveal his true feelings.

"You could always just not turn up…"

He banished the thought from his mind. He would never stand up Zoe, especially on a night like that.

Full of excitement, he lifted the hood of his jacket to shelter himself from the rain.

"Well I hope you make the right choice… and that you're not disappointed."

"Even if it *was* Stuart, and if I'd decided I was going to give him another chance, I wouldn't exactly be running there joyfully. And if it really is a mysterious suitor, I'd be disappointed if he turned out to be a bad copy of Rowan Atkinson," Zoe laughed. "Anyway, I'd better get going, or I won't have time to make myself beautiful!"

"As if she needed it," he thought as he watched her race off to the taxi stand.

Liberty peered at his anxious face and smiled.

"She's a smart girl, she won't fall for him again. Don't worry."

That wasn't what Eric was worrying about at that particular moment, but he nodded and walked off in the opposite direction.

197

He only lived a few blocks from the store, so he decided to walk home to his apartment. By the time he reached the front door he was drenched and that detail only served to worsen his mood. It must be a bad omen.

After a hot shower, he poured himself a rather large glass of wine. He hardly ever drank, but that night he needed to do something to release the tension a bit. Within a few hours, his life would change drastically – both if dinner had a happy ending or if it meant him relocating immediately to Boston. And even though part of him was desperate to pull out of the whole thing, he forced himself to continue with his preparations.

He put on a dark grey suit that was elegant but not too serious. He decided not to wear a tie and chose a light grey shirt instead of the white one he had decided on earlier so as not to look too stuffy.

He even forced himself to wear contacts instead of his usual glasses, and to leave his hair naturally curly instead of smoothing it down with gel. Clover had suggested that he dress casually, maybe even a little scruffily, assuring him that Zoe would prefer it.

He managed to keep his nerves under control until it was time to go to the River Café. During the taxi ride he went over the line in his mind that he was intending to use to break the ice.

"Well, at least you didn't run away in terror, so that's something!" he would say, with fake ironic detachment, if Zoe stayed long enough. And then he would decide what to do next.

And if she ran away… Well, in that case he wouldn't need an opening line, would he?

The River Café was crammed with people. Being the quintessential romantic restaurant, that evening it was packed. Eric had booked well in advance and had reserved a table right next to one of the windows so that they could enjoy a magnificent view of the Brooklyn Bridge and the Statue of Liberty. He knew that Zoe would love it, regardless of whatever else happened.

A few minutes before she was due, he ordered a bottle of French wine but waited to order the food. He could have chosen Zoe's favorite dishes with his eyes closed, but he didn't want to tempt fate…

And three-quarters of an hour later he knew that he had done the right thing.

The wine bottle was already half empty, people were beginning to give him pitying looks and the waiter had stopped coming over to his table, as though resigned to the fact that he wasn't going to order anything.

Zoe had stood him up.

"She didn't stand *you* up – she stood a stranger up," the voice in his brain tried to reassure him – but his heart was saying something else entirely.

Perhaps when she had entered the restaurant and found out who was waiting for her at the table she had decided to get the hell out of there rather than face the situation? Or maybe she had accepted Harris's umpteenth invitation and blown out her blind date?

He imagined her rolling around on a bed with her ex and downed the contents of his glass in one fell swoop.

He felt like a complete idiot.

Feeling terrible, he left a substantial tip on the table, stood up and stalked off towards the door. Crossing the restaurant alone, under the eyes of all the happy couples, only made his bad mood worse.

Outside the rain had doubled in intensity. Blindingly bright and terrifyingly compelling, the flashes of lightning came hot on the heels of one another, reflecting dramatically in the skyscrapers and lighting up a sky thick with black clouds. While he waited for a taxi, Eric stared at the Statue of Liberty across the river: a blue-green ghost in the water, struck repeatedly by bolts of lightning. Just like the statue, he felt invisible and immobile, at the mercy of the elements. But he was certain that Miss Liberty would survive that storm, whereas he felt as if he was about to collapse.

He almost didn't notice the arrival of the taxi or the trip to the Upper East Side. He paid the fare like a robot and then went up to his apartment.

The silence was only broken by the storm that raged outside, echoing his mood. He turned on all the lights to ward off the dark, but as soon as his eyes focused on his surroundings, he turned almost all of them off again.

Even his house was full of her. Zoe had spent a lot of time there: dinners, parties, evenings working. She hadn't left any personal items but she'd helped him decorate and furnish every room, and had personally chosen the dark red sofa and matching curtains. And her photographs were scattered over the walls, shots depicting facets of New York or moments of life during those long years they had known each other.

The sight of her smiling and beautiful in those pictures made him grind his teeth. Only someone as stupid as him could have hoped to charm a woman like her by letting her use him as a doormat for ten years. He ought to have told her where to go a long time ago, gone back to Boston and forgotten about her forever…

"And maybe it's time to tell her to her face," he thought.

In a burst of anger and false courage, he grabbed the phone and called Zoe's home number, one hand pressed over his eyes. Saying what was on his mind would mean freeing himself from a burden. Even if *it* would destroy him later on. But at that moment he was not afraid of anything: he had nothing left to lose.

Almost like divine intervention, the doorbell rang, startling him. Muttering an expletive, he threw the phone down on a bookcase shelf and went to open the door. He wasn't really in the mood to see anyone, but perhaps a distraction would stop him from doing anything stupid.

A roll of thunder chose that moment to make its appearance, echoing the dull thumping of his heart.

He grasped the handle and pulled the door open with a curt gesture. And then froze.

"I shouldn't be here, I know. But I really need to talk to you."

Chapter 11

Even soaking wet and with her makeup running down her face the way it was now, she was so beautiful that it was actually painful.

"Can I come in?" asked Zoe in a whisper. "Just for a moment?"

Eric stood there staring at her.

"God, I'm a *disaster!*" she said, sounding mortified and pulling her jacket around her. "The rain turned into a sort of monsoon as I stepped out of the cab." She was wearing a black dress that covered her down to below the knee but which showed off every curve of her body.

Eric couldn't utter a word. Within him, contrasting emotions raged: disbelief, anger, hope, confusion.

Had he drunk so much that he was actually having hallucinations? What the hell was Zoe doing at his place?

A small part of him was glad to see her, but the other part – still angry at having waited in vain in the restaurant like an idiot – almost wanted to shut the door on her.

Yet another deafening roll of thunder, loud enough to rattle the windows, echoed around the room, and suddenly the power went off, plunging the apartment into almost total darkness. It took their eyes a moment to adjust to the unexpected lack of light, and when he managed to make out Zoe's wet, weary face again, Eric silently cursed himself, took her by the arm and dragged her inside.

"Sit down, or don't. Suit yourself," he said flatly, heading into the kitchen. There, he filled a glass with the wine that he had left on the table before leaving: he didn't know whether he wanted to use the alcohol to clear his thoughts or to dull them sufficiently to stop thinking altogether.

"Listen, I'm sorry for just turning up here without warning," said Zoe from behind him.

"So why did you, then?"

"Actually, I don't really know. It was a last minute impulse." Zoe looked at him, slightly uncomfortable. "Am I disturbing you?"

"Want some wine?" Without waiting for an answer, Eric gave her a glass and, with a trembling hand, filled it, and then – the way illuminated by a continuous succession of flashes of lightning outside the large windows – walked off back into the living room, leaving her there alone.

"Are you okay?" asked a perplexed Zoe as she followed him in.

"Does it matter?" he snorted. He collapsed onto the sofa as though his legs were suddenly unable to support his weight, and stared at his glass.

Confused, Zoe sat down beside him. "Are you angry?"

In response, he laughed. A laugh so completely devoid of mirth that she raised her eyebrows in surprise.

"Oh, yes. I am very angry"

"What happened? Don't tell me your better half managed to get you mad on Valentine's Day…"

Eric ignored Zoe's slightly sarcastic tone but began to seriously reflect on her words.

"My better half… Is she really better? She's not sweet at all, that's for sure."

"Do you want to talk?"

"No."

Zoe sighed. "It's obvious that I've picked the wrong time – your head's elsewhere, you haven't got time for me. I'd better go."

Eric saw her stand up and straighten out her dress and then take a step towards the door. At that point he took hold of her hand to restrain her. He'd be damned if he was going to let her just walk out like that on top of everything else!

"Forgive me for not jumping to attention and being ready to sit and hear whatever pops into your pretty little head. But tonight I'm not really in the mood for listening to bullshit."

Zoe went pale in the shadows, shocked by his tone and especially by the anger in his voice, and her eyes grew sad. She sat down next to him and brushed the hair from his forehead.

"God, you're so right... I've been unloading all my bullshit onto you for too long. But it won't happen again. I promise," she murmured, stroking his cheek. "I don't know what happened tonight, but whoever got you into this state doesn't deserve you, believe me."

"You're right, she doesn't deserve me... But my stupid heart doesn't care, unfortunately" replied Eric.

Then, to her complete surprise, he ran his hand through her hair, grasped her neck and pulled her towards him, putting his mouth against hers.

When she'd rung the doorbell of Eric's apartment, that turn of events was the last thing she would have expected. She had climbed into a taxi two hours earlier, braving the storm in the hope of spending a fun evening. She had decided to go on the blind date with her mysterious suitor simply to have something to do other than staying at home watching a tearjerker on TV, but she hadn't been particularly optimistic about it. What would it be but dinner with a man that meant nothing to her, pretending for a few hours that she wasn't alone and desperate: the usual.

While the taxi was making its way at a snail's pace through the traffic, trying to get out of the congestion it found itself in, she had watched the rain beating on the windshield with unparalleled violence and wondered if it really was worth it. The chill of the evening had penetrated her to the bone through the seductive dress she had worn more out of habit than any real intention of seducing anyone, and suddenly she had found herself asking the taxi driver to turn down a side street and drive in the other direction until she told him to stop. The man had seemed sympathetic and, for nearly an hour, had driven aimlessly around the city.

Zoe had thought long and hard and decided that she was going to stop. No more blind dates with dinner in the company of strangers; she didn't want any more relationships that served only to give her the illusion of having a man beside her. If it was real love she wanted, it was time to start acting as though she deserved it.

And then, on an impulse, she had asked the taxi driver to head for the East Side.

She needed her best friend. On a night like that, she felt the need to be comforted by the only person who was able to give her security.

Only it was not her usual sweet, tender Eric who opened the door, but a cold, angry and half drunk man.

A man who was kissing her with barely restrained lust.

Taken totally off guard, Zoe froze. Eric's lips were hard and the kiss he was giving had nothing in common with the fairy tale one she had dreamed of months before. On the contrary, it seemed almost like a punishment. But why?

Was it some other woman he was actually trying to punish…?

She stiffened in anger and pushed him away. "How much have you drunk? Hey, I'm not Stephanie!"

"I know damn well you're not. And don't worry, I'm not so drunk that I don't know what I'm doing – the way *you* did on New Year's Eve."

The way you did on New Year's Eve?!

That must mean that…?

Zoe had no time to reply or to think, though, because Eric's mouth was once again pressed against hers, this time with less coldness but with the same forcefulness, and her mind began to cloud over. She kept superimposing the image of that night in Times Square over what was happening now until the two kisses eventually began to merge into one.

So it was all true… She hadn't dreamed any of it…

Something inside her seemed to swell and then suddenly explode into dozens of small pieces, each of which seemed to find its proper place. She felt a heavy weight slipping from her shoulders, all her doubts vanishing, while only one desire began to fill her heart: she wanted to kiss Eric Morgan, and this time she wanted to remember it perfectly.

She put her hot, trembling hands to his face and returned his kiss as gently as she could. She felt the tension in Eric's body evaporate and his lips soften, and at that point she felt as though she could recognize him again. He no longer seemed angry or determined to take revenge. He just seemed to want to devour her.

It would really be a pain in the ass if she fainted with joy right now.

She felt as light headed as if she had been inhaling helium – she couldn't think straight, all her senses were focused on the contact with those soft lips, and her own reaction surprised her more than a little. Her heart was pounding in her chest as violently as the storm outside, the blood was flowing in her veins like a raging torrent and her skin was getting hot at an alarming rate.

Was it really Eric who was kissing her? Her best friend? The shy, intelligent and surprisingly sexy guy she worked with?

A lovely feeling of finding herself face to face with a stranger swept over her. Eric's familiar scent was comforting, his passion was turning her on, and the whole situation was complete insanity. But it was an insanity that she was in no hurry to recover from.

She put her hand into his wet hair and pulled him to her, but at that moment the sudden, blinding return of the electric power made them both freeze.

Zoe opened her eyes to find Eric's profound, clear eyes staring back at her. They were so close that their noses were touching and only an inch or so separated their lips. On his face was an expression so intense that it made her feel dizzy.

"Bad timing," he murmured, with a hoarse and sensual voice that lit a thousand sparks on her skin.

He was right, the lights had come back on at a very inconvenient time. Had it been fate putting a providential stop to this madness or just a coincidence?

She had to make a decision: to go back to what they had been doing or to move away before it was too late.

Kissing Eric could be dangerous, especially given the strange emotions that he had somehow been arousing in her lately. And moreover, he was with another girl…

The thought struck her like a baseball bat, but for none of the right reasons. She should immediately extract herself from that triangle and feel guilty about what she was doing to another unsuspecting girl. Instead all she could do was feel fierce jealousy.

This was *her* Eric, and she wasn't planning on sharing him with anyone.

Looking into his slightly misty eyes, Zoe sent her better judgment to hell and bent over to turn off the lamp next to the couch.

"Are you turning off the light to forget who you've got in front of you?" he asked.

"I'm turning off the light to avoid you getting distracted," whispered Zoe.

With the room once again immersed in twilight, she put her arms around his neck and kissed him, sighing with pleasure when she felt Eric's lips surrender to hers with no trace of hesitation.

The abruptness of the first kiss was inexorably replaced by a languid passion. Eric didn't seem to be in any kind of rush, and he savored her so slowly and so deeply that it took her breath away. His hands on her body were delicate, but they knew exactly how to touch the right spots. In a state of stunned euphoria, Zoe felt as though she had been plunged into some parallel reality from which she had absolutely no desire to return.

He had always been there, right beside her. How many other times could she have enjoyed these wonderful feelings, if only she had been able to imagine them?

Had Eric always thought of her that way, or was it just a momentary impulse inspired by the wine?

A thousand thoughts flowed through her mind, some wonderful and some horrible. Maybe they should break off that wonderful kiss and have a talk to try and work out what was really going on…

But Eric drew her to him, pulling her onto his lap, his hands moving lazily under her dress, touching her thighs where her stockings ended and pushing higher and higher, his caresses becoming more and more daring.

Zoe put all thoughts of talking things through out of her mind.

All in all, the explanations could wait.

Chapter 12

An oblique ray of sunlight fell across the bed, caressing the crumpled sheets and stubbly cheek of the man asleep between them.

It was too early to get up and go to work, but Zoe was already up, fully dressed and gripping her phone tightly in her hand. But she couldn't take her eyes off the sleeping figure.

One of his arms lay outstretched on the mattress where not long ago she herself had been, his face was partially hidden by the pillow, and his bare, uncovered limbs contrasted with the whiteness of the sheets. The expression on that face which she so adored was so relaxed and satisfied that it gave her a shiver of pleasure to see it.

In her mind's eye, she saw the image of the hypothetical awakening they might have had if she had only stayed in that bed: a sleepy look while he focused on her face, a tender smile spreading over his soft lips and a hoarse voice wishing her good morning as he bent over to kiss her…

Her stomach tightened and, consequently, so did the hand she was holding the phone in. The powerful desire she felt to see that scene come true was the reason why she had slipped out of the warm bed and hurriedly gotten herself dressed.

The images of the night before came flooding back into her mind, making her blush.

She would never again doubt Eric's talent for lovemaking.

He had made her tremble with desire. Had been careful, slow, curious, untiring. He had taken everything he wanted and given all of himself in return. She couldn't remember when she had ever had so much pleasure in a man's arms in her life, and all without resorting to any kind of erotic trickery. The sweetness of the guy had won her over after the first few kisses, and the rest had been a wonderful, exciting discovery.

But what did it all mean?

The question troubled her deeply. Feeling this euphoric after a night spent with someone she'd just met would have been a lot simpler. Feeling like she was walking on air thanks to a guy she had always known and with whom she had shared the joys and sorrows of daily life – that was scary.

If things didn't work out, everything would be over between them.

She was terrified.

Her tender bosom buddy, her fussy co-worker, the sarcastic critic of her lifestyle, was right there, fast asleep, oblivious to what was going through her head. What would he think when he eventually woke up? Would he be puzzled? Would he too feel confused and frightened? The night before he'd been drunk and angry, maybe it had been that which had set the train of events in motion…

Still, Eric had said things that left her breathless, and confirmed that the kiss she thought she had dreamed on New Year's Eve had really happened.

How could he have dissembled like that? And why had he done it? To protect their friendship? Or because he wasn't interested in going any further?

The memory of the passion they had shared that night leapt into her mind: well it was a bit too late now for not wanting to go any further.

She shivered inside her still damp coat.

They would have to talk and clear things up. The sex had been great, but it mustn't in any way destroy their relationship. She could not lose Eric.

"So why don't you climb back into that bed and wait for him to wake up so you can see how things actually are?" suggested her conscience.

Because what she feared most was precisely Eric's reaction when he did wake up. If he had behaved as though he felt guilty or shocked for having allowed his passion to overwhelm him, Zoe wouldn't have been able to stand it. She would no longer have been able to pretend that it was all just a dream, the way she had been doing.

She needed to get some fresh air and be on her own for a while before seeing him again in the shop in a couple of hours time. That would be long enough for her to prepare for any eventuality and, at the same time, to clear her head.

But she couldn't just disappear without a word.

She walked over to Eric's desk, feeling a deep intimacy as she rummaged through his things. The fact that she knew exactly which drawer to open to find a notebook and a pen underlined just how much time she had spent with him in that same room over the years, mostly for work. She had never imagined that she would find herself one day ecstatically rolling around in that bed with him. Let alone after having been carried away by passion on his couch…

Feeling her clothes almost evaporate on her body, she bent down to write a note on a piece of paper which she then laid on the empty pillow. A pillow that still bore the imprint of her head.

As she rose again, she found herself staring at Eric through an imaginary viewfinder, studying his features and amazed once again by how handsome he was.

She had felt such intense pleasure in undressing him the night before, revealing the agile body that had been giving her sleepless nights lately. Making contact with his warm skin had been a shock, but it had been the soft, extremely sensual and yet respectful way that he had touched her the whole time which had been the coup de grace. After the first moments of overwhelming passion, Eric had treated her like a precious jewel yet somehow had still managed to make her burn like a firebrand.

Making love to him had been like putting on some particularly comfortable, warm clothes only to find that as well as giving you a sense of security and well-being, they also gave you immense pleasure.

How had she managed not to fall for him all these years?

She was afraid to answer her own question. Whatever the reason they had not arrived at that point before was, now it would involve a drastic change in their relationship. And given that Eric was the pivot on which so much of her life turned, she wasn't sure that the change would be for the better.

She rushed out of the beloved apartment before she broke down in tears.

*

While shivering in the bitter cold of the morning, she stood waiting in the street for her taxi to arrive and felt a powerful anxiety growing in her chest. A crazed terror took possession of her, threatening to crush her.

She had told herself that she was ready to fall in love again, but was it actually true? Eric wasn't like the stupid pretty boys she'd been dating the last few years, he was a real man – serious, intelligent, caring and honest.

She couldn't disappoint him. Just the thought of it was intolerable.

But she didn't want to go through what she had gone through with Stuart again either, denying herself and putting up with everything simply to be loved. She knew deep down that Eric would never take advantage of her weaknesses the way her ex had done, but who could guarantee that?

Did these reflections mean that she was really in love with Eric? Or had it just been some kind of chemical reaction? Might her desperate need not to be alone on Valentine's Day meant that her feelings had gotten blown out of all proportion?

No!

Her mind recoiled at the thought. She had made love to Eric because he – him, Eric himself – had made her *want* to – not just because he was the only man who'd been available at that particular moment. She had run to him the previous night instead of giving Stuart a second chance or getting to know her mysterious suitor. That had to count for something.

Eric was essential for her. What mattered now was understanding exactly in what way.

A few minutes later, the taxi dropped her off at her apartment, where she had a hot shower and put on dry clothes. Before going to the store she looked at herself in the mirror, and saw that there was something different about her. The confident, sexy woman had vanished, giving way to the confused and fearful girl she had always tried to hide from the world. Eric was the only one who had ever looked behind the mask and found the real Zoe.

He had an advantage over her... Especially after last night.

When she finally got to Giftland, she was so agitated at the idea of seeing him again that her hands were shaking. She wished that Clover, the only one she could really talk about the subject with calmly, had been there, but her friend was in Paris and wouldn't be coming back for a couple of days.

Liberty, who had arrived early as usual, was there to welcome her inside, and looked fresh and rested as after a long sleep. Her boss had spent a romantic evening which had probably ended with sex too, so why didn't she look as devastated as Zoe did?

She went straight behind the counter, took off her jacket and decided to try and pull herself together, breathe slowly and stay calm.

Hey, she thought – it's Eric that I'm going to have to face when he eventually turns up, not some heartless monster. Shy as he was, he would probably be even more uncomfortable with the whole thing than she was. She convinced herself that the whole thing would end in a good laugh while Eric's ears went bright pink, so there was no need to panic.

"A night of sex, what's the big deal?" she thought. It probably wouldn't have any consequences at all. So why did she feel her heart jump in her chest at the thought of it?

"Are you okay?" asked Liberty, while she fumbled with the coffee machine.

"I had sex with Eric."

Zoe dropped her bombshell, expecting to see Liberty's eyes go wide and her cup fall to the floor.

Her friend, however, just shrugged. "About time. It took you longer than I'd predicted, but the timing was perfect. I bet that you don't hate Valentine's Day from now on. It'll always fall on the same day as your anniversary. Isn't that sweet!"

Zoe was the one whose eyes grew wide. Fortunately, she had no cup of coffee to drop.

"Lib, what the hell are you talking about?! Can't you see what a state I'm in?"

"Come to think of it, I can... Was it *that* terrible?" asked Liberty with a worried frown as she walked toward her office. "I hope it's not going to make things uncomfortable here in the shop."

"It wasn't terrible at all, it was wonderful!" said Zoe as she followed her upstairs, dropping into an office chair with an expression of complete desperation on her face. "And that's the problem."

Liberty sighed. "The longer I know you two, the less I understand you."

"It's all so weird... I mean, until yesterday I just thought of him as my teddy bear – and then today it's like my body is still electric with passion!"

"Hey, listen, I'm not Clover: spare me the juicy details, please!"

"I'm not going to tell you the 'juicy details' – that's *personal*," Zoe muttered, running her hands through her hair.

"Well how about that, that's a new one! Once upon a time you used to give fairly detailed reports."

She was right. But that was because with the other men, Zoe had never actually cared much about what had happened. With Eric, though, things were completely different.

Liberty noticed her distraught air and sat down beside her. "I don't understand what the problem is."

"The problem is that I got it all wrong! I shouldn't have gone over to his place last night, and I shouldn't have taken advantage of his mood. He was angry, maybe even drunk. He was acting weirdly, and I let myself get carried away and we ended up in bed together. But it shouldn't have happened!"

"You let yourself get carried away? You mean that you jumped on him?"

"I means that I let him do it! I was miserable, and soaking wet from the rain, he was wet and pissed off about something, probably that idiot girlfriend of his… and so I tried to comfort him. And then he kissed me, and I…. Well, I just couldn't resist! There was that really bad storm, and the power went off, and we were in the dark, alone, on Valentine's Day… It was a time bomb waiting to go off!"

"So are you saying that it was just physical chemistry?"

Zoe, more and more confused, shook her head. She didn't know herself what she meant.

"I don't know… I mean, who's to say that it didn't all just happen by chance? I'm so fond of him, and I felt alone and I went to him, but I certainly never imagined… I've never thought about getting together with him, not seriously… I mean, we're talking about *Eric*! The know-it-all with the glasses, the guy who's more interested in books than in women! Maybe I got him confused. Isn't that what he's always said about me? That I make men stupid when I get too close to them?"

"Yeah, but he's always thought he was different from those kinds of men."

"And in fact he'd never thought about me like that either, but last night he was angry and drunk and I was on my own and feeling sorry for myself… Just like always, for that matter! Oh, Lib, I've totally screwed up! He didn't deserve it! He wasn't himself, and I should have acted like an adult and stopped him… And now we can't be friends any more!" Zoe babbled, covering her face with her hands.

"Are you *sure* that Eric didn't want to? Drunk or not, I can't really see him being at the mercy of his instincts," said Liberty, after a moment's thought.

Zoe spun around to face her. "What do you mean?"

"I mean that Eric's overprotectiveness is really sweet, but it's something he only does with you. And he does it so much that it seems like more than just being fond of you as a friend."

"Are you saying he might have a secret crush on me?"

"I wouldn't be surprised. And the fact that you two ended up in bed together seems to me to be confirmation of the fact. I don't think he's so inexperienced or naive that he'd have sex with you just to fill up an evening or to let off some steam. Do you really think he'd be capable of that?"

"No…" said Zoe, looking at her and taking a deep breath. "But what about me? Why did I go to bed with him, in your opinion?"

"I think that since that ridiculous calendar for Sydney Andrews you've started to look at him with different eyes. In that moment you suddenly saw him as an attractive man, whereas before he'd always just been 'Eric, your best friend'. The combination of all the affection, complicity and profound understanding that already exists between you two with a healthy new physical attraction just completely KO'd you."

"He deserves a woman who wants him without having seen him naked."

"And haven't you always thought he was great, even before seeing his attributes?" Liberty rolled her eyes, then touched her friend's hand gently. "Unfortunately, there's no predetermined order for falling in love with someone, and love at first sight isn't always the best choice, believe me. Sometimes a relationship that starts slowly and gets stronger over time is better."

"So are you saying… Are you saying you think we should be together?" asked Zoe in a whisper. The thought made her dizzy, but she couldn't tell if it was because of the joy or the confusion.

"It's not up to me to tell you who you should be with, you have to figure that out yourself. What happened is definitely going to change things between you, but if there are no major feelings at stake between you, you should go back to being friends, sooner or later. And if there are… well, you two would be better off getting everything out in the open once and for all."

Zoe took a deep breath and stood up.

"You're right. The affection between us will let us face this thing like a couple of adults," she said, trying to convince herself. "I'm going to wait for him downstairs."

He would be arriving at any moment, so she forced herself to calm down.

Liberty was right, there were no rules about the way you fell in love with someone. It just happened. Some relationships began with love at first sight, others with the people involved not even liking each other, and others still with a great friendship. And the same thing could happen to her and Eric. They were young, healthy, always together. Perhaps it was inevitable that, sooner or later, something would happen. She just had to ask herself a few questions and answer them honestly.

Was she attracted to Eric?

Yes, without a doubt. She had always thought he was cute, even though he worked hard at not letting anybody realize that he was. And after discovering how attractive he could be if he spent a little more effort on his appearance, her opinion of him in that regard had improved markedly.

Did she trust him? More than any other person in the world.

Could she imagine being in a relationship with him? They'd always got on great before they'd been to bed together, so why shouldn't they after?

What did she feel for him? She adored him, always had. Right from day one, she had liked that guy, always bent over his books yet always with something smart and witty to say for himself. Despite that nerdy appearance, behind those glasses there was a hot temper, tempered by a reassuring sweetness and immense patience.

She realized, in retrospect, that she had never taken an important step without him.

In anticipation of her move to New York, she had persuaded Eric to want to live there rather than in Boston. When she had found a job at Giftland, she had got them to give him a job too so he'd be with her. He was the one she ran to when she had good news to share, as well as when she felt lonely and uncertain about life.

She'd always thought she wasn't good enough for him, and therefore not even his type. She, who hadn't even graduated from college and who knew only how to enchant men and take photographs, could never have held the attention of a guy like Eric for long. But she'd never actually thought about that, simply because their friendship had given her everything she needed – more than any other loving relationship.

Romance always complicated everything, that's why she had clung so tightly to that dear, sweet friend. Eric would never disappoint her, he was there for her and he always would be there for her – he would never stab her in the back, he would never abandon her.

And finally she realized why no other man had been able to conquer her.

No one could hold a candle to a guy like Eric. She had mistakenly thought that Stuart Harris could, but the only thing they had in common was the fact that they were both graduates. If back then she could have even imagined that Eric might like her, Stuart would probably never have entered her life.

That realization made her heart start pounding.

The truth was that, without knowing it, she had always been in love with Eric – a pure love, without ulterior motives, something that went beyond physical attraction and sex. It was the kind of feeling that kept two people close even when their bodies started to age and orgasms were just memories, a bond that dug deep into the soul like a rivulet of water destined to grow as it went along instead of a powerful and invigorating wave that left only sand and debris in its wake.

That must be why she had felt vaguely threatened every time she had seen him going out with other girls, and why she was so jealous of Stephanie…

The girl that he had loved in his youth and who that night had betrayed, because of her.

Biting her thumbnail so hard she chipped the polish, she stared out of the window without really seeing anything.

Eric must feel like a monster. Whatever he had felt, or still felt, for her, it was not in his nature to get involved with a girl without being really interested, and last night must be weighing heavily on his conscience.

Was *that* why he was so late?

Lost as she was in her thoughts, she hadn't noticed the time passing. It was now ten o'clock and there was still no sign of Eric.

Maybe he needed to recover from the shock of last night, she thought, with a sigh. She couldn't really blame him.

Work kept her busy until lunch time, by which time his absence was really starting to make her nervous.

What had happened? Why hadn't he arrived yet?

Liberty had come downstairs a couple of times to ask her the same thing and to help out with the clients, even though the shop was pretty quiet now that St Valentine's Day was just a memory.

Summoning up her courage, Zoe tried calling him, but his phone rang and rang and no one answered. What could have happened? Could he be sick? Had something happened to him on his way to work? Anxiety slowly turned in panic as one horrible scenario after another flashed through her head with every passing minute. Suddenly, the idea of facing him after last night frightened her less than the thought of losing him for any other reason.

Liberty tried to reassure her, telling her that if he had had an accident, the hospital would already have called, seeing as he'd put her down as the person to call in case of emergency, but it didn't make her feel any better. Liberty even tried to joke about it, saying that Eric was probably so embarrassed about everything that he'd climbed aboard the first plane to some unknown destination just to avoid meeting her, but not even that could reassure her.

She was about to walk out of work and go to Eric's house when Liberty, who had retired to her office, suddenly came back downstairs. Her expression was so gloomy and full of veiled concern that it immediately put Zoe on the alert.

"What's happened?" she asked, taking a step forward.

"He's alive, if that's any consolation. He's just sent me a fax."

"A *fax*?" Zoe blinked in confusion. "What does he say?"

Liberty stared for a moment at the paper she held in her hands then raised her eyes to Zoe's. "That this is his resignation, with immediate effect."

She felt as if a truck had driven over her, crushing all of her vital organs. Her head throbbed painfully, not just from the hangover from the previous night, and her muscles had gone so stiff that she couldn't stop trembling.

She had never felt more angry, bitter and disappointed in her entire life.

*

That morning, when he had opened his eyes and seen the empty bed beside him he had let out a groan of despair, thinking he had only dreamed the whole thing. It wouldn't have been the first time that he had lived out his love for Zoe in his imagination, but he immediately noticed a couple of things that reassured him.

The pillow on the left side of the bed still bore the imprint of a head, and the fruity scent of Zoe hung throughout the room, on the sheets and on his skin.

He hadn't imagined any of it, it had all been quite real.

As soon as he saw the note lying on the pillow, though, his anxiety returned. Sitting under the covers, he rubbed his face with his hands before reading the few words it contained:

I need to get changed and get my feet back on the ground. See you later in the store. Zoe xxx

Get her feet back on the ground... What did she mean? Was she so happy after last night that she felt as if she was walking on air, too?

Or did she just want to forget all about it and get back to reality?

It seemed almost impossible. After ten years of waiting and shattered dreams, he – Eric Morgan – had actually managed to go to bed with Zoe Mathison, the most courted woman in New York! But precisely because it all seemed so absurd, that note prompted him to get up and get ready to go out in a hurry. Perhaps the store wasn't really the perfect place to clear the air, but they wouldn't have to talk much for him to get an idea of the way things were. He knew Zoe so well that he would be able to tell from a single look at her face whether she was happy or unhappy about what had happened between them.

The words he had heard her saying to Liberty rang in his ears, tormenting him. It had not been his intention to eavesdrop, but when he arrived at Giftland he had heard their voices coming from Liberty's office and had set off towards them as if drawn by a magnet...

"The problem is that I got it all wrong! I shouldn't have gone over to his place last night, and I shouldn't have taken advantage of his mood. He was angry, maybe even drunk. He was acting weirdly, and I let myself get carried away and we ended up in bed together. But it shouldn't have happened!"

Her words had made him freeze.

Could Zoe really think that for him it had just been sex for the sake of it? That he was stupid enough to go to bed with her just because he had been drinking?

But it was what she said next that was the coup de grace.

"I don't know… I mean, who's to say that it didn't all just happen by chance? I'm so fond of him, and I felt alone and I went to him, but I certainly never imagined… I've never thought about getting together him, not seriously… I mean, we're talking about *Eric*! The know-it-all with the glasses, the guy who's more interested in books than in women! Maybe I got him confused. Isn't that what he's always said about me? That I make men stupid when I get too close to them?… He'd never thought about me like that either, but last night he was angry and drunk and I was at on my own and feeling sorry for myself… Just like always, for that matter! Oh, Lib, I've totally screwed up! He didn't deserve it! He wasn't himself, and I should have acted like an adult and stopped him… And now we can't be friends any more!"

He had heard her sounding more enthusiastic after nights spent in the company of perfect idiots. After she had been in his arms, though, she had seemed mortified and scared at the idea of them no longer being friends…

Without waiting a moment longer he had left the shop, his stomach in a vice-like grip and full of anxiety.

He knew it. What had he expected? That a woman like that would really want a guy like him? She'd had sex with him out of pity, in the name of their friendship… To *console* him! What an idiot. How could he have thrown ten years of his life away by falling for a person who thought he was a nobody, a loser with too many hormones? Did she think he was so pathetic that he wouldn't have been able to resist the idea of a bit of healthy sex? Or perhaps so stupid that he couldn't tell two women apart once he'd had a couple of drinks?

She was right about one thing, though: they could not go back to being friends. For his part, the chapter entitled Zoe Mathison had to be permanently closed that very day.

Once he got back home he wrote a letter of resignation to Liberty immediately, even though he waited a while before sending it. He had decided to stop working at Giftland and to go back to living in Boston with his parents, as far away from Zoe and all the memories of her as possible. But taking the first step was harder than he had expected. He had been hoping for too long to get to that point, and now that at last he had held her in his arms, it was damn hard to get used to the idea of letting go of her for once and for all.

He felt like a coward, but he had no alternative. He would never be able to feel any better if he stayed in New York, where he would always have been terrified that he would bump into her in the street. He had to put some distance between them and hope to forget her in a hurry.

The phone rang several times during the day. Probably worried by his absence, Zoe and Liberty tried to call him on his mobile and on the landline, but every time Zoe's name appeared on the display, he felt angrier than before.

His eyes fell on the Valentine's gift that Stephanie had thrown at him after he had left her, and he felt doubly stupid. He had let a beautiful girl who was actually interested in him slip through his fingers so he could chase a ghost, someone who had never considered him a man. And that cute little teddy bear that, with him in mind, Zoe had chosen for Steffy had been a perfect metaphor for the whole story.

A soft toy in Zoe's hands, that's what he had always been and what she had always seen.

Almost choking on the anger and bitterness he felt, he sent the fax and lay down on his bed – though not before having thrown aside the scented sheets.

He had been lying there for a while when he heard the phone ring again.

He let the answering machine answer, and prepared himself to hear Zoe's increasingly worried voice again – but it wasn't her who left a message.

"Bonsoir, mon ami!" He raised his eyebrows at the sound of Clover's cheerful voice. "You didn't call me, you bum! You promised to tell me exactly what happened last night but you didn't – you're not a man of your word!" she chuckled. "I hope this means, like Cade says, that you and Zoe have been involved in something so interesting that it's made you forget about everything else. You've certainly got to make up for lost time! Anyway, call me when you can, otherwise I will get Zoe to tell me all the juicy details!"

More annoyed than ever, Eric grabbed the phone. "Great idea! Call Zoe so she can tell you what happened!"

"Eric! I didn't think you were at home…" Clover seemed puzzled by his tone of voice. "Are you okay?"

"No, I'm not okay. And you know what? It's partly your fault!" snapped Eric, gripping the receiver. "You and your stupid romantic ideas and your sentimental assumptions, you brainwashed me! You stopped me from giving up on Zoe, you kept telling me that there was hope – well there wasn't any, and you didn't understand shit!"

"But…"

"I ended up looking more pathetic and more ridiculous than I ever have in my *life*, Clover. Zoe doesn't want a guy like me, I've thrown ten years down the toilet. But you're not the only one who's to blame. Only a loser like me could have believed the words of someone as optimistic as you and hung on to a stupid dream all this time. I should have gone back to Boston a long time ago, but it's not too late for me to go and end it here. And I hope I never have to see any of you again!"

He hung up, breathless from anger. He already felt guilty for having blasted poor Clover with his despair, but he hadn't been able to help himself.

Angrily, he unplugged the telephone and lay back on the bed, staring at the ceiling.

It was time for him to turn the page and start behaving like a man, but ten years of crumbled hopes were a lot to digest in a single day, so he decided to wallow in self-pity until he felt completely empty.

*

Clover stared at the phone despondently. Eric's furious words had surprised and confused her, leaving her with an unpleasant feeling.

"Something wrong?" asked Cade, coming into the bedroom.

Clover broke away from the window, which gave onto an incredible view of the illuminated Eiffel Tower, and gave him a sad look. "I don't know… Eric was furious!"

"Things didn't go the way you expected?"

"This can't be right!" Clover sat down on the big double bed, wringing her hands. "I was *sure* it would work between them."

"Did he tell you what happened?"

"No. But he said he never wants to see any of us again."

Cade sat down beside her, stroking her back. "Wait until he's calmed down, maybe then he'll tell you what went wrong."

"If Zoe has screwed it all up because of that idiot of an ex of hers, I'll never forgive her!" Clover muttered, crossing her arms over her chest.

"You think she's still in love with Stuart?"

"Of course she isn't! She's in love with Eric, she just hasn't realized it yet! And she will regret bitterly disappointing him, if that's what she's done, because she will *never* find a guy who's better suited to her!" Her eyes flashing in the dim room, Clover stood up. "I'm going to call her and give her a piece of my mind."

Smiling tenderly, Cade grabbed her hand and pulled her back down onto the bed. "Honey, leave it. They're big enough to look after themselves."

"But I was sure that it would have worked out for Eric, I talked him into telling her everything and now he hates me!"

"Knowing him, he's probably already regretting what he said." Cade massaged her neck, forcing her to look at him. "You were sweet to try to help him, you're a good friend and he knows that. It was time he faced up to the situation. And if things didn't work out, well, he'll get used to it."

"He wants to move to Boston so he doesn't have to see her any more." Clover let Cade's fingers calm her, but her eyes were sad. "That's why I have to talk to Zoe. I want to know why she is throwing away her best chance to be happy."

"Maybe she's afraid. We were too, do you remember?"

Clover thought back to the two weeks when she and Cade had been separated, thinking that it was all over between them, and sighed.

"Do you think that they'll be as quick as we were at realizing they're made for each other?"

"If they love each other as much as we do, they won't hold out for long," said Cade, kissing her on the tip of her nose. "Now let's enjoy our last hours in Paris, all right? You can tackle the problem when we get back to New York."

"I think I need something sweet," muttered Clover, hiding her face in his neck.

"You mean sweeter than me?" smiled Cade.

"Yeah, you are pretty sweet. Maybe if you were coated in chocolate…"

Clover's mischievous look earned her a long kiss, then Cade pulled her to her feet. "Let's go. Zack recommended a few pâtisseries that do the best chocolate, and those macaroons that you like so much."

"I love that guy!" sighed Clover, dreamily.

Cade lifted her up and slung her over his shoulder, with her head hanging down towards the floor, making her scream.

"Come on, I was joking!"

"Too late, I'm carrying you through the hall upside down. And if there's a photographer out there, you can say goodbye to that sweet ickle fairy image the journalists invented for you!"

Clover laughed heartily. "I don't care about my reputation. But you'll look like a caveman!"

"I'll be fine."

When Cade opened the door and started off down the corridor, Clover stared up at him. "Are you really going to go through with this?!"

"Sure. You're going to need to find a very convincing reason for persuading me not to carry you out of the hotel like this."

"The blood's going to my brain. Is that convincing enough?"

"Afraid not."

"What if I promise to keep you up all night...?" she said in a seductive voice, stroking his back sensually.

Cade gave her a pat on the butt. "I'd already planned on that."

"I could always refuse to participate."

In response, he touched her leg with a finger which he ran all along its length to the hem of the woollen dress she was wearing. He chuckled when he felt her shudder and pressed the elevator call button.

Once inside, Clover spoke again. "And what if I promise you never to say another word to Zack?"

"Now there's an idea I like."

Amused, Clover shook her head, making her long red hair wave. "No, I'm sorry... I just couldn't do that!"

"There are seven floors left, you better decide your destiny pretty fast."

"Oh God, Cade! How can you be jealous of Zack? Ok, he's handsome, but since I met you I've become immune to other men, and you know it!"

"Hmm... And why do you think that is?"

"Because I love you, sweet cheeks. What else?"

Cade set her back down on the ground and put his hands on her hips.

"Correct answer," he murmured, his eyes full of love, before kissing her.

Chapter 13

She was on the verge of exploding. Her confusion after having sex with Eric had turned slowly into anxiety and then into panic before finally settling on sadness. And after the sadness, inevitably, had come the anger.

Forty-eight hours of silence. She had never waited so long for a phone call from a guy in her life.

She did not know what to think. Eric wasn't answering her phone calls, or those of Liberty; his flat seemed to be empty, at least judging by the fact that nobody opened up to her insistent knocking, and no one had heard from him for the last two days.

What the hell was going through his head? Why this sudden disappearance, and why the resignation? Could it be that he was so stupid and shy that he couldn't face showing himself? Or was there another reason? Why couldn't they resolve things like a couple of mature adults?

She was on the verge of actually contacting Eric's mother in Boston when the shop door opened and Clover, who had returned from Paris, walked in. Zoe saw the wary expression on her face and did not waste any time.

"You've heard, then?"

"About Eric, you mean?"

"He quit, did you know?"

Clover's eyes widened, and she banged her palms down on the countertop.

"Would you mind telling me what the hell you did to him?!"

"Me? *Me*?!" shouted Zoe, attracting the stares of a couple of customers. Livid with anger, she lowered her voice. "First, that idiot takes me to bed and then he disappears for two days without a single word, and it's all *my* fault? All those unasked for put-downs of my awful exes, and then he behaves worse than all of them put together! If I catch sight of him, I'll murder him myself!"

"He took you to *bed*?" Clover blinked. "So you didn't just crack up laughing when you turned up at the restaurant and saw him, then?"

Zoe frowned in confusion.

"The *restaurant*? What are you talking about?"

Clover hesitated. "Wait a minute, would you mind just telling me exactly what the hell happened? Maybe it's the jet lag, but I'm not understanding anything."

"On the evening of Valentine's Day I was in a mess. A small part of me wanted to accept Stuart's invitation to dinner, hoping – mistakenly, I know – that maybe we could give it another try. But in my heart I knew that I would never be able to forget what he'd done, just like I knew that what I felt for him wasn't really love. So I turned down his invitation, told him not to call me any more, and I got ready to go out to the River Café, but… well, I just felt really stupid spending the most romantic night of the year with a complete stranger who I might not even like at all. And after wandering around aimlessly for a while, I found myself getting a cab over to Eric's," said Zoe, her arms crossed in front of her chest. "But when I got there, he was angry and drunk. I thought maybe he was sad because of Stephanie, but he wouldn't tell me anything. I tried to comfort him… There was the storm, and the lights went off, and one thing led to another and we ended up having sex."

"So you didn't go to the restaurant, then…"

"No, but what's that got to do with it?"

"And what about the morning after it happened?"

"I left before he woke up," said Zoe, biting her lower lip. "It all seemed so crazy! We were friends, and then suddenly we were lovers… I thought I'd better clear my head before I faced it all. I left him a note telling him that I was going home to change and that we'd meet here. But he never turned up, and at two in the afternoon his resignation came by fax!"

Clover seemed dazed. "I don't get it."

"Oh, me neither, believe me! It's been two days and there's been no trace of him, he's not answering the phone and it looks like there's no one at home. I'm planning to call his mother to see if he's in Boston, but I don't want to scare her for no good reason."

"I spoke to him," sighed Clover, her elbows on the counter and her face in her hands. "He was so pissed! He says he never wants to see us again."

Zoe felt her stomach drop. "But why?"

"I don't know! I thought you must have reacted badly to the thing with the restaurant and that you'd turned him down, but now that you've told me how things actually went I do not know *what* to think."

"Clover, what the hell has the restaurant got to do with it?!"

"Oh *God*, you're slow on the uptake sometimes!" Clover raised her eyes to the heavens and then looked her in the face. "Eric was the mystery man!"

"What?" said a stunned Zoe. For a moment she couldn't seem to grasp the concept, but then the reality of the situation collapsed in on her.

It had been *Eric* who had sent those tickets? And the gifts, the balloons and the roses… He was the man who she was supposed to meet at the River Café?

"Is this a joke?" she asked, her voice trembling and her heart thudding dully in her breast.

"Damn it, Zoe, Eric has been in love with you for ten years! How the hell could you not realize?!"

"And how do you know?"

"I noticed a long time ago, and I asked him and he admitted it to me. But he made me promise not to tell anyone – he didn't want you to know."

"Why?!" she blurted out in frustration. She could feel the anger returning.

"Because he was sure he didn't have a chance with you and he didn't want to ruin your friendship. He always said that if he'd confessed everything and you'd turned him down, he would be forced to leave New York and move back to Boston to get over it. That's why I though you must have said 'no'! He was so angry. From the way he spoke, I thought you'd humiliated him!"

"I didn't do anything!" Zoe cried, her voice breaking. "I mean, apart from standing him up at the River Café, but I didn't know that it was him who was waiting for me… and anyway, I still *was* with him at the end of the day!" She ran a hand through her untidy hair in an attempt to calm herself down, then ran into Eric's office and closed the door.

How could she never have noticed anything? And why hadn't he spoken to her about his feelings? Or taken the opportunity to when she had kissed him in Times Square on New Year's Eve?

Suddenly, all the presents that Eric had delivered to her anonymously over the last few days made perfect sense: the

Red Velvet, as well as being her favorite dessert, was the first thing they had eaten together at the university cafeteria; the plush hamster looked like the one she had given him for his twenty-third birthday; the pendant was a reference to the star that Eric had bought for her online in honor of her move to New York...

Nine red roses, plus one – ten roses, one for each of the years they had known each other...

They were all perfectly obvious to her now, each with a special meaning that only she could understand.

How could she have been so stupid? And what about him? How had he managed to hide it so well for all these years?

They had wasted so much time...

But why the hell was Eric so angry now? What could possibly have made him react like that? She had left him with a satisfied smile on his face, dammit, and now he didn't want to see her ever again...

She thought of all the years they had spent together, tried to look at every situation through different eyes, and soon the tears were flowing down her face.

She must have made him suffer so much, she realized. All those times when she'd told him about her flings, the two years with Stuart, those dinners for Valentine's Day, Christmas and New Year when she had forced him to play the part of her boyfriend! Eric had always put up with it all in silence, while she took advantage of his kindness, mistaking it for friendship...

While she had been desperately searching for someone to love her, she hadn't noticed that he'd been by her side the whole time...

Clover and Liberty joined her shortly afterwards.

"How can we help?" asked Liberty, sitting down next to her.

"I don't know," said Zoe, shaking her head disconsolately. "I feel so sad and bitter about what I've just discovered and about all the time that we've wasted. And I'm mad at him! He can't just walk away like this, for no reason, after all we've been through together."

"We must be missing something. It can't just be because of the note you left him," said Clover, thinking aloud. "Did you make it sound like you regretted it?"

"No! What I wrote might have sounded shocked, but it certainly wasn't regretful."

"What do you feel for him?" her friend asked her, straight out.

Zoe turned her grey eyes to her. "I need him, that's all you need to know. I can't face analyzing my feelings right now, not in this mood. But before he disappeared I really had realized how important Eric is to me, and I wanted to talk to him about it."

"So did you tell him?"

"How could I, if he won't answer the phone?"

"You could leave him a voicemail message"

"No way, I want to tell him right to his face." Zoe got up from her chair and wiped her eyes. "If he's such a coward that he doesn't want to face me then he's not the man I thought he was. Tell him that, when you call him!"

Zoe left the room and Liberty and Clover stared at one another helplessly.

"What do we do now?" sighed Clover.

"If those two don't get this issue sorted out quickly I'm going to fire the pair of them," muttered Liberty, tugging at the hem of her elegant skirt.

"We have to find a way to get them talking. They are meant to be together, and he has waited so long, damn! It *can't* end like this, not now that it was just about to actually begin for real!"

"I think that they should sort it out themselves. If Eric really wants her then it's time for him to man up. He's not an insecure little boy any more, and I really don't feel like making excuses for his behavior."

Clover was walking back and forth across the office, tapping her lips with a finger. "He never gave up, not even when she momentarily lost her head over that idiot Harris. He might be angry right now for some reason, but he'll come back, I can feel it."

The more pessimistic Liberty shook her head. "Weak men can be really stupid sometimes. Their self-esteem is more important than anything else and walking over other people's hearts doesn't mean much to them. Maybe they don't even realize it, because they're so focused on themselves."

Her friend's bitter tone made Clover curious, and she interrupted her pacing to look at her.

"Are you sure that everything's ok between you and Justin?"

Liberty frowned. "Yes – why?"

"I don't know, you've been sounding pretty bitter when you talk about men lately."

"Justin has his head screwed on, and he's serious and responsible. He doesn't have any weaknesses and he knows what he wants. I really can't complain."

Clover gave a puzzled nod. "If you say so." She was about to add something else when they suddenly heard Zoe's voice – sounding hysterical.

"What the hell are you doing?!"

Curious, Clover and Liberty ran into the next room just in time to see Zoe being lifted up bodily and dragged off by an almost unrecognisable Eric.

"What the...?" laughed Clover.

"About damn time!"

"Where is he taking her?" asked Liberty as she watched her colleague put Zoe on a motorcycle parked in front of the shop and then set off at top speed.

"Wherever it is, I hope it helps them fix things" said Clover, putting her hands to her heart. "How romantic! A love kidnapping!"

"At that speed, let's just hope he doesn't kill her," muttered Liberty, as she prepared to serve a customer who had just entered.

Clover rolled her eyes. "Honey, there is *anything* in the world that *doesn't* make you breathe a sigh of pure joy?"

"Hey, I'm just a naturally joyful person!"

"Yeah, right..."

*

"Stop, damn it!"

Zoe unleashed another flurry of punches against Eric's back, trying to slow down his mad rush through the city streets. It had been almost twenty minutes since he had burst into the store and dragged her away on the bike that she had never seen before, and he still hadn't said a word to her.

She had tried to make him communicate in every way she knew, starting with flattery and threats then moving on to punches and kicks, but nothing had distracted him from riding the bike, and she had to be careful not to overdo it if she didn't want to risk them both ending up on the asphalt.

What the hell was going on in that dumb head of his? First he disappeared and handed in his notice, then he swooped down into the store acting like a bad boy and kidnapped her during working hours! She barely knew him any more.

She had only just managed to see his face before he forced her into the thick biker jacket and full-face helmet and dragged her out of the shop, and she'd barely been able to believe her eyes. That neat, perfect boy she had always known had been replaced by a shabbily dressed man with dark rings under his bloodshot eyes and several days' growth of beard. There was no trace of his glasses, he was acting completely differently to the way he usually did, and even his way of dressing seemed to have changed.

He looked worryingly like Eric's evil twin.

The joy that had flooded through her when she had seen him come into the store had turned into disbelief, and then into irritation. But despite the domineering way he was behaving, she was still happy to be breathing his scent and couldn't wait to get off that bike and hug him tight... after having given him a piece of her mind, obviously.

She stopped banging on his back and sighed loudly, resigned to waiting for him to grow tired of that little game. With her eyes fixed on the landscape whizzing past them, she focused on the speech she intended to make to him, even though she didn't really know where to start. She was afraid to tell him how she felt, given recent events: Eric seemed unpredictable now, and she had never been great at communicating her feelings – especially when the stakes were so high.

Feeling the bike begin to slow down, she looked around her, increasingly bewildered. She didn't know this part of town, but it was clear that it wasn't a particularly nice one, and the only building she could see looked like a motel.

He'd returned from the dead after forty-eight hours and taken her to a motel?!

Eric stopped the bike in the parking lot, dismounted and took off his helmet. Zoe stared at him.

"What are we doing here?"

Without answering, Eric locked the helmets to the bike and helped her dismount, none too gently, then towed her off towards the entrance. Zoe obstinately tried to stop him, but to no avail.

"Eric, for God's sake, will you just stop for a moment? I don't want to go in there, I want to talk to you properly! Hey, did you hear me?"

He stopped so suddenly that she crashed into his back, and turned to look at her. His face was so serious it gave her goosebumps.

"You want to talk? Fine. Come inside."

"Couldn't you have called me? Given me a time and place and asked me to come to you? Did you really have to bring me to a place like this?" continued Zoe, feeling Eric's grip tighten on her wrist. "Listen, unless you let go of me right away, I'll scream! I'll say that you've kidnapped me and that you want to rape me!"

"And I'll add that to all the other humiliations I've gone through because of you."

Zoe went silent. Twinges of guilt and anger went through her as, with blood boiling, she waited for Eric to get the key to a room. Once she was safely inside the sparsely furnished room, however, she exploded.

"You! You are… *impossible!*" she snapped, wriggling out of his grasp and giving him a shove. "I've never been so angry with you in my life!"

"Maybe because it's the first time that I haven't been kissing your feet," said Eric, seemingly unperturbed. "You'll get used to it."

"What does that mean? That from now on this is going to be the way you treat me?"

"Why, don't you like it?" Eric's burning eyes rested on her as he advanced towards her. Zoe stepped back until she was against the wall, but it was a mistake. Eric put a hand on the wall each side of her, imprisoning her. He was so close that she could feel his body heat. With that cold, insolent expression, tough-guy clothes and without his glasses, it felt as though he was a stranger. But his scent was the same as always: familiar, fresh and clean.

That particularly comforted her. She looked up into the green-blue eyes she knew so well and softened her tone. "I want the old Eric back."

"What for? To be your flunky? The butt of all your jokes? The confidant you describe all your sexual conquests to?"

"You're making me feel like a horrible bitch," whispered Zoe, bowing her head to escape his gaze. Eric lifted her chin, stopping her.

"Maybe it's not your fault. You need something else."

With a sudden movement he took her by the hips, pulling them against his own, then he bowed his head and kissed her so urgently, so voraciously, that it was almost brutal. It was a type of kissing that Zoe knew well – but it wasn't Eric's kissing.

Eric's hands moved to her butt, squeezing it emotionlessly, and then moved to her breasts, while the almost punitive kiss continued and her body was crushed against that of Eric, whose excitement was palpable.

This wasn't him. This was the way all the assholes she'd dated over the last few years behaved: that cocky bullshit, motorbike bravado, kisses devoid of feeling, the macho fondling, the squalid motels. And he knew it perfectly well because he had always had to listen to her telling him about it.

Always.

If she had had any doubts about her feelings for that wonderful man, that was the moment when they could have vanished altogether.

Even though she kept them squeezed tightly shut, her eyes filled with tears. One managed to force its way out from between the dark lashes and roll down her cheek until it eventually came into contact with Eric's skin.

The instant it did, he froze. He broke away from her as if she was burning, stared at her face – now bathed in tears – and backed away in horror.

"Eric," murmured Zoe, taking a step forward. But he shook his head, rubbed his face with one hand and sat down on the edge of the bed, running his fingers through his hair. He looked so desperate that it almost made her heart break.

She approached the bed and slipped between his legs, running a hand through his soft brown curls.

"Look at me," she begged.

"You were right about everything. What an idiot I am," he said, without looking up. "It is understandable that you don't want me."

"That's what you think."

"No, it's what you think." Eric stared at her, his expression a mixture of resignation and anger. "I heard what you said to Liberty two days ago. I felt so pathetic…"

Zoe gasped.

"What?"

"You didn't realize I was there, did you? But I was, I got dressed in a hurry after I woke up and I came into the store. I wanted to see your face and try and work out if that stupid note meant that you were as happy as I was about what had happened or whether you were already regretting it." Disappointedly, Eric shook his head, pushed her off him and stood up. "You think I'm just a poor loser who happily throws himself at the first pretty girl he meets. It's obvious, isn't it? Someone like me couldn't afford to waste an opportunity like that."

"It's not like that!"

"It was Valentine's Day, I was drunk, you were feeling lonely… A stupid mistake that we shouldn't have made, right? You're not made for someone like me."

Zoe shook her head vigorously. "I didn't know *what* I was saying, I was just talking things through! I was surprised and confused, and I was afraid that it meant our friendship was over!" She took another step forward, searching his eyes. "You never said anything to me! You've kept what you felt about me for all these years hidden, letting me humiliate you and hurt you and take advantage of you! You tried to make me think that kiss in Times Square was just a drunken dream! And now you're blaming me because I was a bit surprised?"

"Kept it *hidden*? *Really*?" laughed Eric mirthlessly. "Christ, the only thing missing was me actually drooling when you walked into the room!"

Zoe remembered those words. They were the ones Eric had used when he was talking about his first love, Stephanie…

Her soul in turmoil, she looked at him. "So you mean you were talking about me then? *I* was the girl that you fell in love with at university, not Stephanie…"

"She turned up at the right time, but the truth is that I honestly didn't even remember having met her," sighed Eric. "And for the record, I had already split up with her when I started to send you those stupid gifts."

"How could I have imagined that you were in love with me? I didn't even think that I was your type!"

"Oh come on, who are you kidding…"

"It's the truth!" Zoe almost stamped her foot in irritation. "All I am is beautiful! Is *that* why you're in love with me? You, with all your degrees, your scientific brain, your principles, your elegance… what use is someone like me to someone like you?"

Eric's shocked look sent shivers down her spine, but she went on. "I never thought I was up to your standards, Eric. I felt like the pretty airhead on some TV show who goes out with the football players and the bad boys because they are the only ones who don't care about being with an intelligent woman. All the girls you've dated have been so smart, and so serious. I thought that was the type of girl you were looking for!"

"I had to force myself to go out with them. I felt as if I was cheating on you!" said Eric, slumping against the door and staring out the window. "I've spent ten years just hoping that you would notice me."

"And I've wasted ten years dating assholes, just because I couldn't find anyone who gave me even half of what you give me!" Zoe walked over to him and put her hands on his chest. "The only one I ever really fell for was Stuart, and you know it. The only guy even slightly like you that I've ever dated."

"If you wanted to insult me, you've just succeeded," he snapped sarcastically.

Zoe smiled, sensing her Eric under the hard shell that he was affecting. "You know what I mean," she murmured. Then she turned serious. "And you also know how I felt while we were together. I felt so inferior compared to him that I almost cancelled my personality just to make him appreciate and love me. I never want to feel like that again. The only one I could be myself with, and who seemed to love me and appreciate me in every way, was you, and I… I would never have done anything to complicate what we had."

"Are you telling me that you were secretly in love with me?" he asked skeptically.

Zoe shrugged. "Maybe I just hadn't realized it."

The silence that greeted these words threatened to make her heart fall right out of her chest and onto the floor. Timidly, she raised her face to peer at Eric's expression, and the intensity of the look he gave her was shocking.

"Well?" she asked uneasily.

Eric raised an eyebrow, his face now relaxed now but still wearing a serious expression. "I'm waiting," he said, his arms crossed over his chest.

"Waiting for…?" Eric's challenging look almost made her blush. "Do you want me to make you a declaration of love? Here?"

"Why not? I sent you cards and gifts every year for Valentine's Day, not to mention last week, and I think that I've just opened myself right up to you." He shrugged, a mischievous twinkle in his eye. "Do try to be convincing, though: I've been dreaming of this moment for so long that my expectations are pretty high."

"Isn't it the man who's supposed to do these things?" she muttered, looking around her. "Maybe the way I put it a little while ago wasn't a *classic* declaration of love, but I felt like I made it clear to you all the same. Do you *have* to embarrass me? If you're hoping that I'm going to get down on my knees…"

Eric's silence provoked a sigh from her. She closed her eyes for a moment and looked within herself for the courage to open her heart to someone in a way she had never done before.

"I love you, okay? How could I not? You're my best friend, the only one who understands me, who appreciates me, who makes me feel good. You're the person that I run to when things aren't going right, and even when they are. It took me a while to realize it, but love has many faces, you've said so yourself… If it meant not losing you, I'd have accepted the face it had before," she said in a single breath, adding "but to tell the truth I like the new one better."

Chuckling, Eric took her in his arms. "That'll do," he smiled, and then kissed her with all the love that he had been repressing for the last ten years.

The feel of those soft, sweet lips, their flavour and the delicate firmness of their embrace tore a groan of happiness from Zoe, who returned it hungrily. Being in his arms was like coming home, returning to an intimate and safe place. But much, much more exciting…

"I can hardly believe it's true," whispered Eric, his lips on her mouth and his forehead pressed to hers.

"Neither can I, but I'm not going to let you change your mind."

"Why would I?"

"Because I'm unbearable. Are you sure that you won't kick me out after the first week?" she whispered, with a pout.

"I've put up with your worst sides for the last ten years for absolutely no personal gain," he joked, stroking her back and at the same time holding her against his chest. "Given this new formula, I reckon I can put up with at least another ten."

"Hey, a night of sex with me is worth plenty, honey," she winked. "You're going to have to double your threshold of tolerance!"

"We've only done it once, I still have to assess its real value," he continued in the same tone, nibbling her ear. "I'm going to need at least one night of sex for each year that I wasted lusting after you to make a complete assessment of the issue."

"Technically we did it twice," she said softly, tilting her head to make it easier for his lips, which had started to move delicately along the hot skin of her neck.

"That was the same night, it doesn't count. If we count the individual times instead of the days, we'll end up halving the amount of time for a perfect understanding."

"I'm getting confused. You're the brain, you keep count," Zoe muttered, closing his mouth with a kiss.

Her heartbeat soared. It seemed incredible that she was there, leaning against the door of a motel, flirting and swapping sexual innuendo with her best friend – Eric, so passionate and seductive that she almost didn't recognize him.

"You want to make the most of the room?" he asked in a whisper when they separated to catch their breath.

Although tempted, Zoe shook her head. "I want to go to your place. And this time, I swear that I won't run away when we're done," she whispered, giving him a very intent look.

Eric stole another kiss before he led her out of the room.

While he handed back the keys he put his lips to her ear. "We should have stayed longer – they'll get the idea that we've already finished, and that's not good for my self-esteem."

Zoe chuckled softly, then squeezed his arm, and with an ecstatic expression, said "You were great! I've never felt more satisfied than this in my whole life!" loudly enough for the guy behind the counter in reception to hear her. "Tell me you'll stay with me tonight."

Eric's ears grew pink with embarrassment and Zoe felt her heart fill with emotion.

"I'm relieved to know that you're not the motorbike and leather jacket type," she said, once they were outside. "I love it when you're uncomfortable… You're so cute!"

Eric grunted a reply while he placed his helmet on his head.

"Where did you get it?" she asked as she climbed onto the saddle.

"It belongs to a friend of mine."

"I didn't even know you could ride one."

"There's a lot you still have to discover about me," said Eric with a wink. Suddenly, he turned serious. "I'm sorry I went so fast before. I was angry, but that's no excuse for being irresponsible."

"It was worth it. In fact, seeing as I now have an overwhelming desire to discover all of your hidden sides, how about not wasting any more time and taking me home?"

Eric revved the engine and Zoe laughed and clung to him.

And while the bike raced through the streets of the city, she had the feeling that she had finally found her place in the world.

Epilogue

"You're happy, right?" said Zoe with a smile to Clover while she struggled to take her eyes off her boyfriend.

"Very" her friend said, a satisfied expression on her face. "I knew he was the right one. It took you long enough to figure it out, but finally you two are together."

"Hey, he wasn't exactly Speedy Gonzales himself, am I right?" muttered Zoe, shaking her head. "If I think about how much time we've wasted…"

"Well I don't consider it a waste of time. At the end of the day, you are together. And you were more in tune with each other than a lot of other couples I know."

"You're right," sighed Zoe, her eyes shining like never before. "He's taking me to dinner at the River Café tonight, seeing as our hot date for Valentine's Day got blown out."

"You know, you wouldn't think Eric was the romantic type, but actually he is."

"Yes, in his own weird way – he's not mushy, and that makes him even cuter. And he's so adorable when he's embarrassed… God, I could just kiss him to pieces!"

"I think that college student over there feels the same way," whispered Liberty, who had walked up behind her, into her ear.

Zoe turned to the counter and her eyes narrowed when she saw the flirty way that the girl – who was wearing a skirt that was *way* too short – was behaving with Eric.

"Excuse me a moment," she hissed, and marched off in their direction.

Eric smiled when he saw her but carried on explaining to the girl in front of him how the intricate vintage music box worked. "It's a perfect gift for your friend if, as you say, she likes collectibles. This is a truly unique piece."

"You almost make me want to keep it for myself," giggled the girl.

"Think about it – if you decide to keep it, you can always come back here to see if you can find something else for your friend," said Eric, kindly.

"Maybe you're right. The way you talk about this music box has almost made me fall in love with it. But maybe if you could give me some more details…"

"I'll be happy to help you if you need any more information," cut in Zoe, a falsely angelic smile on her lips.

"Oh no, that's fine – your colleague is already doing a great job of helping me."

"My boyfriend is very sweet, but he doesn't know as much about the vintage items as I do," said Zoe, turning in the direction of Eric and patting his arm. "Go back to your work, honey. I'll deal with her," she said in a soothing voice, before planting a kiss on his mouth.

While Eric walked away, a confused expression on his face, Zoe turned her eyes back to the girl, trying not to glare at her too much. "So, what do you want to know?"

"Look, I've decided: I'll take it," the girl stammered, pulling out her wallet from her backpack. "I don't really need to know anything else."

"I totally agree. When you see something unique, the best thing to do is snatch it up before someone else steals it out from under your nose," said Zoe with a wink.

Once the girl had left, Zoe joined Eric and Clover in the office.

"You went over there to mark your territory like a rottweiler! Bravo!" laughed Clover, who was perched on the edge of her desk.

Eric looked at her with incredulity.

"Hold on, let me get this straight: you were *jealous* of that girl?"

"She was flirting with you absolutely shamelessly! Jeez, how old was she, eighteen? They start young, these girls today," Zoe muttered, approaching him. She looked at him with a critical eye, then shook her head. "No, that's not going to work."

"What do you mean?"

Zoe stared at the collar of his dark shirt, which was unbuttoned at the throat, and hurriedly did it up.

"Since when have you gone around dressed like this? Do you really need to be flashing all this flesh to the other girls? And what about your hair? Couldn't you have kept it combed this morning?" She put her hands on his head in an attempt to tame the messy curls that gave him that mussed look that she liked so much. "You used to keep your hair so perfectly combed it looked like plastic."

"You said that you like it better like this," he protested in puzzlement.

"And where are the glasses?"

Zoe looked around, spotted them on the desk and grabbed them, sticking them on his nose. "Okay, now you're perfect."

Clover, chuckling in the corner, intercepted Eric's amazed glance and shrugged. "Who the hell understands her?" she mouthed to him.

"Zoe, you gave me a forty-five minute sermon about how I never used to make the most of my appearance and told me that all I needed to do to make myself better looking was wear

a sexier shirt, leave my hair messy and wear contact lenses...
and now you're changing your mind?" asked Eric.

Zoe smiled at him gently.

"This just shows how much I like you, even when you look
like the teacher's pet!" She flung her arms around him and
kissed him briefly.

"Hey, I don't want you to change, let's be clear about that."

"And she especially doesn't want other girls looking at
you!" Snorted Clover from behind her.

"Yeah, that too," agreed Zoe.

His arms around her, Eric laughed.

"So does that mean that I have to make myself look ugly
every day just to reassure you?"

"'Ugly' isn't quite the right word, but if you could avoid
batting your eyelashes at half-naked young girls I would be
grateful, yes."

Eric shook his head.

"Zoe Mathison jealous over me! There must be something
in the air that's making her crazy."

"I was already jealous, but I couldn't make it too obvious,"
smiled Zoe. "Anyway, now that I've finally got my hands on
you I have no intention of letting anyone take you away from
me. The less people notice you, the better."

"The holidays have been really generous with us this year,"
said Clover, looking at them. "Christmas brought me Cade,
Valentine's Day brought the two of you together... What's the
next one?"

"Easter, I suppose" giggled Zoe. "Too bad that Liberty is
already taken. We could have prepared a giant egg with a
hunky male stripper in it and have it delivered right here!
What a gift that would have been? It'd have knocked her off
her feet!"

Eric grimaced. "That sounds more like something *you* would have wanted to get."

"Maybe once upon a time, but not any more," said Zoe, looking at him carefully with a mischievous expression on her beautiful face. "But seeing you climb out of a huge Easter egg dressed only in chocolate wouldn't be a bad idea…"

Eric cleared his throat in embarrassment, and Clover laughed heartily.

"We should all go out on a date together," suggested Zoe. "We are all in couples now, it would be fun. Me and Eric, you and Cade, Lib and Justin." She looked over at Eric with a smirk. "We deserve an official night out with our friends after the disaster a few weeks ago."

"Finally I will have someone equipped with a reasonably high IQ to talk to," he nodded, looking at her out of the corner of his eye. "By the way: that scene that you made before with that poor girl – can I do that too when the next slimeball comes in here and tries the moves on you?"

"Of course you can," said Zoe, hugging him tightly. It felt as though she was living in some beautiful dream from which she hoped she would never wake up.

Eric Morgan had always given her everything she needed as a friend, and it turned out he gave her even more as a boyfriend. Letting him act jealous was the least he deserved: she'd have fly posted all of downtown New York, if only she could, to cry out to all and sundry that this guy was hers and hers alone.

She suddenly felt a hint of anxiety, and she looked into his eyes. "Promise me you'll stay with me forever," she murmured. "I don't care how, I just want to know you'll always be there."

"I always have been."

"And you won't hightail it to Boston the first time we have a problem, right?"

"No," said Eric with a gentle smile.

"And what if I make you angry?"

"You always make me angry!"

Zoe ignored his sarcasm. "And if I disappoint you?"

"What are you doing, covering your back?"

"I just want to be sure."

Eric looked into her eyes, gave her a quick kiss, then shrugged.

"Maybe I could go to Boston…" Zoe stiffened, but he tightened his grip. "But I'm sure that it wouldn't be long before I came back here." He rested his forehead on hers and looked into her eyes with profound love. "I've waited so long… How could I have managed if I hadn't been sure that you'd be worth it, don't you think?"

"You're probably right," she sighed, feeling her fear slip away.

"Hey, I'm the brainy one, remember?" joked Eric. "I've done my calculations, so you can rest easy."

Zoe gave him a gentle punch on the shoulder.

The click of a camera made them turn around. Clover was holding the old Polaroid instant camera that she always kept on her desk and looking at them with a tender smile on her face.

"Your first official picture as sweethearts," she said, waving the photo.

Zoe turned in her direction. "You could have used my camera instead of old that thing, we might have got a decent picture!"

"What do you care? It's a keepsake, not a photo shoot!"

Eric glanced at the photograph and snorted in amusement. "God, we look as though we're stoned out of our gourds! Check out our faces!"

"Drug addicts of love," winked Zoe, planting a kiss on his mouth. Then she reached over to Clover. "Thank you for taking that, I will treasure it."

"No way, this is mine," said Clover, walking over to the big noticeboard on the wall behind her desk upon which were pinned dozens of photographs similar to the one in her hand. It was a sort of a collection of all the most successful gifts she had found over the years – the ones she was most proud of.

"I did play a small role in all of this and I'm going to take the credit that I deserve!"

Zoe gave way. "It's true, you were great. Your courtship plan for Valentine's Day was a stroke of genius, even if we did screw up part of it."

"Not entirely, since I managed to bump the reservation at the restaurant," Eric corrected her. Then he turned to Clover, with a gentle smile. "I owe you a lot. You're help's been so precious, and I don't just mean in the last few days, I mean always. If I didn't give in more than once that was thanks to you and your unshakable optimism."

"Hey, don't make me cry! For the last few months I've been getting emotional about happiness." Clover joined them, hugging them both in a single embrace. "I love you guys."

"We love you too."

"Ok, this is all very nice, but I would like some of you to actually go back to work now. If it's not *too* much trouble."

Zoe and Eric sat up straight and Clover smiled at Liberty's ostentatiously bored voice as she walked past them absently.

"Come on over here, Ice Lady," Clover called out, pulling her by the hand and dragging her into the group hug.

Liberty stiffened slightly, and snorted. "Since you fell in love you've all become such a drag. How long do you think this honeymoon period is going to last?"

"You tell us, you've been in love longer than we have," said Zoe.

Slipping away from their arms, Liberty straightened her suit jacket. "It should wear off in a hurry, then. Thank God"

Clover frowned. "But I don't want to stop feeling like I'm walking on air every time I think about him!"

"Me neither," said Zoe, looking at Eric, who smiled and squeezed her tighter.

"I've been drifting aimlessly for years and now that I have finally found me a decent one, it's going to be while before my euphoria fades."

Liberty shook her head. "God help me! I've spent years being pummelled by Clover's cartoon optimism and Zoe's sex kitten exuberance. I used to like being able to count on Eric's pragmatic sarcasm, but I note with regret that you seem to have turned his head." She looked at him sternly, but could not entirely prevent a hint of sweetness appearing in her green eyes. "Hey, just don't turn into a shrinking violet, all right? I still need someone to keep them in check when I'm too busy to do it myself."

"You can count on me," smiled Eric, winking at her.

Clover pointed at her boss threateningly. "I know your cynicism and sarcasm is just a mask, even though I will never understood why. But one day I'll work it out and I'll find something to loosen you up. And at that point, your photo is going to end up on that wall together with all the others."

"You can dig all you want, you won't find anything," smiled Liberty, walking away.

Clover followed her. "You're wrong – there is always something precious under the surface of each of us!"

"In my case, it's probably crude oil!"

While the sound of her colleagues' voices grew distant, Zoe abandoned herself in Eric's arms. "How long do you think they'll keep that up?"

"How long is it until closing time?" he joked. "When Clover makes up her mind about something she's pretty much unstoppable, as you know. But Liberty is even more stubborn than she is, so I'm afraid it might go on indefinitely. The afternoon is looking like it's going to be a long and exhausting one."

Zoe touched his neck with a finger, a mischievous expression on her face.

"We could make it more interesting, you know?"

"What you have in mind?"

"Oh, I have *dozens* of ideas. The problem is that you have to be naked for all of them, and I very much doubt that you would let me strip you off anywhere in the store, with Liberty only a few steps away..."

She felt his arms tighten around her, squeezing her to that exciting – and excited – body which Zoe was now anxious to see and touch at all times of the day and night. She just didn't seem to be able to get enough of the guy – and they had plenty of lost time to make up for.

Eric's face didn't change, which meant that it took Zoe a moment to understand the meaning of his answer.

"You're right – with Liberty only a few steps away, I wouldn't be comfortable. But if there were a couple of doors between us... You know your darkroom? Nobody goes in there without your permission..."

"Eric Morgan, I never imagined that you were so brazen!" Zoe pulled back from him, amazed, amused and, in spite of herself, intrigued. "I'd never have expected to hear *you* propose a quickie in the darkroom! But I like it – let's go!"

She grabbed his arm and began to drag him toward the door, but Eric held back.

"Hey, wait a minute. If you say it like that it sounds sad, and meaningless. 'Quickie'… That's a *horrible* word for a few moments of passion with the woman you love! It's never going to be 'quickies' or anything like that with me. I'm not like your exes."

Zoe grabbed him by the hair and yanked his head down so that she could kiss him ardently. She worked hard at driving him half-crazy with lust, and when she knew she had him in the palm of her hand, she moved her lips slightly away from his and said, "So do you want to keep talking, you dirty little nerd?"

"No," said Eric huskily. "We can talk later."

Zoe giggled and dragged him quickly upstairs.

We hope you enjoyed this book!

Cassie Rocca's *A New York Love Story* is available now!

Buy it now
http://headofzeus.com/books/isbn/9781784978891

More addictive fiction from Aria:

 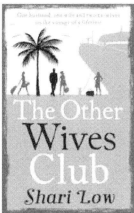 

Find out more
http://headofzeus.com/books/isbn/9781784976996

Find out more
http://headofzeus.com/books/isbn/9781786692009

Find out more
http://headofzeus.com/books/isbn/9781786694300

Thanks

To think that it was only yesterday that I used to walk around bookshops, daydreaming about one day seeing my own name on the cover of a novel… and now here I am with my second!

Please don't wake me up!

I never know whether I should be grateful to God, to destiny or to the universe in general for all this, but certainly some of the credit goes to the people around me:

The ones who first gave me life as well as those few but wonderful members of my family who have always encouraged me to try.

To all those I met later, because they found themselves watching from close-up the transformation of a shy, almost invisible girl into a girl who is… well, still shy, but who now has a 'famous' name.

To all those who actually turned this dream into a reality: my publisher and the people he assigned to work with me, who have followed me and believed in me every step of the way.

To all those who keep it alive: my readers, who trusted me right from the beginning and every day inundate me with affection and enthusiasm.

I hope I always deserve your esteem.

About Cassie Rocca

CASSIE ROCCA is a writer of Sicilian origin who has lived in Genoa since the age of three. In everyday life she is a child-minder, a job which gives her plenty of ideas for her modern fairy tales.

Find me on Twitter
https://twitter.com/CassieRocca?lang=en-gb

Find me on Facebook

https://www.facebook.com/CassandraRoccaScrittrice/

Also by Cassie Rocca

 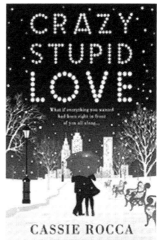

Find out more
http://headofzeus.com/books/isbn/9781784978891

Find out more
http://headofzeus.com/books/isbn/9781786698995

Visit Aria now
http://www.ariafiction.com

Become an Aria Addict

Aria is the new digital-first fiction imprint from Head of Zeus.

It's Aria's ambition to discover and publish tomorrow's superstars, targeting fiction addicts and readers keen to discover new and exciting authors.

Aria will publish a variety of genres under the commercial fiction umbrella such as women's fiction, crime, thrillers, historical fiction, saga and erotica.

So, whether you're a budding writer looking for a publisher or an avid reader looking for something to escape with – Aria will have something for you.

Get in touch: aria@headofzeus.com

Become an Aria Addict
http://www.ariafiction.com

Find us on Twitter
https://twitter.com/Aria_Fiction

Find us on Facebook
http://www.facebook.com/ariafiction

Find us on BookGrail
http://www.bookgrail.com/store/aria/

Addictive Fiction

First published in Italy in 2017 by Newton Compton

First published in the UK in 2017 by Aria, an imprint of Head of Zeus Ltd

Copyright © Cassie Rocca, 2016

The moral right of Cassie Rocca to be identified as the author of this work has been asserted in accordance with the Copyright, Designs and Patents Act of 1988.

All rights reserved. No part of this publication may be reproduced, stored in a retrieval system, or transmitted, in any form or by any means, electronic, mechanical, photocopying, recording, or otherwise, without the prior permission of both the copyright owner and the above publisher of this book.

This is a work of fiction. All characters, organizations, and events portrayed in this novel are either products of the author's imagination or are used fictitiously.

9 7 5 3 1 2 4 6 8

A CIP catalogue record for this book is available from the British Library.

ISBN (E) 9781786698995

Aria
c/o Head of Zeus
First Floor East
5–8 Hardwick Street
London EC1R 4RG

www.ariafiction.com

25588972R00151

Printed in Great Britain
by Amazon